MILLTOWN

a novel

Shane Joseph

Milltown
Copyright © 2019 Shane Joseph
All rights reserved
Published by Blue Denim Press Inc.
First Edition
ISBN 978-1-927832-40-5

This is a work of fiction. Resemblances to persons living or dead, or to organizations, are unintended and purely co-incidental.

Cover Design by Joanne Kasunic.
Cover photography by Ken Solilo
Typeset in Windlass, Cambria and Garamond

Library and Archives Canada Cataloguing in Publication

Title: Milltown : a novel / Shane Joseph.

Names: Joseph, Shane, 1955- author.

Description: First edition.

Identifiers: Canadiana (print) 20190053631 | Canadiana (ebook) 20190053658 | ISBN 9781927882405 (softcover) | ISBN 9781927882412 (Kindle) | ISBN 9781927882429 (EPUB)

Classification: LCC PS8619.O846 M55 2019 | DDC C813/.6—dc23

The evil that men do lives after them; The good is oft interred with their
bones.
- William Shakespeare.

Other works by Shane Joseph

<u>Novels</u>

Redemption in Paradise
After the Flood
The Ulysses Man
In the Shadow of the Conquistador

<u>Short Story Collections</u>

Fringe Dwellers
Paradise Revisited
Crossing Limbo

Prologue—12th March 2008

Sam Selvadurai walked the deserted boardwalk, looking out on the lake and across to the lighthouse, and asked that imposing beacon whether he had come to the right place. There was no answer. The lake stared back at him, frigid under blue March skies, a layer of thin ice suppressing bubbling wavelets that brushed against frozen ones on a dune-like beach covered with a sprinkling of fresh snow.

Despite his misgivings, he could smell the freedom in this country; he inhaled deeply, letting the cold creep inside him, refreshing, numbing, ridding his doubts about coming to live in a small town where his foreignness stuck out like that lighthouse at the end of the pier. Out here he would lose the anonymity of Toronto, where he had been classified as another "ethnic."

There were a few people out at this mid-hour of the morning; dog walkers and joggers and middle-aged men and women looking far from trim. An old woman, hunched and bundled in an overlong coat, pulled a shopping cart along the boardwalk a few steps ahead. She laboured under her burden. As Sam moved to overtake her, she looked sideways at him over a tightly wrapped scarf. Panic crossed her face and she stumbled, sending the cart and its contents spilling into the snow.

Sam instinctively went to her aid, holding out his hand. She looked up at him apprehensively, refusing the offered help, mumbling under her breath and looking around for someone else. But no one else was in the vicinity, and, after jerking her head frantically about her, she reluctantly took his extended hand.

"Are you hurt?" he asked.

"What?" Her voice was croaky and hoarse.

Cigarette smoker, he thought.

"Are you all right?" he enunciated slowly.

"You speak English?"

He suppressed a smile. "Can I get your things?"

She straightened her clothes, then felt all over her body for injuries while he righted her cart and returned her spilled groceries into it: tinned beans, a cabbage, bacon, a packet of hot-cross buns, two bananas, a box of cereal, and eggs that looked cracked.

"I'm afraid your eggs may be broken."

"You speak English," the woman repeated, shaking her head. She took back possession of her cart and began slowly limping away.

So much for gratitude, Sam thought.

He turned left onto the pier and walked down to its end, right up to the lighthouse where the wind was stronger and the ice broke against the rocks. With his back to the wind, he looked towards the town. The sun warmed his face.

Milltown, population 20,000 and growing rapidly. Church steeples rose in places over the trees—they were all represented here—Catholic, Anglican, Presbyterian, Baptist, United, even the Jehovah's Witnesses. Malani was sure to find a home in one of them, having attended a Methodist school back home, even though she was a Buddhist. There was no temple for him, but he had lost his faith in the gods after all that had gone on in Sri Lanka. The town hall stood tall in the downtown core, while evergreens sprouted between the smaller buildings. By next month there would be more leaves, as those gaunt stalks on the eastern shoreline—maples, oaks, willows—burst into bloom. Such sturdy trees, unlike the ones back home, they rarely stirred no matter how strong the winds howled in this cold country. Sam wondered if that was why Canadians were taciturn and composed, unlike his native countrymen who wore their hearts on their sleeves and ended up killing each other.

The chemical plant and its myriad white buildings ran down to the water on the western edge of the town. Too close to the water, he thought. The plant worried him. Recent newspaper reports in Toronto had focused on this small town; they had cited the rise of cancers in the area.

But then, back home, people had died anyway—taken out of their homes in the middle of the night, asked to say a word in Sinhala, and if accented, doused with gasoline and set on fire. Sam had been forced to witness his own house in Colombo go up in flames; the fact that his wife was a Sinhalese and a Buddhist was no exemption—it may have spared his life, perhaps—but all their earthly possessions had succumbed to conflagration during that night of terror.

He shivered. Was there evil in this country too? Hidden behind this benevolent townscape? Lurking in the nooks and crannies of homes, in the hidden recesses of people's hearts. The lighthouse would know, for its beacon shone upon everything and everyone during its circulatory night vigils. This lighthouse *must* know the story of this town. If he could only tap into its fount of secrets.

He started back towards the town, dodging empty beer cans and the random used condom left behind before the cold weather had driven the town's cleaners into hibernation. Luxury condominiums were rising up by the marina, some units still under construction. These signs were what had alerted him to the changing demographics of this place—the new entrants, mostly transplants from the city looking for cheaper lakefront property—would also be looking for the diversity of culture and food they were used to in Toronto. There were no ethnic South Asian restaurants in town. When he had first come here last summer on a scouting mission, Sam had staked out a corner on Main and Ontario streets. With preparations nearing completion, he would soon be opening South Asian Delights—a full service restaurant—his dream. He would finally be his own boss after years of being pushed around—after the mobs had arrived and pulled him out his sleep, plunging him into the nightmare of the displaced.

Why did I terrify that old woman? What's wrong with me? He caught sight of his reflection in a store window: brown coat, checked red scarf, well worn leather gloves giving way at the fingers, round face with a bushy salt and pepper moustache, portly figure (he'd put on some weight since coming to this country, thanks to all the fast food), golf cap hiding his balding pate but failing to hide the flecks of grey hair that fell down in oily curls over his collar. Dress shoes, badly salted and wet—he'd never bothered to buy winter boots, a legacy from the old country where sandals and chappals were de rigueur. It must be the golf hat in this weather, he thought, or the shoes. He didn't much care for appearances; the more nondescript you were when faceless government assassins were picking victims to toss in the fire, the better.

He looked inside an ornately decorated shop window displaying giftware: candles, multi-coloured soaps, potpourri, polka dotted vases, tea sets, cutlery in brass, silver, and bronze, tea kettles that looked out of fairy tale books—frivolities to his frugal mind. And yet, despite their losses in Sri Lanka, material acquisitions had re-accumulated over time, like flotsam gathering under the rocks at the entrance to this frozen harbour. Upon coming to Canada, they had bought more "stuff" than they ever needed. The apartment in Toronto had been bursting at the seams when the movers arrived. At this moment, Malani and the children were unpacking and arguing about what went where. Sam had begged for a breather, for some exercise to deal with his blood pressure, and had come out here to collect his thoughts.

The hairs on the back of his neck began to crawl, and he swivelled around. Was he being watched? People were going about their business on Main Street. He shrugged the feeling away. He was over-reacting.

Yet, as he made his way towards his new home, the apartment above the soon-to-be opened South Asian Delights, he did not doubt that evil lurked here, just as it did back home. If only that lighthouse could talk.

One

A rt Hamilton swivelled in his chair and looked out at the lake through the ceiling-to-floor windows of his cavernous office. Another blue March day, and the ice was melting—climate change was firmly in place. When he was a kid, he remembered skating on the lake well past March Break. A dark-complexioned man was helping an old woman with her fallen grocery bag out on the boardwalk. Immigrants were slowly starting to trickle into this former United Empire Loyalist enclave. Many of them had money—cash. And they wouldn't say how they had earned it or got it out of their countries.

He recognized the man. Selva…what was it…Selva-Dorai? Had leased the corner block on Main Street, next door to the accounting firm. Poor Steve Spade had been hard pressed to sell out. But business was business. Steve was months behind on his rent and had always assumed that his status as an icon of the town—Spade's Burgers and Beer—would immunize him from his obligations.

Spade was not his concern today. Art reached inside his drawer and pulled out the red file. This deal was too lucrative to be true: organophosphate compounds—a principle component in insecticide manufacturing. The US client was manufacturing the insecticides for export to the Third World—something Art had never dabbled in before—but the manufacturer down south had impeccable credentials. Well, almost. They did not want to manufacture the banned organophosphates on their home turf. As long as Art could deliver the compound safely across the border, the client would ensure that the border authorities did not ask awkward questions, and he was willing to make advance payments on the shipments—a far better solution than

Art's current thirty-day grace period on receivables. But, and there was always a *but*: organophosphates were also used in the manufacturing of nerve gas back in the old days. The scrutinizers, employees, lawyers, accountants—they all needed to be brought onside with appropriate smoke-screening. He was the only one who could pull it off. The revenue would fund the last phase of his waterfront condominium development; bring another eighty units on the market. This was doable, and he was going to do it—like all the other times before. Besides, it was good for the local economy.

He fingered the business card picked at the last Chamber of Commerce event. Jane Garner—she was attractive—late thirties, alert, brunette, great body, intelligent, and a crooked smile hinting that she was willing to stretch limits. Jane had recently moved to Milltown from the city and had bought an accounting practice from a retiring sole practitioner. The South Asian guy had triggered off thoughts of Jane, as she was located next door to the restaurant. Art needed a new accountant for this deal; his regular one was too conservative and asked too many questions. He picked up the phone and dialled long distance.

"Hello, Tom. How's it going? Good. I got a job for you. Woman by the name of Jane Garner, formerly of Argyle, Forbes and Associates in Toronto. Can you get the dirt on her? The usual—family status, why did she leave, any shit she's covering up. I need it by Friday."

He hung up and rose to pace the office. Tom was a good guy, discreet and rigorous, ex-cop.

Art adjusted his starburst tie in the mirror. He liked what he saw: six feet of hockey playing chunkiness, steel grey hair, long and wavy down to his collar, sharp nose, wide mouth, piercing eyes, grey Armani suit. He stretched and looked out the window once more. Milltown sprawled before him, half of it already his. Let the other half be, he had said as he cast further afield into other reaches of the county—he needed competition, and a smart businessman never drew attention to himself unless he had to for marketing purposes. What he owned had come in slow increments, built on the profitable hardware store and the money-losing mill the town got its name from. Art had inherited the mill at the tender age of twenty-three when his parents died in a car accident on their way down to Florida for the winter.

He had shut the mill within days of taking the helm, and block by block, he built the Hamilton Empire.

He walked back to his desk and put the red folder away. As he was about to shut and lock the drawer, he noticed the picture in its frame resting at the bottom. Against his inclination he drew it out: Martha and Andy hugging each other outside the Skyline at Niagara Falls, smiling. They both had lived on the edge, and he had pushed them over, or so some of the town-folk said.

Niagara Falls, Martha's hometown, Francolini country, where they had met at university, where they spent their honeymoon, and where she threw herself over the falls, plunging Andy into his one-way journey to Hell.

He pushed the picture back under the papers and locked the drawer.

Time to lock away non-productive thoughts; his wife and son had been the negative influences in his life, the forces that had strengthened and caused him to overcome, to achieve what he had today. He did not want to be associated with losers, God bless their souls.

It was time to go and see his friend, the mayor.

***

"It's tainted, we can't sell." Mayor Frank Morgan said, throwing the report on his desk. "And it's municipal property adjoining your plant. If this gets to council..." He left the rest in the air.

Art Hamilton retrieved the environmental report and scanned it. "Would it ease your mind if my company bought this lot? It will help in our expansion."

Frank's eyes blinked. "Why didn't I think of that! I've had a sleepless night on this."

Art slipped the report into his jacket pocket. "Leave this with me for a few days. I'll speak to our property manager. As buyers, we won't insist on an environmental report for an adjacent lot."

"And you'll provide a competitive bid?"

"How about a ten percent premium to what's on the table to keep your council happy?"

Frank laughed. "And just when I thought I had a problem…"

"I am glad you called me." Art settled himself into a comfortable armchair.

"Now all I have to worry about is how fast you are expanding in this town. I get asked these questions. And the people you bring in…"

"What do you mean?"

"You've got to watch out who you rent to on Main Street," Frank said, averting his eyes from his guest. He walked over to the side cabinet and wiped a speck of dust off the collection of tropical stuffed birds perched on top of it.

"Oh, come off it, Frank," Art said, tossing his head back and leaning into the plush cushions. "We need diversity in this town. Milltown could be the next Oakville if we plan it right. We need art galleries, high end-boutiques, exotic restaurants. We need to re-open the old Odeon playhouse and bring in some road shows."

"And all I get from my constituents is that more foreigners are coming in and that we should have done something to prop up Spade's business."

"You are going to win this election, Frank. Don't get sidetracked by the noise."

Frank's face puffed with delight at Art's words. He was a bald man in his late fifties with beady eyes, always looking up because his five-foot-two-inch frame did not give him an alternative.

"I see you've expanded the birds," Art said, changing topics.

Frank lovingly stroked one of the creatures at the end of the row of stuffed birds lining his credenza. "I received this Mynah from Simon

Smith following his visit to India. And the parakeet, I got at an auction in Toronto."

Art had lost count of the collections that Frank owned. The mayor's house was full of them: elaborately sculpted daggers and swords; ships in bottles of all sizes and colours; maps of varying degrees of cartographical accuracy, some slightly more than parchments; Chinese porcelain vases; bronze Buddhas; sets of redundant encyclopaedias thanks to the Internet. Frank was always open to "gifts" which made him easy to work with.

"Rick Jones has decided to run against me," Frank said, turning away and sitting in his enormous chair flanked by the oversized Canadian and county flags. He rested his chin in his hands, elbows on the glass-topped desk.

"My drunkard brother-in-law…" Art replied under his breath.

"He's still got some fire left. Remember he almost won the first time."

"Almost-won or also-ran? He's tried everything—provincial, municipal, even federal politics, and he always 'almost wins.' Come on, he's nothing but wind. Stale wind that no one buys these days."

"Well, he's got some of those old-timers from the mill that you closed down on his side."

"What could I do, Frank? They make flour cheaper than any of us can in those sweat shops overseas. I had to get out when the getting out was good. Condominiums and chemicals make better sense."

"That's where Jones gets his fuel—'more for the rich, less for the poor' and all that stuff."

"I said this before—you need to cut out the noise. You are going to win this election. You have my support behind you, Frank."

Frank looked up wearily, and a faint smile crossed his face. "Thanks for your support, Art. You are a loyal friend. How's Andy doing?"

Art rose and walked over to the window. He kept his back to Frank.

The mayor carried on blissfully unaware that his guest was tugging the brocade curtain involuntarily.

"It's great that they transferred him to Sunnyside. You could visit him and all. Imagine being in Alberta or BC or one of those outlandish places."

"Hmm."

"You get out to see him recently?"

Art turned from the window, trying to act calm. But seeing Frank's ebullience fade, he knew he wasn't succeeding. "Not much. There's no way back for that kid."

"What a shame."

Art cleared his throat. It was time to get down to business. Business cleared away the cobwebs, focussed the mind. "I have a deal coming up."

He saw a shadow cross Frank's face.

"A big order for the chemical plant."

"That's good news, Art."

He could see that Frank was waiting for the punch line. "I want you to keep the councillor, Doug Spade, and the environmentalist pack on your council off my back."

Frank was trying to read Art's face. "You mean this does not measure up to standards?"

"We always work to standards, Frank. It is *intent* that I don't want misinterpreted."

"You are not manufacturing explosives for terrorists, are you?" Frank started to laugh, partly to release the tension.

"No. But given young Doug's idealism, he could spin anything to his advantage."

"He's the people's choice. The one to replace me as mayor in a few years. Just what are you manufacturing?"

"Compounds for pesticides. I'm shipping it down south."

Frank let go a deep breath. "Ah. I feared worse."

"Not with people growing 'green' these days. I want you to keep Doug off my back."

"Can you get Rick off mine?"

They laughed.

As Art turned to go, he said, "Don't worry about the Asian restaurant—if there is any fallout, I've got a clause in the agreement that allows me to cancel the lease. The man may be a good cook, but he is not very sharp on legal fine print."

"I thought you'd have something like that up your sleeve." Frank grinned, standing up and extending his hand.

"As for Rick Jones," Art continued, "a well-timed exposé in a 'letter to the editor' in the Milltown Gazette should remind our citizens of his past drunken shortcomings. I'll phone Ed at the Gazette and see what we can do."

"Thanks very much, Art." Frank shook Art's hand with both his. "I knew I could count on you."

"You worry about Doug for me, will you?" Art went out, brushing against Sue Miller, Frank's attractive assistant, who was coming in with a bundle of mail.

Two

Sue squeezed past Art and entered the mayor's office. "Hi Art," she said hurriedly. She felt his eyes burning her from behind as she deposited the heavy bundle of mail, all sorted for Frank: those for signature only, others for action, some complaints (they were usually at the bottom as they affected his mood for the rest of the day), and plenty of support letters for the mayor's upcoming re-election campaign (these sat on top).

She disliked Art, his son, and all the things they stood for, yet her position as the mayor's confidential secretary forced her to tolerate him.

"Have a good day, you two," Art said, his eyes boring into Sue as she bent over the desk baring her cleavage. She let him look; this was the one weapon still available to her, for how long she could not tell.

After Art had departed, she turned her attention to her boss. He, too, was eyeing her with his usual lascivious smile. She had worn a thin white blouse today with a pastel pink bra underneath. The rest of her meagre wardrobe was in the wash. She knew this would get his attention: not so much a fashion statement as a cock teaser.

"Your coffee is coming up in a minute," she said, arranging the magazines on the coffee table. *Savour your first sexual fantasy of the day with a hot cup of java.*

"And what's the news today?" Frank had already dived into his mail.

When she returned with his steaming mug of coffee, he was staring at a notice in his hand.

"What the fuck is this?" He waved it at her, reaching for his coffee as if for a lifejacket.

"Oh, that," she said dismissively. She had deliberately placed it there to get his reaction. "You couldn't expect Rick to have fans anywhere but at Macy's Pub, could you?"

"But free drinks? He'd have the whole damned town in there! Who is bankrolling him?"

She loved to watch him squirm. "They say the displaced workers have got some union funds from the city."

"I've got to go down there and have a word with Macy. After all I've done for him."

"It's a free country, Frank. Besides, you think Macy will turn down a gig like this at his crappy watering hole?"

The mayor placed the notice inside his action file and leafed through the rest of the papers. "Sometimes, the way you sympathize with Rick Jones, I wonder whether you are in his camp or mine."

"You forget he was married to my best friend. *Your* best friend, Art's, sister-in-law, if you recall."

He sighed and drained his coffee. "Yes, I wonder whether I made a fatal mistake hiring you."

Then she did what gave her the biggest thrill of the day. She steeled her face, walked over, and shut the door to the outer office. Swallowing deeply so that the bile would not gush up, she went up to him, swivelled his chair around, and drew his bald head between her breasts, rubbing them gently into his face. "Are you dissatisfied with my performance to date, Your Worship?"

He moaned, opened the buttons of her blouse and sucked greedily on her bra-encased nipples. "Ha, ha…very satisfied, yum…yes…"

She suddenly pulled back, formal again, leaving him groping at the empty air between them. "Your next appointment is in fifteen minutes, and these constituents usually arrive a few minutes early."

He shot up in his seat as if struck with a bolt of electricity and started straightening his tie. Suddenly, the exigencies of office crashed down on him. He looked hungrily at her—this was the boldest she had been with him.

Sue chuckled inwardly.

"I'll make sure you have a few minutes before I show them in." She tucked her breasts securely inside her bra, buttoned her blouse and walked out of the room.

In the outer office, she poured herself a cup of coffee and sat down to compose her thoughts before the visitors arrived. Bob and Billy in their baseball uniforms smiled back at her from the photograph in the centre of her desk. Bob, the coach of the junior team, and Billy, their only son, all puffed up in his catcher's pads and guards. In the background, the white buildings of the chemical plant stood as a grim reminder. She felt unworthy of Bob just then, after cavorting with the mayor in his office. But the feeling of shame soon dissipated and was replaced with one of iron purpose—*you do what you have to do to get to the bottom of things, and if enticing the man behind the throne to get to the answers is the only way, then you do it!*

Bob and Billy would have to understand. Women had done it over the ages—Sheba, Salome, Wallis-Simpson, and Mata Hari. She shivered. All those femme fatales had paid a price in the end. Was she on the same slippery slope? The mayor's bald head between her breasts had also released an ache for Bob, who had loved doing exactly that, especially when she had graduated to the D cup. But Bob was gone, his body riddled with a cancer that could only have come from one of those white buildings in the background of the picture, where he had spent so many hours of his day and rarely talked about at night, because, like her, he had a strong work ethic and would take any measure to get the job done.

After she ushered the visitors into the mayor's office, Sue went through the notes and letters left for her by Frank from the previous evening. The mayor worked late when he was not attending civic functions, and there was usually a pile of correspondence waiting for her when she arrived each morning for work. The man's life was his job, especially as his wife, Frieda, lived in Florida for half the year and was down in Toronto for the other half, ostensibly attending to a feeble mother in a nursing home. Frank liked it that way, he had said to Sue, now that the children were married and had moved out of the province.

Sue sorted Frank's scribbly notes on various papers for interpretation and typing later. Next, a few bills that had to be authorized, then the RSVPs to call in for the various functions: a wedding, the Lions Club annual general meeting and social, the Women's Shelter gala, the Hospital Foundation charity event. The mayor did not cook at home for he was never home in the evenings.

Two sealed envelopes caught her attention. Frank did some of his personal correspondence, especially the ones he did not want her to read. The first one, addressed to his daughter Carrie in Alberta, was one of Frank's infrequent letters to his offspring, usually enclosed with a cheque for debts owed at the other end. The second was to a firm called Green Line Water Coolers Inc., which immediately rang a bell.

Sue glanced back at the closed door of the mayor's office. Glasses chinked inside. Frank had pulled out the sherry, despite it being an hour before lunch. She would be uninterrupted for awhile, she figured. Using her portable steamer and the fine letter opener, always kept locked in her drawer, she pried open the envelope.

Dear Sirs,

Thank you for your letter of 18 Feb 2008 and the accompanying report. Let me assure you that we will take the necessary measures to remedy municipal lot # 110 before the sale is affected. We will communicate with you when this matter is rectified and trust that you will continue to hold your offer to buy the property.

Yours truly,
Frank Morgan
Mayor
Milltown

Sue's palms got clammy. Green Line Water Coolers—they were the American manufacturers who had expressed an interest in setting up a Canadian operation next door to the chemical plant. And how come she had not seen their letter and the accompanying environmental report in the incoming mail? Was Frank rifling through and intercepting mail before she got in to work?

She rose and quickly made a photocopy of the letter, slipping the original back in the envelope and resealing it with glue.

***

Sue took the long route home after work that day. The sun had gone down, and the wind had picked up off the lake. She needed exercise to rid her head of her stress, and she gritted her teeth against the wind and strode fast to increase her heart rate. She knew the route and could follow it with her mind on other things. She cut through a side street off the town hall that took her down to the water. From there, she would head east along the boardwalk, past the town limits, then up the hill, past the lake-side houses before cutting inland again, crossing the railway tracks and arriving at her semi-detached bungalow—thirty minutes of fast walking, a good substitute for the absence of sex, she figured.

The sex bit bothered her. Ever since the night Frank Morgan had given her, his new secretary, a ride home from the office Christmas party, driven her onto the pier instead, parked a distance from some of the other misted-over cars where teenagers were making out, put his hand on her thigh, and told her what a miserable marriage he had.

She had considered the job as personal assistant a promotion, a way out of the town's administrative office and into the inner sanctum of municipal power, another step in her "mission." But when the mayor's cold and tentative hands gripped her leg that night, two weeks into the job, she realized that it came with obligations beyond the call of duty.

"Don't you get lonely, Sue?" Frank had asked. "With Bob gone and all?"

16

She looked helplessly out of the misting window, the outside world going opaque with their steamed, alcohol-laced breath.

"Sometimes." She wondered how it would feel the morning after if she just let him go all the way with her. Something in her, her Catholic upbringing, held her back. She wanted to open the car door and run. Then she thought of Billy and of her role as sole breadwinner. And of her "mission." Was it a mission or simple revenge? Dwelling on it gave her a headache. She just preferred to set a course and follow it through to the end.

"It's the same with me," Frank was mumbling. "I'll be discreet."

She felt his hand move up her leg. He was plucking at her panties. She stopped his groping ice-cold fingers. "No, Frank—not like this. We've both had too much to drink."

A car in front started its engines and roared past, back towards the town, its headlights sweeping the mayor's car. Despite the thickly misted windscreen, Frank ducked instinctively. That broke the spell.

"Take me home, Frank," Sue pleaded.

Frank reluctantly started the car. "You'll give some consideration to what I said?"

After a brief silence she replied, almost in a whisper, "Yes."

"I'll be discreet," he repeated as he dropped her off at her home. "Good night!"

That had been nearly three months ago. Frank's entreaties and invitations had started to ramp up from there. First, there had been invitations to go into Toronto for the weekend, which she put off because she had a good excuse: her local curling team was in a tournament that ran on the weekends, and her absence would be noticed. The invitations switched over to his cottage on the Kawarthas, normally unoccupied in the winter. She had turned down those, too. When he began to get snappy and curt with her, she let him pet her heavily in the office one day, when they had both been working late; the janitors coming in had short circuited their horseplay before he got too hot. This was her way of keeping him warm but not boiling him over. Now, she occasionally repeated this "therapy," like she had done today, to keep his libido high and interest piqued. But she knew it was only going to be a matter of time before he wanted more.

Today's gift of the letter confirmed to her that the promise she had made to her dying Bob could, and must, be delivered swiftly. All was not well in Milltown. Beneath the veneer of small-town Canada, and Milltown's reputation as one of the best little towns to live in—if one could believe the tourist brochures, that is—there was a cancer spreading, taking the town's stoic hearts away in their prime, like it did Bob.

Her footsteps slowed as she crested the hill. Large crumbling houses from the 1800's sat in large laid-back lots in this part of Milltown—the landed gentry, the merchants, and the transplants from Toronto who had either inherited or snatched up these properties during the last recession. She could not dream of buying one of these places now. Perhaps if Bob had been alive, there may have been that possibility, but not now. She walked past #80; that was one house she was familiar visiting, especially when Brenda was alive. And she wouldn't mind its present occupant's hands wandering around her naked body in lieu of Frank's. Just the thought of Rick still gave her goose bumps—the old Rick, not the sad soul who currently resided inside his still-athletic but rapidly emaciating body.

Dogs barked as she went past. Those ferocious Great Danes—Beelzebub and Mephistopheles—Bill and Phil, as they were affectionately known. They must be aging, too, or they must be the second iteration of those majestic dogs. Rick used to strike a commanding figure when he strode down Main Street on Sunday evenings in his black sweater and pants with those two black monsters on either side; he reminded Sue of an avenging charioteer in an old Cecil B De Mille movie.

The strumming of a guitar wafted to her ears as she stopped by the gate and looked for signs of life inside the house. A silhouette of a man framed itself behind a blind on the ground floor—shaggy long hair, cigarette dangling from the mouth. The guitar wailed a sad song, accompanied by the dogs with their barking. A "Shut up!" rang firmly and the dogs were silenced. The guitar player rose, setting the instrument aside, and the light went out in the room.

Sue hurried along, memories of Brenda filtering through her mind. Brenda, fragile, slightly off-centre, like her older sister Martha. They said it ran in their mother's side of the family—something about the Jewish mother surviving the concentration camps as a child where the Nazis had performed experiments on her.

Beautiful Brenda and Sexy Sue, as they were known in high school, falling for the handsome young lawyer who had just moved in from Toronto, leaving their high school sweethearts lost and loathsome for this smart aleck who had romantically interrupted their lives.

The boat, *The Seagull,* was what had done it. Rick Jones was a sailor and had sailed into Milltown in this plush boat that docked permanently in the marina, where he entertained the town's high society almost every weekend. He had his food catered from the branch of Francolini's, Brenda's father's gourmet restaurant newly opened in Milltown, where Sue and Brenda worked part-time. The night Brenda was scheduled to serve food and drinks aboard the Seagull, she had asked Sue to come along. The pay was good, Rick was known to be a generous tipper, and there were always free drinks after the party.

The crowd aboard had been wild, rich, and drunk under a cloudless sky and a full moon that shone like a spotlight. A woman fell into the water midway during the party. Rick looked overboard at the screaming, gurgling woman, then stripped down to his waist nonchalantly—what a hairy chest—and dived in to rescue her while the other party-goers hiccupped and wondered what was going on, including the drowning woman's aging and corpulent husband. Rick saved the hapless woman in the nick of time and administered the kiss of life to her back on deck, in full view of the embarrassed husband.

After the last of the guests had departed, and as Brenda and Sue were finishing stowing away the left-over food and beverages, an energized Rick invited them for drinks on the deck.

"Let's go sailing." he suddenly said.

"We have to get home by midnight," Brenda, prim, proper, and calculating, said out aloud.

"Nonsense. You are off duty, and I'll tell your boss that you girls did a fabulous job. The night has just begun—just look at that moon."

They did not need a lot of convincing. Before long, they were sailing out on the lake under a still glistening moon with clouds on its periphery and listening to strains of Burt Bacharach on the stereo.

"Want to swim?"

"We did not bring our swimsuits."

"Who needs them?" He laughed and headed for the stern. The boat was locked, riding the low waves. The girls saw him in silhouette in the moonlight, ripping his shirt off once again, dropping his pants, and with a whoop he was flying off the gunwale, splashing into the water. He called out, "The water is actually warm. Come on in."

Brenda looked at Sue and shook her head. "This is a bit too much, all in one night."

"I'm going in," Sue said, surging with excitement. How often did they do crazy things like this in a sleepy town like Milltown? The moon went behind a cloud.

Sue stripped off her dress and thought of diving in her underwear. Then she caught herself: she did not want to go home in wet, sticky under-garments. Off came her bra and panties as well, landing in a heap on top of her dress on the deck. The moon came out of the cloud at that point and Rick was watching her closely as she sought cover by diving overboard quickly. The water was bracing, rough, and knocked her breath away. She surfaced gasping. "It's coooold…" she managed to gasp, then tried going into a rhythmic crawl to keep warm.

"I'll race you," she heard him say and saw him swimming towards her. She was a good swimmer and had made the school swim team two years in a row. She tried to outdistance him, but his strokes were strong. When he caught up with her, they were several hundred yards away from the boat and the swell was stronger. Somewhere in the distance she heard Brenda calling after them.

He reached her, and his arms circled her, exploring her quickly. Even under the turgid water she felt her pulse rise and the damp release between her legs. He squeezed her breasts and glided his fingers over her nipples that were full to bursting. He kissed her without invitation while she was still gasping with the delight that his fingers had unleashed, and she had no recourse but to hold onto him lest she go underwater.

Then he was holding her with one hand and using his free arm to steer them back towards the boat. "Paddle with me," he commanded, and she soon got accustomed to his stroke and used her right arm to pull along with him, their bodies locked together.

When they neared the boat, Brenda had gone indoors. Rick swung himself onboard easily and reached down for Sue. They stood on the deck, naked, laughing, water dripping off bodies warm from exercise and sexual excitement.

"Here, I brought you some blankets." Brenda's icy voice broke the spell.

They wrapped themselves in the blankets and Rick went in search of brandy to warm up.

"You could have drowned," Brenda said. She had suddenly developed a scowl. She did not speak for the rest of the way home.

When the boat neared the pier, Sue saw the lights of the old Buick glinting at them. Bob! What was he doing out so late? She pulled on her sweater over her damp clothes—lying on the open deck hadn't kept them dry.

Bob was standing, hands inside his faded jeans pockets, baseball cap askew, cigarette long having gone out. He was squinting as if trying to figure all this out. Rick jumped nimbly down from the boat and secured the mooring.

"Hi!" Rick said nonchalantly at the scruffy stranger standing with hands in pockets. "Looking for someone?"

"Is my Sue on board?"

My Sue!

Sue felt like she wanted to jump overboard and stay there. Brenda's cold look and face shouted *Bitch* silently.

"Oh sure." Rick continued surveying Bob. "Sue! Someone for you."

"I'm coming, Bob," Sue said, jumping onto the dock. "Mr. Jones took us out for a sail. How come you're here to pick me up?"

"I finished early at the plant. Thought I'd give you a surprise. You're all wet."

She tried to hide her dampness by tugging the sweater tighter around her, but instead she started shivering. Bob pulled off his denim jacket and placed it around her shoulders, and she felt comforted by the smell of his sweat, cigarette fumes, and that other smell that came from the chemical plant, a sweet, acidic odour she had come to associate with Bob.

She took his hand and drew him away from the others, keeping her head bowed, ears hot with embarrassment. "Let's go home, Bobby. Good night, everyone!"

As she got into the Buick, she saw Brenda triumphantly take Rick's hand and pull him towards his red Cadillac parked in the lot opposite the boat.

Sue sighed at the memory as she headed home. Brenda never let go of Rick's hand after that first night, not in their dating that followed, not through their marriage with its stormy ups and downs. Eerily enough, the only time Brenda let go of Rick's hand was when she jumped into the water five years ago, drunk and daring, trying to replicate. . .replicate what? What Sue and Rick had done on that first night when they went out sailing?

Bob never talked during their ride home that day. He just did his duty as he had always done in the two years he had been her steady date. He took her to the front door of her parents' house, gave her a kiss (on the cheek, that day) and bid her good night.

Leaving the memories behind, Sue crossed the railway lines that carried all of Canada's freight back and forth across the land and headed into the lower-middle class section of town—apartment buildings and townhouses for retirees, single parents, service workers, and others for whom boats and lake-side cottages were only a dream.

She passed Billy's school, Milltown High. This was the one part of her walk home she did not like. There were pivotal incidents that changed lives: when Kennedy was shot, when Armstrong landed on the moon, 9/11. Life was never the same after one of those kinds of days. Well, the incidents of a year ago at Milltown High had been a turning point for her, for Billy, and for many people in this town. She shivered as she passed the school. Could she blame Billy for never wanting to go to classes after what had happened? Going back to the classrooms, the library, the playground, and the gym, where blood had been spilled in the most gruesome manner, trying to pretend that nothing was wrong, that this could still be a place of learning? Did all of what had happened have its genesis in those cruel mind-altering experiments performed on Mrs. Francolini over half a century ago?

She was grateful to turn onto the short walkway up to her townhouse. Billy was not at home, probably hanging out with his friends after work at the new mall, if he had any friends, that is. He'd be in around ten o'clock; he came home to eat and to sleep—that was a relief. In the meantime, she could content herself with a quiet dinner by herself, a glass of wine, and a couple of hours of TV sitcoms to drive away memories, mayors, and missions that had plagued her today.

Three

The Selvadurais sat down to dinner amidst opened boxes in a house that gave off foreign smells mixed with their own. Urethane from the plumber, who had fixed the leaky faucets prior to their moving in, blended with the smell of chicken curry Malani had scrambled together in pots and pans hastily unpacked from cardboard boxes. The rotis bought from a Sri Lankan restaurant on the way up from Toronto yesterday would be gobbled up tonight, and no doubt, none were to be had in the local grocery store.

Mahesh and Saro ate quietly; they looked sad and introspective now that their frenetic activities for the day of staking out their shared bedroom, carving out their respective territories inside it, and putting their personal stamps on them, were over. Sam had peeped in on them during the afternoon: Mahesh's desi-rap and basketball posters had gone up on his wall, and Saro's Avril Lavigne concert pictures, along with her batik art were on her side of the room, giving her brother competition.

But now, as the family lingered over this traditional meal—a strong reminder of the way things used to be—the reality of their move into a small white town appeared to be sinking in. . .for all of them.

"Tomorrow, first thing, we have to go to the high school and finish their enrolment," Malani announced, ladling equal portions of leftover curry into everyone's plate.

"Can I have some more rotis?" Mahesh enquired, looking around.

"You will have to wait until your father's restaurant is running. Our kind of food is not available here."

Sam beamed. "That is why we came—to create a unique niche."

"I hate the colour of the walls in my room," Saro said.

"The people who lived here before must have been rednecks," Mahesh said.

"Why do you say that, mister?" His mother wagged her finger at him. "Do you think you come from royalty?"

"Purple walls!" Saro rolled her eyes. "Duh."

"And Billy Ray Cyrus scratched into the wall, above my bed," Mahesh replied, scraping his bowl with the last piece of roti.

"You can always paint over it if you don't like it," Sam said. "The restaurant downstairs was a beer and hamburger joint—what do you expect?"

"Meat and potatoes, meat and potatoes—I'd better get used to eating it," Mahesh said.

"And I'd better get used to colouring my hair blue and red and wearing silver bangles and leather boots," Saro said.

"You will wear nothing of the kind." Malani bristled. For a moment she looked at Sam and a wave of helplessness crossed her face. Then the fire resumed in her; the fire that Sam loved so much, the fire that had held him strong through all the hot spots they had been in during their itinerant lives.

Sam rose from the table and started clearing the plates. "Yes, I think that's enough of complaining. We are here now, and we are going to stay here. No more running."

"That's a relief," Mahesh said. "At least I might end up with a school friend who will remember me."

"If you make any in this place, that is," Saro said.

After dinner was cleared away and Saro had helped her mother wash and dry the plates, Malani poured tea and brought her husband a cup. Sam was setting up the stereo system in the living room.

"You know—I don't know why they had to dismantle everything in this system. I am getting so confused with these wires," he said.

"Why don't you get Mahesh to set it up? He took it apart. Mahesh! Son, come and help your father put this thing together."

Mahesh came in grumbling. "I have schoolwork to catch up on," he muttered under his breath.

"But first help Daddy set up the stereo."

Sam was amazed at how quickly Mahesh connected the wires and flicked switches to test everything. In ten minutes, he was done.

"There—it's fixed." Mahesh flipped the remote a couple of times switching from CD to tuner and gave a nod of satisfaction. "Now, remember—no shuffling the rack without CDs in it and saying nothing is playing!" He ambled off to his room.

"You need to get these children to do more," Malani said. "You indulge them too much."

Sam sipped his tea and remained silent. He decided to change the subject. "Put a CD on, will you. That Englebert one."

Malani put on the Englebert Humperdink CD, their favourite. It reminded him of the good old days back home. Suddenly this brief respite, soon to be lost when the restaurant opened, was something to hold onto. It seemed to be ebbing away from him, just as the tea lowered in his cup with every sip.

He put down the half-empty cup, rose and opened his arms to Malani. "Come, dance with me."

She looked surprised. Sam kept his arms outstretched. They never danced anymore. Not since leaving the old country.

"Dance? Are you crazy? We are not young anymore."

"But why not?" he insisted. "For once we can stop running and try to live the lives we had. Before all that bad stuff happened."

"How can I think of dancing? I'm more worried about how we have disrupted the children's schooling by pulling them out in the middle of the year."

"They are bright kids. You know that. They have always figured things out when we have moved."

The fire in her eyes dimmed, and she looked worried, vulnerable. "You think they will be okay, Sam?"

He went over to her, pulled her up to him, and embraced her. She resisted momentarily, looking over her shoulder self-consciously as if the kids were going to burst in on them. Then she yielded and rested her head on his shoulder. He moved slowly to the music, and in no time, they had both fallen in step to the "The Last Waltz."

"Whatever their concerns may be—they are secure kids. They have us."

She held him tighter as they moved about this strange room they would mould into their home, each pre-occupied with their thoughts, not wanting to think of what tomorrow would bring.

***

In the middle of the night, he awoke. Malani was snoring lightly. They had made love after a long dry spell that night. The tension of the move was over, and he felt that wondrous connection to her again. He bent over her and kissed her cheek, and she murmured in her sleep, breaking her snore. She always responded like that to him.

He rose and drew on his sarong, pulled on a sweatshirt, and felt around for his bedroom slippers. The uncarpeted wood floor was cold and creaky; they would have to carpet it one day when there was more money. He passed the children's room, relieved that their lights were out; Mahesh was known to be up late in the dark with his earphones on, listening to rap downloaded off the internet. Sam tiptoed downstairs to the ground floor and entered the restaurant through the "staff only" door.

This was his moment of glory—the crowning achievement of his life's striving—and he wanted to savour it alone. He put on the dimmer lights, just bright enough to see objects in the room, but not strong enough to attract attention from the street. The tables and chairs were in place; he had gone for rattan as it reflected the east—his world. The furniture belonging to the former owner—comprised of faded green and red booths and beer-stained wooden tables with names, dates, hearts, and expletives notched into them—all had to go. Spade's Burgers and Beer had to be wiped out in order for South Asian Delights to be born. He had brought in a crew of movers from Toronto to make the switch and had seen worried and angry looks on some passers-by.

"What's happening to Spade's?" one old-timer had enquired aloud.

"Oh, some foreigner is buying the place," another man, leaning heavily on a cane and sucking a cigar, rasped out loud enough for Sam to hear as he supervised the movers.

The first old man shook his head and ambled away. "Everything's changing these days. Can't say what they'll do next."

Sam hoped that he could surmount the small-town mentality—he had to. He had wanted to run after that old man and say to him, "Do you know how much change *I* have been through?"

He shrugged off the recollection and went into the kitchen. The contents in this area had consumed all his savings: brand new cooking ovens and refrigeration units gleamed back at him in the half-light. Very soon they would be greasy and used, but he would clean and polish them every night after closing time—that was the mark of a professional chef. The equipment at Spades had long exceeded their life-spans, yet old Spade had pitched them as being in excellent shape and got indignant when Sam declined to buy them.

Sam had designed the kitchen himself, this was what he had learned in hotel school in the old country but had never had the opportunity to put into practice because he had always worked for someone else. And where had he *not* worked: from the Hilton and Oberoi chains back home, to fast food joints on arrival in Canada; then moving up slightly when employers knew what he was capable of—Greek restaurants, French rotisseries, Italian bistros—he was glad for the city's multiculturalism. He made the mistake of moving up to head chef in a popular Sri Lankan restaurant in the heart of Toronto and getting the moniker of "Sam the Man—the chef with a taste of home." His reputation had made the restaurant money and brought in many new patrons, but it had also brought in those two men who strode up to him while he stood at the bus stop late one evening after work. They had promptly told him that he should be making a contribution to the struggle back home.

Up to that point, Sam had dodged the "struggle" by being invisible within his ethnic community since coming to Canada. His other jobs had also kept him out of that orbit. As "Sam the Man," he was in the spotlight again.

"I am hardly making any money here, *baba*," he pleaded with the men, who wore hoods and thick coats and spoke with accents from the home country.

They ignored his excuses. "You have a Sinhalese wife, also. You had better show some support."

Sam bristled, despite the danger he faced. "*Adey*—the Sinhalese people burned my house down in Colombo. Now my own people are harassing me?"

"We are not harassing you, unless you *want* to be harassed," the tall one with a hooked nose said. His shorter companion kept looking around in case someone should overhear the conversation.

"What do you want?" Sam asked finally, in disgust.

"Ten percent of your earnings—that's all. Just like giving to the church. After awhile you will not feel it."

"Do you provide tax receipts?" Sam felt the bitterness well inside him.

The tall man grabbed Sam by his collar and tightened viciously. "*Adey*—don't fuck with us. Cash—that's what we want. Or your beautiful wife will not need to put on make-up anymore. Remember that."

The tall man tossed Sam back against the shelter, and the two men quickly melted into the night.

That was the incident that had prompted him to pull out of Toronto. To pull out all his savings, sell the house, and plunk it all on this restaurant. In a perverse way, he was glad for the "push" those men had given him or else the restaurant would have continued to be only a dream. Would they come looking for him in this small town full of white people? Hardly likely, he reasoned, given that they had lots more fish to go after in the big city—thousands of dumb immigrants from the home country arriving in Canada each year, thinking that they were escaping Sri Lankan politics forever. Silly buggers!

A rustling outside the front door of the restaurant brought Sam out of his reverie. He had come out of the kitchen and was making his way upstairs when he had heard the sound.

There! There it was again—as if a cat was scratching at the front doors.

His slippered feet making no sound, Sam tip-toed towards the front entrance, only to knock into a table and shatter the silence. He saw two figures pull away from the door, their shadows caught by the street light as they crossed the window.

Sam threw open the door and stepped out, the cool night air causing him to shiver. But the crudely painted sign, "PAKI—GO HOME!" made him shudder even more. He ripped the sign off the door as running footsteps echoed down the street. He stepped out onto the sidewalk, the torn sign in his hands. A dark shock of black hair and a receding hockey jersey sporting the Maple Leafs was all he could see. Sam felt weak in the knees and sat down on the steps of South Asian Delights.

The restaurant dream was starting to look like a nightmare.

Four

The youngsters, all in their late teens and dressed in blue overalls, moved in single file. The guards hung back, except for the supervisor, a grey-haired stocky man, spewing words of well-intentioned wisdom to his charges as he led them to the worksite. The wire fence, fifteen feet high and concave at the top, armed and ready to emit the alarm at a touch, ran all around the grounds.

Andy Hamilton, newly released into the day program from his solitary confinement and medication regimen, had difficulty focussing in sunlight and the cool temperatures of April. He huddled along at the end of the line, listening to the two guards chatting in low whispers, their truncheons swinging like engorged phalluses at their sides. They were grumbling about the pay and the shift schedule. Andy grinned—they were all in prison. The guards, too.

The inmates circled a half-complete concrete structure. The supervisor was explaining the art of interior walling; there were buckets of white paste and sheets of drywall leaning up against the outer concrete facade. No houses were ever built here—it was like play dough camp for young adults: one day it was dry-walling, the next roofing, then window installation, then siding, eaves troughs, shingling—all intended to impart employment and life skills to these kids who had fallen off the path and ease them back into the larger, unforgiving world some day.

Andy looked vacantly at the budding maples and sycamores that bordered the property. Tall lindens lined the driveway that led to the giant white gates that led to...freedom?

There is no freedom—we all live in our private hells. The inmates, the guards, even the supervisor. Mom. Me.

That familiar feeling of hopelessness started to surface, and he began to panic. He knew where that feeling led him—the desire to control, to dominate. And he had just earned his ticket to the outdoors; he could not fuck it up again. They'd put him in the dungeon for longer and shoot him with higher levels of those drugs that left him not knowing whether it was night or day. He shook his head and forced himself to focus on the supervisor's face that was swelling like a balloon in front of him.

Someone nudged him from behind.

"You okay, kiddo?" It was Henry, the toothless guard and ex-wrestler, with stringy hair hanging to the edges of his balding head. Henry was his ally, his friend. Henry slipped him porn magazines that he could jerk off to.

Andy grunted and tried to focus on the supervisor, who was now looking his way, too. *Don't stare at me, you prick—you know what I could do to you.* It would be so easy to give up control, to give into that urge to feed himself with these bastards who tried to dominate him. He involuntarily reached down for a split piece of two-by-four that lay among the debris of the worksite.

"No, you don't, kiddo." Henry's fist closed like a vice on Andy's hand. Henry pulled him out of the group and called back to the super, "Me and young Hamilton here are going to have a little chat—get him re-oriented."

The supervisor winked at Henry and returned to addressing the rest of the group.

"You silly prick," Henry hissed when they were out of earshot. "Do you want to go back in the bin?"

Andy remained silent. Henry, he trusted. Henry relied on his father for money. Henry would look after him.

"Wanna go indoors?" Henry asked after they had walked around the perimeter once.

"Yeah."

"This time only, okay? You have to get out with the rest of the kids soon, or they'll transfer you someplace else, and nobody will find you."

"Who wants to find me, Henry?"

"Your dad cares for you. You know that."

"Oh yeah?" Mention of his father got him mad. He did not understand why Henry was doing this. "My father pays you to keep tabs on me—that's all."

"Your dad's a busy man. This town owes him a lot."

"He owed Mom a lot."

"Oh, go on—feel sorry for yourself."

Andy lashed out, swinging with his left hand. But Henry had moved to get behind him and grabbed him in a hammerlock, pushing down. One of the guards blew a whistle, and two others stumbled out of the main building, running with truncheons in hand.

The lead guard came up. "Need help with this little shit?"

Henry had progressed to lock in his grip with a half nelson added to pin his charge down well and good. "Nah—I've got him under control. Kid's a bit hyper—probably got his meds screwed up. Leave me be with him for awhile until he cools down." As if to make his point, Henry tightened his grip, making Andy cry out in pain.

***

Later that afternoon, Andy sat on his bunk and stared into nothingness. Letting the mind go blank was a solace. He wished he could stay like that forever. The drugs helped do that, he knew, but coming out of them was so yuck: his stomach ran and his head hurt, and he felt woozy—he just craved the next dose, so he could go back into oblivion and peace.

But they had started to lessen his meds; they said he needed to be less dependent. The therapist had started to work with him, to train him to meditate so he could blank his mind without the drugs. He managed it sometimes, like now. But for how long? Almost in answer to his question those images started to re-appear, repeating tapes that seemed to play out forever.

His mother and father are fighting again. How old is he in this dream? Seven or eight? She is throwing things at his father, and Andy is hiding under the kitchen table, watching two pairs of adult feet scurry about the room.

"You are sleeping with her," his mother yells and throws a pan at his father.

"She's my secretary, and she's attractive—that's all," his father returns. "If you are that stressed out—go to your mother's for awhile."

"Go to my mother's! That's all you can say every time. 'Go to the priest. Go to your mother's. Go to your sorority.' Why not you go to a shrink and check out your rampaging libido?"

Andy puts his hands over his ears as he does not want to listen to the shouting anymore, his head is splitting. Then he remembers running out from under the table and shoving his father in the crotch, throwing him against the sink.

"See what you are doing to this poor little boy?" his mother yells triumphantly.

Andy picks up a fallen glass and flings it at his mother. "I hate you, too. Why can't you just be happy?"

As his mother takes the glass on her breast in shock, Andy spins on his heels and darts upstairs and shuts his bedroom door.

The images cut off with the shutting of that door, and Andy stirred in his bunk to a ringing in his ears. It was the bell for lunch going off— mercifully releasing him from the maze-like caverns of his mind. He remembered that he had apologized to his mother afterwards, cried at her bedside and said how sorry he was; he even let her stroke his head as he lay beside her. But his father he had never apologized to—he never could.

Five

The high school boys were in the change room after phys-ed class. Roars, hoots, and braggadocio punctured the air in unending waves. Billy Miller was late for his evening job at the supermarket, so he sat on the bench, packed his things, and tried not to get into any long conversations.

A patter of wet feet, straight out of the shower, naked, with a proudly dangling cock on display—Jack towered in front of him.

"Yo, Billy—you were great today, man. The shot from the three-point line was brilliant. When are you trying out for the team?"

"Wrong conversation, Jack. I've got work to do."

"You're always working, guy," Ted piped out from the locker to Billy's left. Ted had rusty hair and was the guard on the basketball team.

"Or checking out chicks," Jack countered, towelling his cock slowly. No matter how hard Jack tried, Billy had never seen that damn thing come erect.

"We are never getting out of this town, Billy—better enjoy life, guy," Ted said.

"*You* should talk," Jack said, dolloping deodorant—he had inordinately long hair in his armpits and a relatively hairless chest. *Selective shaving.* "How do you manage hockey *and* basketball?"

"Strict scheduling," Ted said. "And no girls. I mean, not seriously, yet."

Billy swung his gym bag over his shoulder. "Well, I'll leave you guys to check out the sports scene in Milltown."

"Hey, Billy—"

"Yes, Jack?" Billy paused, his hand on the door of the change-room.

"How you making out with that Indian chick?"

"Sri Lankan," Billy corrected.

Jack shrugged, pulling on his pants. "Indian, Sri Lankan—what does it matter—they're all the same."

"Shh!" Ted put his hand up to his mouth. "I just saw her brother hit the showers."

"Fuck him," Jack said loudly. "I hope his sister's not as smart-alecky as him."

"She's great," Billy replied. "And now, I have to go."

"You kissed her yet?" Jack called out. "Fucked her?"

Billy left the questions unanswered and pushed through the door.

He got into his mother's aging Chevy Cavalier. He was grateful for the loaner from his mom, especially as she had to walk to work at the town hall. He had fifteen minutes before his shift at the loading and stacking job in the supermarket. He wondered whether he would have time to swing by South Asian Delights. The car took a few cranks before starting up—he had to check that starter motor before it packed up. His mother was no good with cars; she had left it all to his father and now to him. He missed his father on these occasions; Bob could fix these things in seconds. In fact, this car was the one his father had bought second-hand for his mother eight years ago, and Bob may have even tinkered with the starting mechanism, leaving his imprint on it.

He cut down Mather Lane onto Jarvis and headed south for half a mile before taking a left onto Main Street. The lake peeped out in between the shops on Main—dark blue with foamy caps on the edges—still pretty in the fading light. He couldn't imagine living where he could not see water. The lake had been a constant companion in his life. His parents had brought him down every weekend in the summers to play on the beach. And he would run into the water unconcerned, letting the chill waves take him, always knowing that his father would be behind him in case he got caught by a sudden undertow. He had been an ace swimmer in his class but had to decline lifeguard duty on the beach due to his part-time work and his studies. He had bowed out of a lot of things since his father passed away—sports—well, hockey had been out of his affordability range, but not trying out for basketball had hurt. And so, he had given in to his mother's desire for him to get out of Milltown, go to university in Toronto or another major city, if he could, by getting grades needed for a scholarship. Then, like a beacon in a misty and barren port, Sarojini had arrived in Milltown and was now upsetting his focus and his long-term plans. She, too, was the difference he was seeking from the humdrum of this town's life.

He cut the engine on Main Street and let the Cavalier coast to a stop opposite the restaurant. Parking was plentiful as it was after 5:00 p.m. The lights inside were garish—reds, oranges and blues—but subdued. The place was mostly empty. Macy's Pub, three doors down, was already warming up with regular patrons swinging in and out of its doors; Billy suddenly recalled that the Maple Leafs were playing Ottawa tonight. He looked up at the Selvadurai's family quarters above South Asian Delights—the curtains were drawn.

Sarojini lived in a walled fortress. She came to school and she went home, that was all anyone saw of her. She was a year younger than him, in grade eleven. Yet when he had seen her participate in the interclass debates, her speech, though accented, was fluent, and she had made no bones about tearing apart smart-aleck Jack on the subject of gender equality. *No wonder Jacko is pissed off at her!* She did not participate in any other school activities or sports. It only added to her mystique. She gave him the urge to scale the fortress that sat above the restaurant and rescue the exotic damsel within.

He'd have to pluck the courage to talk to her privately one of these days. All they had done was exchange pleasantries in the company of other school kids who were common friends. He knew she was interested because whenever he had caught her glance, she had taken in a breath and looked down or away. And yet that hostile brother of hers…

On impulse, he got out of the car and crossed the street towards the window frontage of the restaurant. He looked in through the window quickly. A man, Sarojini's father, stood behind the bar pouring drinks. An elderly couple sat in a corner of the restaurant, the empty platters of their recent meal still to be cleared away. Another man—he recognized Rick Jones—sat at the other end, alone as usual. The rest of the restaurant was empty. A woman, Sarojini's mother, he thought, came out of the rear of the restaurant and went towards Rick with a tray of steaming dishes. The father brought a beer on a tray over to Rick and cleared the empty bottle away, smiling, bowing, being very courteous. No sign of Sarojini. Billy saw the father look at him gaping through the window. Sam Selvadurai frowned. Billy straightened up and turned around to walk back to his car.

He sucked in his breath immediately when he saw Sarojini crossing the street and heading towards him. She was carrying several grocery bags yet walking briskly. He blushed, caught off guard at her sudden appearance. She seemed emboldened at the sight of him opposite the family's restaurant, as if he were now on her turf.

"Do you want me to translate the menu for you?" she asked him, a smile playing on the sides of her face.

"Er, no…I wasn't thinking of eating. I have to go to work."

"Then what are you doing here?" Her smile widened.

"Well, checking it out. Maybe I'll come another time."

"That's good."

"Yeah, I suppose I *could* come another time," he repeated to himself.

She put one hand of bags down and pointed to the menu card in front of the heavy oaken door. "The string hoppers and chicken curry are very nice. My favourites."

"Can I order take-out?"

"Sure. You will have to call ahead though, because it takes time to prepare."

Then he blurted out something that even surprised him. "Will you come out with me for a ride in Presqu'ile Park if I order string hoopers and curry?"

"Hoppers—not hoopers." She studied him intently, her smile evaporating. She looked inside quickly at her father who was staring at the two of them. "I'll think about it," she said and hurried indoors.

He lingered long enough to see her set down her load, exchange her coat for an apron, pick up the grocery bags again, and go around the counter and into the rear of the restaurant.

He walked back to his car on wobbly legs. She hadn't said no. That was what he clung to. Had he been nervous when he asked her? He had practiced this move so many times, but the suddenness in which he was called on to deliver it had put him completely out of step. He was damp under the arms and his palms were sticky on the steering wheel.

His drive to the mall on the edge of town was occupied with a storm of memories. He had a feeling of déjà vu. Why did he always seek out these inaccessible damsels? The last time it had been Jen. Look where that had ended up. The schoolyard flashed before him. Running to save her. Pulling her blood-spattered body into the gym and shutting the door. The shouts from outside, "Billy you bastard, I am going to get her and you. You can't hide her from me forever." Cradling fair Jen's head in his lap, willing her to keep breathing, despite the globules of blood coming out of her mouth every time she exhaled. Looking frantically for something to defend himself and Jen with. Nothing available. Then the screaming of sirens and squealing of brakes outside, the shattering of the gym door lock with repeated shots fired at it. And Jen, not breathing anymore...

He shook himself awake. He was in the supermarket parking lot, having driven on auto-pilot, pre-occupied with his memories.

And now, here was another precious girl, protected by scowling fathers and brash brothers. He slammed shut the door of the Cavalier and walked into work.

✳✳✳

In the restaurant, Sam began putting away his bottles at the bar. That would be it for tonight. No one came in past 7:00 p.m. in this town on a weekday, he was now beginning to realize that 5:00 p.m. was rush hour here—dinner time.

The elderly couple had left, carefully counting cash and coin to settle their bill. They had complained that the curries were too spicy. *Aney baba!* He had watered it down so much and yet it was too spicy? He was damned if he was going to compromise the flavour any more.

Sam looked eagerly at the tall, gaunt figure in the corner, now on his third beer, scarcely having touched his food that would very soon be a cold and soggy mess.

"Another drink for you, sir?" Sam asked.

"Sure. Make it a scotch on the rocks this time, will you," the man said absently.

"Shall I warm up your food for you sir. This food is best eaten warm."

"Not to worry—it's very good. I'm enjoying the aromas."

He looked like a friendly man, although the hooded eyes revealed past disappointments. The expensive felt jacket had been dressy once, but it was frayed at the collar.

After serving his guest's drink order, and mindful of his privacy, Sam picked up the free community newspaper that kept appearing on his doorstep every day and glanced through the headlines. Running the restaurant had left him no time to figure out what was going on in the outside world. According to the news, the town was expanding: the next phase of condo development on the waterfront had received council approval to proceed and the chemical complex was adding a new extension. The statement from Art Hamilton in the article said, "We have received a rush of new orders and need more production space." Art did not elaborate on what those orders were.

"It's a tough slog, isn't it?" the man at the corner table suddenly spoke up, twirling the scotch in his glass.

Aware that he was being spoken to, Sam looked up from his newspaper. "Yes, business is slower than I expected. I hope the summer will be better."

"Don't count on it. We don't like change here. You represent change to them."

"But people like you are still coming in. It takes time."

"Yes, I was change to them once, too. But they never could get it." He started picking at his food.

"What do you do, sir? For a living, I mean…if you don't mind me asking."

"I'm a lawyer. Here's my card—if I can find one. Ah, here's one." He fished out a crumpled card and put it on the table.

Sam walked over and took it. *Rick Jones LLB*, it said.

"Well, I am honoured to meet you, sir. I might require your services one day."

"Your landlord treating you okay?"

"So far, so good."

"He chews people up when they get in the way. Watch him."

"I have had no problem, so far, only some vagrants who painted my doors before I opened for business."

"I heard about that at Macy's. They were raising a pint to celebrate the miscreants who'd done it. Those bastards were sending you a message that they don't like change. This curry is excellent, by the way. Please compliment the cook, your wife, I take it?"

"Yes, sir. I will tell her."

Rick Jones started digging into his food a bit more rapidly, and Sam felt comforted. Two other male customers walked in just then, they looked like out-of-towners, of mixed Eurasian race, for they stood on the sidewalk staring inside before stepping in. One of them chimed as soon as they entered, "Well, I never expected an Asian restaurant here. And a Sri Lankan one at that. What luck!"

Sam got busy serving them, and when he next looked up, Rick Jones had left cash on his table, including a generous tip, and quietly disappeared. He had picked through all four dishes but eaten very little of each.

The new arrivals bolted down their food like they were taking a break at a Toronto food court between meetings and talked loudly about how they were thinking of buying some lakeside property shortly. This was good news for Sam: he needed more customers like this to take up residence here.

"This is one of the last places for good real-estate, everything west of the greenbelt is gone already," one of the guests proclaimed, burping, as he slid his Platinum American Express card into the bill tray.

Please come soon, before my cash flow runs out. Sam returned to his newspaper after his guests hurried out, mouthing compliments as they left. Within minutes, they roared past, heading down Main St. in a Lexus.

An article in the letters to the editor caught his eye. He let out a deep breath as he read it, glancing at the empty table where his lone customer had sat drinking and eating until very recently:

Dear Editor:

<u>Rick Jones—a repeating old record.</u>

How many times must we entertain this "has been" in our electoral process? Sure, anyone has the right to run for election in this free country of ours. But there comes a time when people must know when to get off the bus and not waste taxpayers' money or attention. Milltown's very own Rick Jones, dropout from the Federal, Provincial, and Municipal electoral cards several times in previous years (the last time due to alcohol related depression) is planning to run again. Again? Doesn't he get it? Radical epiphanic leaders don't exist anymore, or if they do, they are just tooting records that were popular in the times of Paul the Apostle. Have we not had legions of Jimmy Swaggarts and Eliott Spitzers to remind us that one does not convert to "Messiah" overnight while remnants of tragic flaws remain behind to discredit one the moment one preaches to the contrary? My advice to Mr. Jones—now that he has fallen off his horse of prosperity and shameless wealth—is to stay there and not pick up the flag for the poor and downtrodden yet again. He just does not know when to quit and will probably never learn.

Joe Saxon
Unemployed Accountant
Most recently employed at Hamilton Mills.

Six

Macy's Pub was full. The beer flowed abundantly, the TV monitors were tuned to maximum volume, and Sue had difficulty juggling the mugs in her hand. It was on nights like this that she hated doing this second job three times a week. But the tips were good, and she needed every dollar. Besides, with what she had discovered lately at the office, she did not know how long she would be holding down her day job.

She had thought of calling in sick for this shift. Frank was going to be making his election pitch to the regulars in the pub tonight, and she was not looking forward to witnessing it. Typical of Frank to show up during a hockey game and show how "regular" he was. This was also the mayor's counter to the "drink-up and listen-up" session that Rick Jones had hosted a week ago, which had been poorly attended. Rick should have picked a game night. You couldn't go wrong with the Leafs and the Sens.

Sue put down four mugs on a table inside one of the booths. A chunky guy in a baseball hat and Oilers sweatshirt—whom she recognized as a worker in the chemical plant—grabbed her hand and pouted a kiss. "Hey Sue, think of going out one of these days?"

"I don't do married guys, Chuck," she countered and quickly turned away to a patron at another table who was trying to catch her attention. She heard a muted "Dyke" grunted behind her. Her decision not to entertain local men, especially married ones, since Bob had passed away, had earned her names like "Frigidaire," "Ice-Maid," and "Cockteaser," to name a few.

A roar went through the room as the Leafs scored seconds before the second period ended.

She went behind the bar and mixed a couple of whiskey sours and a screwdriver and drew three mugs of assorted ale from the taps. She rang up the tabs to keep score. The noise was deafening as the period-ending whistle blew, and everyone charged back to the bar for refreshments. She was flooded with requests, and she had to write them down to keep score. Old Macy, his belly pushing up behind the bar was pontificating and holding forth at the other end.

Then Sue saw what the extra commotion was about. Frank Morgan had timed the perfect entrance at the whistle so as not to deflect his audience's rapt attention from the game. And he had brought along his companion, Art Hamilton, for support.

Seeing Frank and feeling Chuck's hot paw still on her hand made her feel sluttish. *I don't do married guys! Yeah, right!*

Frank was being mobbed by the crowd at the bar, and he was in his "hello, boys" mode, joking at the Senators' fumbling of the puck in the last period. "Did you see that play?" He had obviously been watching the game closely on some portable TV before making his grand appearance. If he saw Sue, he ignored her. She felt relieved and concentrated on filling her drinks orders.

Art came up to the bar and said, "Sue, a round of drinks for everyone here."

"It'll take a while," she said. "I'm busy with this round."

Macy, at the other end of the bar, frowned at her and butted in. "It will be done, Mr. Hamilton, no problem." He started hauling glasses onto the bar and shouted, "Hey folks—drinks on Mr. Hamilton." Another rush surged towards Macy.

Frank jumped up on a table and raised a foaming flagon. "Folks, I know how important this game is to you, so I will be quick. If I am elected for this new term, I promise to open a new hockey arena at the abandoned municipal property beside the chemical plant. Mr. Art

Hamilton here, who has been generous with drinks tonight, has promised to buy the property and to co-sponsor the construction. Think of it—very soon your kids will get all the ice-time they need—no more will they be running off to Toronto or Ottawa to realize their dreams—they could do it right here in Milltown."

A roar of approval and raised glasses, sloshing beer all over the place, drowned out Sue's panicky thought. She felt sweat trickle down her sides. Complimentary beer mugs were being handed over to everyone and a toast to the returning mayor went up.

"Over my dead body, Frank!"

The voice coming from the doorway cut in during the lull when everyone was busy downing their toast. Heads turned, and in the doorway stood Rick Jones: faded maroon felt jacket opened to reveal a black shirt with the top buttons undone, greying chest hairs—still luxuriant—poking out, washed out denim jeans, and boots.

Sniggers began in the background. Sue heard pernicious ones, like, "Give it up, Rick." "Have another drink and shut the fuck-up, Jones." Eventually, they subsided as Rick continued to stand there like an accusing finger, staring Frank down.

Art smiled artificially and walked over, taking Rick by the shoulder. "Come now, Rick, this is Frank's party. You had yours last week. It's not good business for competing candidates to be at the same function."

Rick shook Art off. "I came in for a drink. This is still a public place isn't it? Or is this joint going to be renamed "Hamilton's Pub" one of these days? Like just about everything else in this town."

Art gesticulated to Macy, the fixed smile still on his face. "Give our Rick, here, a drink, Pat."

"I'll pay for my own." Rick moved to the bar, and people made way for him. He took up a position just in front of Sue.

"Hi Sue. It's been awhile." His hard stare softened, and for once she could see the deep sadness in his face.

"Good to see ya, Rick. Yes, it has been awhile." She wanted to reach out and touch his hand, take him away from this hostile place where everyone was ready to crucify him.

He took a sip of the scotch that Macy placed in front of him and turned around to face the crowd. Sue could see his salt and pepper curls skirting the edges of his jacket collar, which, at this proximity, was really showing its age. "So, you are building a hockey rink eh, Frank. How many jobs do you think that's going to bring to the town?"

Frank, still standing on the table, shot back, his face flushing, "It's not always about jobs, Rick—it's about the quality of life. We don't want kids on the street doing drugs out of boredom. We want them busy and active."

Rick turned to the patrons. "Tell me, how many of you can afford those luxury condominiums going up all over the place? How many of you guys are buying shacks out in the country and commuting on icy roads to work in town because there is no more affordable housing here? How many of you are going to be too drunk to drive back tonight because you live too far now? How many of you are driving without licenses because they were revoked long ago?"

An uneasy silence took over. The final period of the game had begun on TV, but Macy had turned the volume down during the break, and no one was paying attention anymore.

"Hamilton—" Rick had switched his gaze over to Art who was standing on the fringe of the crowd, his smile, having evaporated, was replaced with a scowl. "Did you give Joe Saxon his job back, so he would write that piece about me in your newspaper? Is Joe here tonight?"

"Joe's in Florida this week," someone offered at the back.

"An unemployed man goes to Florida—you really pay well for your journalism, Art." Rick said and downed his drink, wrinkling his face.

Art Hamilton's face flushed a deep red. "You've overstayed your welcome, Rick. Now that you've had your drink, why don't you leave?

And let me give you a piece of advice—advice you have never taken in your catastrophic political career. We don't like confrontation in this town—anywhere, for that matter. If you were less combative and insulting, you might make a better politician."

Rick tossed a crumpled note on the counter and made for the door. "And be a 'yes man' to big business, Art? Like your gopher, Frank, here? Dream on, buddy."

Sue slipped out the back door just as Rick stood on the sidewalk looking to cross the road. She stayed in the shadow of the alley and called out to him.

"Rick!"

He turned, caught sight of her, and smiled, "Sue—"

"Shh! I've got to go back. But I have to see you about something."

"Why, sure—let's go to my place. Right now."

She remained in shadow. "No, I have to get back. I'm still on shift. I'll pop by on my way home. About midnight. Stay up."

Then she slipped back into the pub.

***

He was waiting for her past midnight when she hurried up the hill after her shift to his darkened house, which was illuminated only by a dim light in the living room, throwing his shadow picking at his guitar upon the drawn curtains. The dogs barked in the back yard somewhere as she pushed through the creaking, rusty gate.

The porch light went on, and he stood in the doorway, the black shirt further unbuttoned; the hair on his lower body was darker. He made no excuse to cover his semi nakedness but waved her in unselfconsciously.

She entered the musty house; books in piles lined the corridor leading into the living room. Faded blue curtains shrouded the windows and newspapers and magazines were strewn over the scratched hardwood floor. She moved a pile of papers and sat down on the worn leather sofa, its springs complaining under her.

"Drink?" he asked, moving over to the bar, which strangely looked stocked and clean, as if this and the well-oiled seat, upon which reposed the sleek guitar, were the only places Rick habituated in the room.

"Water would be fine."

He poured himself a scotch and a glass of water for her. As he handed her the glass, she saw his hands tremble. Either excitement or the DT's, she thought.

"You put on a good show in there tonight."

He laughed. "You didn't come all this way to tell me that, did you?"

"Well, I thought I would pass on the compliment." She looked around the room. "It doesn't look like you get any compliments these days."

He looked glumly at his glass. "You know, you are damned right about that. I have a flawed value proposition. I live in a swanky house from the outside and come across as hollow when I stand up for the poor. But inside…isn't this house shabby? I mean, really poor? Am I not one of them?"

"It could do with sprucing up," she said, not wanting to hurt his feelings. Right now, the way he was staring into his glass, she wondered if he was close to tears.

"I'm selling it and moving into an apartment."

"A luxury condo? Now, that would go down well!"

"No, closer to where your building is."

"That's skid row, Rick—where the single mothers, widows, factory workers on welfare, and ailing seniors live. That wouldn't be good for your image as a politician."

"Well, it's about time we kill the stereotype."

"I wish you luck." Then she remembered what she had come about. She fished out the photocopy from her handbag and passed it to him. He whistled as he read it. "The kids are going to be playing hockey on a piece of polluted land. This is dynamite."

"But we can't use it now, until they actually start building without a clean-up. Not in time to bring Frank down from his mayoral bid, unfortunately. That's what worries me about this letter."

Rick laughed hollowly. "You don't think I've got much hope, have you?"

"Without being disrespectful, Rick, I think you are a loose cannon. Haven't you learned?"

He got up and paced. He flung the curtains in the lakeside windows open, sending a puff of dust in their wake.

"See that house up on the hill. Hamilton's had it in for me for a long time. And he has won every time. It gets to a point where you start losing your patience, and it's downhill after that."

"You have been on a downward spiral long before that, Rick. Long before Brenda died."

"Art blames me for that, too. He thinks Brenda's and Martha's unconnected suicides are related."

"Their men disappointed them—that's the connection!"

Rick turned back from the window and his countenance was haggard, as if her words had pulled and mashed his face.

"I wanted it all, Sue."

"And you did not have a moral bone to anchor yourself to."

He looked like he was about to fall on the floor and faint; he wilted with every cutting remark she made, as if the truth beat him down like nails.

She felt pity and suddenly wanted to reach up to him, take him in her arms like she had done to Bob in his last days, when her late husband had been too ill to sit up.

Rick sat down on the sofa next to her, keeping his distance, staring out the open window.

"Every time I slipped, I paid." He pointed at the Hamilton house. "He hasn't."

"He hasn't slipped yet."

"But he will this time." Rick patted the photocopy on his thigh. He grinned suddenly, his sad eyes lit with a wild enthusiasm she had only seen in his youth. "I owe you."

She rose suddenly. "You have angels in places, Rick—even though you choose to ignore them. Don't screw this one up."

He made to rise, but she restrained him. "I'll let myself out."

She left him staring at the paper.

***

Across the trees and on the hill outside town, with a clear view of the lake, the Hamilton house glowed, its lights ablaze. The wide lane, cut between trees by the main road, wound around half a kilometre, ascended to the furthest point uphill, and came around a bend of tall poplars to face the old American-built, Grecian style mansion. The first owner was an eccentric tobacco planter from New Orleans of Cajun extraction, who had built the house as his summer retreat, something to do with wanting to be closer to his Acadian origins. In the distance, the dark lake lapped the borders of Milltown.

Frank paced the giant study. Art was sitting at his sprawling oak desk smoking a cigar, silently reflective.

"He's going to create trouble, I know it, Art."

Art let out a stream of smoke. He never inhaled; cigars were for effect, and he always kept a good collection of Churchills for guests. But Frank was too agitated to smoke tonight.

"We won't build the rink until after the election," Art said.

"But it's going to happen during my term."

"The builders will be from Toronto. No locals. I'll have the place up and running in a month. And we will rope in the volunteer groups to drum up excitement. Keep the focus off the environment."

Frank stopped his pacing and looked helplessly at Art. "You think this will work?"

"You saw the acknowledgment from the guys in the pub tonight. This is the best thing that's happened to this town. Even the adults will be using that rink in no time."

"Wouldn't it be cheaper and easier to clean the whole place up?"

Art rose from his desk, scowling again. "Now look here, Frank— we are not going into that again. I don't want to give the environmentalists in this town any more fuel."

"Rick Jones has contacts in Toronto. What if he contacts the other buyer?"

"Unlikely. The man's a drunk, okay? He cannot keep his finances in order these days, let alone try to get at me. I wouldn't worry about it."

Frank resumed his pacing, shaking his head as if trying to convince himself. "Maybe I'm over-reacting."

"I'd be more interested in keeping an eye on Sue Miller. She's close to Rick. How much of your confidential work does she handle?"

A sly smile escaped Frank's portly face. "Sue is fine. She knows where her bread is buttered. And boy, do I have all the butter where she is concerned. That stuff between her and Rick is old hat. She told me."

"In that case, you have nothing to worry, my friend. Just go out there and win the election." Art stubbed out his cigar. He wanted to go to bed and hoped his guest would take the hint and leave.

Seven

Billy parked his mother's car around the block from South Asian Delights and sat, palms clammy, heart beating. Would she come today? A week ago, on impulse, he had invited Saro out—again—for a drive in the country, and she had finally accepted. She could only go out tonight as it was her free evening from working in the restaurant. Both her parents would be on duty, so they would not miss her leaving the house for a short while. She made him promise he would bring her back by 9:00 p.m.

It was mid May and election signs dominated Main Street. Frank Morgan's posters outnumbered Rick Jones' by four to one. Yet Billy wanted Rick to win.

Rick had taught him to hit golf balls into the lake when Billy was doing his paper run, years ago. He'd ditch his paper cart and run around the back if he saw Rick's red crumbling Chevy Malibu in the driveway. Rick would pull out his clubs and a bucket of used balls, line them up, and hit one ball at a time off the back stoop, right out into the lake.

"Hey, kid—let me show you," Rick had said the first time when this awestruck thirteen-year-old had stumbled on him in action. Very soon, Billy got the hang of it and was hitting balls further and further into the water, only stopping when a boat went by. At the end of that first summer, Rick gave Billy his old set of clubs. Billy still had them and got out on the public course a few times in the summer when he had spare cash.

A shadow moving in the alley brought him back to the present. Saro, head covered in a scarf, quickly opened the passenger door and got in. "Sorry I'm late—let's go."

He gunned the car, just as a light went on above the restaurant.

"Go, go," she almost yelled as he pulled the car into Main Street and headed out of town.

"Whoa! Calm down. We'll have the cops after us if I drive any faster."

"Worse," she said, looking back. "Mahesh was at the window."

"Have you never been out with boys before?"

"I have. But my parents don't know."

"Why don't you just tell them?"

"I am not sure how they will react. And they have so much on their minds right now. They came to this country for us. At least, that is what my mother says all the time. And our restaurant is not doing so well."

"Well, I bought take-out from you guys earlier—like I promised." The aromatic smells from the parcels in the back seat were already filling up the car.

"Thank you." There was appreciation in her voice, and he darted a look at her. She was studying him as he drove. He stepped on the accelerator, feeling empowered.

"Where are we going?" she asked.

"Up to the old mill. This town gets its name from the mill. It's abandoned now, but there's a great view onto the lake from over there. If we get there before sunset, that is."

He turned off Highway 2 on to a dirt road that streaked between newly seeded barley and corn fields. Old barns, farmhouses, and grain silos slid by as he kicked up dust to turn right on to another paved road that ran parallel to the highway for a few kilometres and then turned inland into the hills.

Saro shook her hair loose from her scarf and began to relax. "Thank you for bringing me out. I have been here almost three months and have only been inside the town limits."

"Your dad does not take you for drives?"

"All my family does is work. We are immigrants, remember? The ones at the bottom of the pile." There was a hint of bitterness in her voice. "My mother said that when she was my age in Sri Lanka, her family had maids, a gardener, and a driver to attend to their needs."

"If it's any consolation to you, I am at the bottom of the pile, too. And I am home-grown."

"Why have you not progressed?" She seemed genuinely puzzled. "With all that this country has to offer, you should have been well-off by now—at least, that is what my father says."

"We were 'well-off' until my father died of cancer. He did not believe in life insurance, and by the time he was diagnosed it was too late to get any. We had just bought a big house in a subdivision in town. Mom could not meet the mortgage payments, so we lost the house. It's the usual hard-luck Canadian story."

"I am sorry to hear that."

He sensed the empathy in her voice but could not turn to look at her as they were twisting and turning around hilly curves.

The road widened into a broken, rutty one and the rush of water nearby came clearly to their ears. Twilight was falling and the lights in Milltown below could be seen to their right about five kilometres away. Billy pulled the car off the road and parked in a grassy verge. "We have to walk from here." He stepped on the foot brake.

He took out the parcel of food and pulled out a blanket from the rear seat. "Grab this blanket. We'll be needing it where we're going." He also took a flashlight from the glove compartment. "It will be dark coming back."

Then he took her hand and led her up the trail. This was his turf and he felt confident. They struck off along an old trodden path that was seeing the new weeds of spring smother it. Mosquitoes bit as they neared the sound of the river. "The river goes downhill here. That's why they built the mill at this elevation," he explained.

He felt her tug on his hand as they walked. "How much further?" Her voice was beginning to sound anxious.

"Just around the bend, here."

An old wooden structure, once a shed, came into view. Its roof had given way in places, and the boards of the walls looked as if they could follow suit at any moment. Debris surrounded the building: old tires, jagged pieces of masonry, rusty metal containers, and the ruins of a pick-up truck, its tires flattened and embedded in the earth.

"This is the mill?" Sarojini halted.

He laughed. "No, this is the caretaker's quarters. Come along, just a bit further."

They passed the shed, and the path broadened into a clearing strewn with rocks and more debris; the roaring river came into view, passing off to their right through the trees, descending below them just ahead. They topped the hill in front, and Saro gasped.

In front of them, down a steep incline, the river narrowed and squeezed through rocks on either side, shooting off in the direction of the lights in Milltown. On the right bank, where the water was at its fiercest, a dilapidated three-storey stone building stood, defiant to the passing torrent.

"That's the mill," Billy said.

They inched downhill to the building. A faded "No Trespassing" sign on the wall looked enigmatic. The walls looked like they would last another hundred years, even if the roof was decayed and crumbling. Some rafters lay strewn around the structure like old fruit forgotten in last season's plucking. The faded wooden double doors were shut, but Billy just lifted the lever and threw open one side. "Come on, I'll show you inside. This is where I used to play as a child."

Even though the dying daylight filtered in from the upper windows that had lost their shutters and panes, the inside was in semi-darkness. Billy waved the flashlight to point out the various features: the cold, dark packing room that still had a few old crates with rats running between them; a four-foot tall slate with archaic chalk writing on it indicating weights and measures of grist processed back in the eighteen hundreds; a mammoth weighing scale with weights scattered around it; the grist room, its walls smudged in white as if workers had taken the remaining output and thrown it against the walls in anger as they departed; and the main pressing room where the giant grinding wheel once stood spinning to the rushing water running underneath. The wheel had been dismantled and moved off to the side, to lean against a wall. The place it had once productively occupied was a gaping hole looking down into the countryside and distant Lake Ontario.

Billy explained. "They built the first mill in 1835. That's the one that ran on hydro power generated off the river. The old millstone and the other artefacts belong to that era. When my grandfather worked here it was more mechanized. They had to computerize if they were going to survive, but they ran out of money."

Sarojini held her breath as she went from room to room. They had to duck their heads in one place when a clutch of bats suddenly struck off from their slumber.

"There is so much history here. Why was it allowed to go to ruin?"

"Money. My grandfather worked in this mill all his life. Mom and Dad tried to organize a fund to turn this place into a museum, but they didn't get far."

"Why doesn't the town council do something about it?" Saro's voice had a bite to it.

"They've got other things to spend their money on. We couldn't get Art Hamilton interested in it. He would have made it happen."

"Hamilton? He's our landlord."

"He owns half of Milltown." It was Billy's turn to show his acidity.

"You don't seem to like Mr. Hamilton," Sarojini said.

"No, I don't. Come on, we have to go outside and have our food. I know just the place by the riverbank where it's not too overgrown."

Suddenly, he wanted to get out and not carry on this line of conversation.

As they retraced their path, Sarojini kicked a bolt in the floor and stumbled, falling to her knees. Billy quickly placed the flashlight on the floor and reached to help her up.

"You okay?"

But Sarojini was swiping the dust and cobwebs aside. "There is a trapdoor here."

"Don't go in there," Billy shouted, then checked himself.

"Where does it lead?" Saro seemed genuinely intrigued.

"Not today. I will take you in there another time." He pulled her to her feet, grabbed the flashlight, and led the way out of the building.

As they stepped into the fading light, he paused as he caught her brushing hair off her face. In those last rays of the sun, with her face in profile, she was beautiful, and he just stared, finally relaxing and accepting why he had wanted to bring her out here—to have her only to himself, to be able to drink in her beauty away from the eyes and desires of others.

She caught him staring and smiled impishly. "Haven't you dated an Asian girl before?"

"Never. . ." he stammered.

Then she arched her eyebrows. "Can I trust you?"

He stammered again, her direct onslaught took him by surprise. "Sure—"

They were very close to each other, and he could feel and smell her breath, tinged with chewing gum. As the wind ruffled her black luxuriant hair, the smell of jasmine wafted towards him. He felt dizzy and his palms broke out in a sweat. He reached out instinctively to draw her to him, but she feinted and swerved out of his grip. Her brows furrowed in anger, and she placed her hands on her hips and pouted. "I thought I could trust you!"

"No, Saro—it's not what you think. I kinda got carried away." He did not want to lose her now. He did not want her to run back to the car and demand that he take her home. "Here, let's go and set up the food, okay?"

The sudden switch of power from him to her, just by her mere act of withholding herself, made Saro seem stronger and even more desirable. In his bid to appease her, he felt that he was weakening. But he could not lose her—she had become too precious to him.

She must have sensed his caving in, for she threw her head back and laughed. "Okay, come along then, we cannot be late. I have to leave in half an hour."

He led her, meekly this time, around the back of the mill and uphill to where the river bank widened onto a grass verge beside the pond that fed the millrace below; the water here was rushing away from them and not spraying the banks with the mist of its charge. They washed their dusty hands in the pond. He spread the blanket on the grass, and she busied herself with opening the food parcels.

Her voice softened again. "It's very kind of you to buy stuff from our restaurant, but I would have sprung for pizza."

"You're kidding?" he said looking incredulously at her. "But your food is delicious! My mouth and eyes water all the time I eat it."

"Not mine. Not when you eat it every day. We have to eat the leftovers. We do not even have a choice."

They occupied themselves with eating for the next ten minutes. Sarojini ate very little, but she watched him, mopping his sweating brow and burping when the chillies hit the wrong spot. He was glad that he had brought along two bottles of chilled mineral water. He ended up drinking some of hers, too. She found it amusing at times and giggled, making him go redder in the face.

The wind blew in from the lake, bringing with it a touch of moisture. Saro shivered and folded her arms around herself.

"You wouldn't be cold if you ate this hot curry," he joked.

Instead, she leaned over to him and snuggled in the crook of his arm. He felt the blood throb at his temples. His cock was starting to get hard, and he could do nothing to curb it, nor did he want to. He quickly tossed the left-over plate of string-hoppers aside, rubbed his hand on a paper napkin, and placed his arm over her, shielding her from the damp. They stayed that way silently until the sun went over the horizon and the dark started settling in rapidly.

"Will you bring me here again sometime?" she asked, her words flowing languorously. "It's very peaceful."

"Sure." He rubbed his head against her silken mane, the white of her scalp where her hair parted in the centre being a sharp contrast to the lush growth that cascaded over her shoulders like an ebony waterfall.

He felt awkward and strange with her, unlike with most girls who were usually curious to find out everything about their date and mostly wanted to talk or fuck or both; Saro was content to lie with him, an aura of peace and harmony emanating around and between them. For a moment he was transposed to a different time, not long ago, when he had been brushing up against another head of hair—blonde—Jen: the one he could not protect. The trapdoor sprung into his mind. A fit of panic seized him, and his heart started to race. Saro broke away and looked at him anxiously.

"Do I make you uncomfortable?"

"No—" he blurted. "No, it's not that." And to convince her, he reached out and pulled her to him desperately. He was going to protect her this time. He reached down, and using the cover of the gathering dusk, kissed her. He was caught unprepared for the kiss she returned, more aggressive than his, her tongue drawing him out, playing with him, coddling him and trailing off with soothing pats to his lips with hers.

"You kiss good!" he exclaimed, blushing.

"You like it?"

"You bet. When will you come out with me next?"

"Saturday, at noon. My parents are going into Toronto for a community function. But I have to be back by four o'clock."

"Sure—I'll pick you up."

"Come along." She had risen and was dusting and folding the blanket. "I have to get back now."

***

The second time he brought her to the mill she asked him about the trapdoor again. He shrugged and relented. "Might as well get this one over with," he said. "Or you're never going to give me a moment's peace."

Saro giggled. "I see that you are used to being harassed by women."

"My mom harasses me a lot, with all the housework and homework and part-time work I have to do. She wants me to be more successful than my dad." He was talking to quell the anxiety of going down the trapdoor. It was not only Saro's curiosity driving him, he realized, but his own desire to wrest a ghost.

"Watch your step," he said, heaving the heavy trapdoor up and easing it on the floor. A rush of stale air hit them, making Saro gag.

"Still want to go down?" he asked.

She cleared her throat and nodded.

He shone the flashlight over a short flight of stairs leading down. It got colder as they descended. The stale air began dissipating quickly and that was a relief. Billy's heart was beating harder, and he was feeling sick to his stomach. He flashed the torch against the south wall—the frescos were still there, faded now, and covered in lines of mould: nymphs in the Garden of Eden as his grandfather had painted them. A metal fireplace encased in dust sat in the centre of the room with its chimney disappearing into the dark of the ceiling. A broken window high on the east wall ushered in a dim ray of daylight. A bookcase, looking of more recent construction, lined the other wall, the hard-bound volumes dusty and falling apart. Billy pulled out a book, and something scurried off behind it in the dark. Moisture had twisted and pasted the pages together—*Ben Hur*, the lettering glimmered in the dark. The musty camp bed against the remaining wall with its side table, the heavy, solid glass ashtray still containing crushed cigar ash at its base, and the lamp that was covered in cobwebs were the only other remaining objects in the room.

"Who lived here?" Saro's voice quivered.

"My grandfather. Thomas Miller. He was the supervisor of the mill and lived in the lodge up the road. When he heard the mill was being shut down, he barricaded himself in this cellar, so that the town authorities could not embarrass themselves by evicting him."

"Do you remember him?"

"No. He died before I was born. He painted these frescos during the three years he spent in here, reading all the books he had never had the time to read during his working life, writing petitions all the way up to the Prime Minister. My dad had just started working as an apprentice at the newly opened chemical plant and used to bring Grandpa his meals and leave them at the door. Grandpa's lungs finally packed up. I never met him but only heard of the stories surrounding him. 'A Miller I was born, a miller I will die,' was his rallying cry, according to Dad. They nicknamed the place Old Tom's Mill after it was abandoned. The bookcase was really broken down, so I built a new one with leftovers I got for free from the hardware store."

"I can understand his reluctance to leave. My parents had difficulty leaving Sri Lanka. Especially Ammi, my mother. She said her folks belonged to descendants from King Vijaya who came to Sri Lanka in the first century. My father had a hard time convincing her to come over to Canada when they started targeting him as a Tamil."

"Is your father not a Sri Lankan too?"

"Yes, he is, and he traces his ancestry to the Indian kings who ruled Jaffna even before the first European colonizers came in the sixteenth century."

Billy fingered another book, then dislodged it from the shelf, sending a fluff of dust into the air. "Sixteenth century—wow! And your dad does not think he belongs to Sri Lanka? This book is called *The United Empire Loyalist History in Canada*—my grandfather's side of the family. And they came to Canada only after 1812. I wish Grandpa had met your dad."

"He should have met the idiots who burned down our house. Maybe he could have drilled some sense into their heads."

Billy was glad the story of his grandfather had taken his mind off the other incidents that had taken place in this room. He felt satisfied. This was the first time since that awful night he had ventured here. And Saro's conversation had helped keep his courage up. Just her presence had been enough.

"We should go back up," he said and shone the flashlight towards the stairs.

Eight

Art checked his suit in the reception room mirror before entering the restaurant. Purple silk handkerchief sticking out at just the right angle from his grey-black suit, thin purple diagonal stripes on a navy-blue tie, tasselled black shoes to round everything off. He ran his hand gently through his well combed and greased hair, straightened his tie, and pushed through the glass doors.

"Good evening, Mr. Hamilton." The petite hostess recognized him instantly. "Your table is ready. And your guest is here."

He followed her, past diners talking in low whispers, to his favourite table by the window that overlooked the harbour. The higher the class of restaurant, he thought, the more discreet the talk, as if rich people had more secrets. Still Fabian's in Port Mossman, the next large town in the county, was Art's favourite venue for private business discussions, away from the prying eyes of Milltown. And their food was damned good, too!

Jane Garner sat facing him, a cocktail already half consumed. She sat straight, her black hair falling over her shoulders, yet the dark business suit did not conceal a deep neckline. She had small, firm breasts; an athletic woman, tall—one could guess, even though she was seated.

"Hello, Mr. Hamilton," she said, rising and extending a firm hand that he took gently in his, feeling the ring—not a wedding ring, he knew. He knew a lot about her already.

"I am sorry I'm late. There was an unexpected glitch at the plant."

She smiled coolly, seeing through his deliberate lie. "I am used to waiting for important clients. I decided to make myself comfortable. The view is pretty from here, even at night."

He ordered a scotch and soda for himself and called for the dinner menu.

"This is unexpected," she said. "I thought we were only having a drink."

"You have to sample the food here," he insisted. "Besides, this may take some time."

She smiled playfully, took a sip from her drink, and looked him over, her intelligent green eyes sizing him up. "In that case, I'll switch off my hourly rate clock for tonight."

Over a dinner of escargot, mushroom soup, racks of lamb, an array of sautéed and herbed vegetables, and wild rice in a lemon and white wine broth, they talked about their mutual businesses— very formal. Jane skilfully dodged questions that got too personal.

She was forthcoming about some of the facts he had got on her: her early apprenticeship on Bay Street in Toronto at one of the Big Four; the partnership move to Argyll, Forbes & Associates; the gruelling hours, jetting about the country; the burnout; and her purchase of the accounting firm of Mason and Associates in Milltown last year.

She did not mention the failed marriage, the son in custody of his father in Toronto, the ruling that she was an unfit mother, never being available to care for her child, the hint of scandal around a deal that had not been deemed kosher by the provincial public accountants' association. But she did drink most of the bottle of reserve Chilean 1995 Carmenere he ordered with dinner. He admired her stony resolve despite his attempts to melt her. By the end of the meal, her steely endurance, despite the alcohol and the casual talk, was beginning to excite him.

They ordered coffee—Spanish for him, café au lait for her—and he decided to stop fencing around.

"I need you to handle a set of books for me. I am setting up a subsidiary."

"And your regular accountant is too busy?" she said slowly, dropping a cube of brown sugar into her coffee and stirring the creamy foam on the top.

Art smiled. "Let's say he is not good at matters that lie outside his comfort zone."

He pulled a draft prospectus out of his jacket pocket. "Take a look at this. Let me know if it will fly."

She gave it a glance, long fingernails coated a deep red, skilfully flipping pages.

"Pesticides."

"Hmm, hmm." He sipped his coffee. "You have a reputation for managing the books of difficult companies."

She placed the papers down on the table. "What else do you know about me, Mr. Hamilton?"

He smiled, studying her over the edge of his cup. "Enough to know that we both live on the edge. That is why I selected you."

She looked out the window. A tug boat tooted its horn and slid out of the harbour. They watched it depart in silence.

"My fee will be high," she said finally, still looking out the window. Then she turned towards him. "I am sure that is not a concern for you."

"Absolutely not. I pay for quality work. And my remuneration is flexible—in any way you want it."

She raised her mug. "Then here's to a good partnership. This dinner was an excellent beginning."

***

Andy jerked off in the dark on his bunk. The lessening of his meds gave him stronger erections, and he had to masturbate, or he felt like shit. He didn't even need the porn mags under his mattress anymore. Warren, in the next bunk, snored; he was on heavy Vallium or else he screamed at night and woke everyone up. Andy turned to the wall as the hot gunk shot out of him. He waited for the quivering in his toes to settle and drew in a yawn. He wiped his hands on the bed sheet—it stunk anyway—pulled his pyjamas up and turned over on his back. Warren continued to snore, and then farted, and the air was a thick mixture of rotten egg and mouldy sperm.

The "lifers," the ones Henry said were unfixable, had come around in the showers earlier today. That punk Butch had squeezed Andy's wet bottom. Butch was thirty pounds heavier and a head taller than Andy. "I'm going to ram my cock up your ass one of these days," he'd said, guffawing and turning to his sycophantic followers for approval.

Every coward needed his band of followers, Andy had realized, since being let out into the general population. His reputation as a killer didn't count. Out here, the gangs and cliques made the rules.

When Butch had his head temporarily turned towards his buddies, Andy lashed out, grabbing the big guy's balls in his hand and squeezing. Butch yelped and sank like a deflated balloon. His followers fell back; one guy yelled for the guards.

"You fucker," Andy screamed, his eyes going crazy with the power he had suddenly acquired. *This big jerk-off is not so big after all when grabbed by the nuts.* "You'll never get that thing up to shove in my ass."

All Andy saw was this squirming cur in front of him, his balls turning soft in his hands; Butch's face was blue by the time a truncheon cracked on Andy's knuckles, making him release his grip. Three guards had entered the showers.

Henry was sweating, getting wet in the spray from the showers, trying to separate them. "You crazy, kid—you are going back to solitary—maybe that's what you wanted."

Andy merely curled his lip at Henry. "He started it."

"The runt wiggled his ass at Butch," one of the sycophants said.

"Fuck off!" Andy shot back.

Butch was huddled in a ball on the floor, struggling for breath, the shower pounding relentlessly on his black hair.

Henry pushed Andy ahead of him. Another guard followed them. "Get your clothes. You're confined to your room till the Super gets here tomorrow morning. Then you are going back into the can." Henry leaned into Andy's ear. "For your own sake!"

In his bed now, Andy wanted his last night in the company of his peers to end. Warren was no company at all, snoring and inhabiting some drug-induced netherworld. Warren farted again in his sleep, and was blissfully unaware of the mounting stench in the room. Solitary was better.

It had felt good taking that big asshole, Butch, down. The sense of power was exhilarating—it had felt just like walking through that school dorm, shooting those fuckers who had humiliated him. The memory flooded back. Down into the yard where the blonde angel stood; the one he wanted for himself, so no one could have her.

"Be my girl," he had commanded her.

"Never," she spat back, daring him in the hot sun while people were screaming and running for cover. And he had shot her. He was his father's son, never take defeat or have anyone get the better of you. He had seen his father crush employees and smaller people, seen him crush his mother too. Andy hated his father, but he had his genes in him, and they made him feel powerful when he crushed people like ants.

And then, as she fell bleeding from the mouth, that asshole, Billy, had rushed out. Billy—his childhood buddy, the one who taught him how to fish and hunt and shoot rabbits in the abandoned farmlands down by the mill. The ass who had been hanging around with the blonde angel. The bastard who had stolen his angel. It was nice raising the gun to pick Billy's head off. He still wondered what happened then. Billy ignored the gun and knelt, cradling the angel in his arms, lifting her up, deliberately turning his back on Andy, carrying her into the gym. *He was telling me to fuck off!* Andy had followed them that time, determined not to be ignored or shaken off, shooting the locks off the gym doors.

"Look at me, you bastard. I'm going to kill you," Andy screamed.

Billy ignored him and continued to wipe dust and blood from the angel.

That's when the fury went out of him, and he dropped the gun, crying and falling to his knees in front of them. This game had lost its interest.

The police had found him there, sobbing.

Andy rolled in his bed. He had been weak that time. If there was a repeat, he would not be such a jerk. That's why it felt good doing really dangerous things like squeezing Butch's balls, knowing full-well that he had run the risk of getting mauled by the rest of Butch's gang. Push the envelope and see what happens. That's what his father did, day in and day out, as he built his empire in Milltown. He'd show his father what he could do.

He heard the key turn in the cell door. The guards had locked him in earlier. Who the fuck was that? Then it dawned on him—Warren had been OD'd for the night. This was part of a plan with the guards in cahoots. He swivelled off the bed, hitting the floor in his bare feet. Two dim figures were creeping in through the crack in the door. The night lamp was useless as a weapon. Andy filled his lungs and let out an unearthly yell, the one he had practised at home, to rattle his father crazy after his mother died. Dad had came rushing in that first time, and for once, Andy had seen panic and fear in his old man. After that, his subsequent nightly yells had become passé, like the boy crying wolf, and his father had smacked him whenever he "misbehaved."

He was not going to get beaten up by Butch and his bunch tonight. Andy upped his screams, enjoying the sound as it ripped through the corridors via the open door. The two figures froze in the doorway, then retreated, slinking away like shadows as lights went on in the hallway. Warren slept through the commotion.

Skelton, the night guard, poked his head in the doorway, shining a flashlight on Andy. "What's up kiddo—bad dreams again?" The flashlight swung around the vicinity and stopped on the wall. "Wet dreams, eh?"

"You'd better not let those assholes in here."

"What assholes?" Skelton asked sweetly. "Seeing ghosts? You scared without Henry to protect you?"

"I'm not scared. Just don't let those bastards in here."

"Maybe you need some Valium—like your pal over there. Shit, it stinks in here."

"I don't need no drugs. Tell your buddies that the next bastard who walks through that door is going to get killed."

"Hey, hey—no tough talk, okay? You've gotta be locked up alone and left to rot, that's what." Skelton bowed his head and closed the door behind him. Andy heard the key turn in the lock. There would be no more intruders that night. Butch and his buddies had blown their chance. Tomorrow it would be back to solitary and the right place to launch the next part of his plan.

Nine

Sam was in a good mood. It was a sunny, warm day, and the crowd on Main Street had increased. These were not the transient types that came in on weekends to sit on the beach with their homemade food and drinks in coolers, the leftovers of which clogged the town's garbage bins after they left. These were local people from rural farms and hamlets, attracted to vote at the election booth that had been set up in the municipal offices, down the street from South Asian Delights.

Sam had seized the opportunity to put out his "free samples" table on the sidewalk. Malani was busy turning out vadais, fish cutlets, patties, and devilled beef for the passersby heading to cast their votes. Many stopped and picked at the bites with curiosity, smacking lips and raising eyebrows afterwards, and accepting the icy, cool Sri Lankan style sherbet to quench their ignited mouths. Sam grinned and dished out his samples liberally, trying to stifle panicked thoughts about the cost of this endeavour when the accounts had to be settled. But this was his rare occasion to showcase himself in front of the locals, especially the ones who did not come into town that often. He heard muffled words like, "Bloody hot…" "but very tasty…" "spicy, hmm…" "I wonder whether we should get some for later at home." All good comments, so he forced himself to smile and dole out more.

Across the street, the long-haired lawyer who had patronized South Asian Delights on more than one occasion, had a table spread out, too, with pamphlets on the environment and going "green." A megaphone hung from Rick Jones' neck, and he would raise it occasionally and shout, "Vote for Change…Vote for Clean…Let's clean this town out." But no one seemed to be paying any attention. More people were interested in the vadais and the fish cutlets and the patties and the devilled beef. And the sherbet, of course. Sam felt like asking Mr. Jones to set his table beside his, perhaps he would get more of an audience. But then, Sam realized, that the Mayoral incumbent was also his landlord's choice, and overt support for the opposition may not be good for business. Finally, he prepared a paper plate of assorted bites, filled a paper cup of sherbet, and crossed the road over to Rick Jones.

"Here, Mr. Jones, I thought you might be hungry with all this campaigning." Sam extended the plate.

Rick Jones looked hungry, indeed, and tired, and his eyes were bloodshot. "Thanks. The sherbet looks good." He downed the cool drink and placed the bites on his table next to the "green" pamphlets.

Sam edged closer. "Mr. Jones…"

Rick had just picked up his megaphone for another reminder on the looming climate crisis to those entering the municipal offices. Seeing Sam, he lowered the instrument, a slight look of annoyance clouding his face.

"Sorry to disturb you, sir," Sam continued. "I just wanted to tell you that I voted this morning. And I voted for you, sir. Just don't tell anyone."

Rick's tired features creased into a grin. "Why, thank you, my man! Not only do you feed me, but you vote for me."

"Shh!" Sam looked furtively about him. "Now I must return to my sample table. I can see the dishes are empty again."

Rick continued grinning. "I guess I recruited one voter, at least. I'm entitled to a break." He picked up a fish cutlet and popped it into his mouth.

***

Later that afternoon, Sam started to take down his table. The promotion had been a success. Three new couples had visited for lunch and several others had returned from the polling station to order take-out. Sam had taken personal care to attend to his new customers with extreme flourish and courtesy, sometimes even leaving his sample table unattended for several minutes. Whenever he returned, the dishes outside were licked clean. He was exhausted but happy. He carried the table inside and took down the "FREE SAMPLES" sign from where he had pinned it to the front door.

Malani was wiping the kitchen counter. She looked thinner than when they had lived in Toronto, and Sam noticed the grey popping around her temples. He went up to her and put his arm on her shoulder. "Mala, I think we are turning the corner. Those customers were so happy. They will be telling others. Soon this place will be hopping. We will be able to afford some real staff instead of bothering the children."

"I hope so." She swept back a wisp of long black hair from her damp forehead. "But the children should continue to work here. That way, we can keep an eye on them."

"They also need to do their sports and have their friends, no? Can't just study and work. We came to this country to give them opportunities, no?"

"Yes—but Saro is taking full use of those 'opportunities.' Have you seen her going out with that white boy?"

"Ah yes, but that is good, no? She is having friends here. She won't be moping and complaining, like our Mahesh."

"Next thing you know, she will be going out on weekends and late evening parties and all that stuff."

"What to do Mala—that is the Canadian way."

"Canadian way or not, we need to bring our children up with the proper values. Look at Mahesh—he does not forget where he comes from. He is proud to be a Sri Lankan."

"But he has to become a Canadian. What for taking that oath and all and saluting the Canadian flag?"

"We must never forget our roots. We came here because we were forced to."

"*Aney* Mala, let's not go over that again. You are Sinhalese and have a country to go back to. Where can I go? Where can our children, half-breeds with the surname Selvadurai, go to?"

"You are not the only one without a home. My own people killed Kamala. Can I ever forget that?"

Sensing the looming argument over Malani's dead sister, one that had occurred on more than one occasion recently, Sam hauled the table into the rear storage room. He returned to the kitchen and helped Malani wipe down the counters. He took the two big pans off the stove, added a liberal dose of soap cleanser and let them soak. Later, he would scrub out the grease. His hands hurt; he did not want to acknowledge that since coming to Canada his fingers had become more arthritic with the cold weather.

"I'm going to take a nap before the evening rush," Mala said and took the stairs to the upper floor.

Evening rush—that was a nice word. Yes, the evenings were bringing in a few more customers. These people were nice, Sam had to admit. They viewed him as strange, and patrons often asked Mala about her multi-coloured saris which still sat well on her buxom body. As long as the establishment was clean and the food exotic, his foreign-ness was accepted. If he had been trying to make burgers and steaks, he may have run out of business faster.

He worried about the children, Mahesh in particular. The boy was a loner, never went out with his friends much, even in Toronto. Mahesh had hated coming to Canada and had cried when they could not go back into their burning home to retrieve his books and cricket gear. He hated baseball—he said it was a cheap form of *Elle*. Why did fielders have to use a glove to catch a ball? Were their hands too soft? Mahesh had started to grow his hair long and read the ancient Hindu scripts, the Upanishads, with a passion. His mother was also pushing him towards the study of Buddhism. Mahesh would be better served to read up on

Canadian history, Sam thought. When Sam had talked to him about it, Mahesh had jumped at him.

"You call this *history?* Two hundred years of white people kicking red people out of their lands? Profiting from two World Wars and now calling themselves the Developed World? Give me a thousand years of history and I might be interested."

There was no arguing with these kids.

Now Saro—she was Sam's pride and joy. A beautiful child, right from the day she was born. She took to music and art from an early age and was always compassionate towards people. She understood the pain that her parents had gone through to come to this country; the shattered and abandoned dreams that they had to put aside first for survival and then for revival in this cold and foreign land. And she helped in the restaurant whenever she could. Mahesh was never around, always pleading that he was studying and getting off without admonishment from his doting mother, leaving the work for Saro.

Ah, well—life is a series of trials, and we are going through one now. Hopefully, with more people coming into the restaurant, with their ability to afford some hired help, their labour would start to ease before his hands gave out.

The restaurant phone rang just as he was about to head upstairs with a cup of tea and the well-thumbed communal newspaper.

Perhaps an advance reservation for dinner tonight!

Sam laid down the cup and grabbed the phone. "South Asian Delights, can I help you?"

The voice on the other side sounded crackly. A cell phone. "*Adey* Selvadurai—you have become a white boy now, hah?" The Sri Lankan accent was raw.

"Who is speaking?"

"Never mind who is speaking. Did you think you could just run away and become a Canadian, huh?"

Sam's palms started to get clammy, and there was a clutch in his throat. He remained silent.

"Your first obligation is to your motherland, *baba*."

"Canada is my motherland. I pay my taxes."

"But you have to pay our taxes, too."

"Listen—whoever you are. I am running an honest business. We are just scraping by. I do not have money for any causes."

"And you listen to us. We will give you three months to get your shit together. Then you *will* pay us. Ten percent of your revenues, understand? Nothing less. Or else those beautiful children you came here for—they will not need looking after again. Got it, *baba*?"

Sam sighed. He felt tired, there was no point in running anymore. "Give me your number. I will call you again when I have the money."

"We know where to find you, don't worry. Three months. Get nice and profitable by then. Then, you pay—got it?" The line went dead.

Ten

Billy Miller stirred as the fly buzzed in his ear like an accusing inquisitor. Beside him, Saro slumbered, her breathing even and contented, the blanket snug around her. The sun was going over the trees and soon darkness would descend, rapidly. He had to get her back home. His mind went back over the last two months since their first outing to the mill.

Saro had not wanted to proceed beyond kisses on that first date. On the third occasion, the time after they had visited his Grandpa's lair, she had relented to heavy petting. Billy had gone home with a cramp in his balls that lasted for three days. When he next met her, he tried to shy away from the petting, believing that she would not go all the way, and just end up giving him ball cramp again. She seemed to sense her hold over him and drew him in, kissing him aggressively, placing his hands on her breasts—he was powerless under the allure of her jasmine scented hair, musky odour, and the throbbing excitement of seeing her flawless breasts revealed to him. In his frenzy, he had come all over her body without even entering her, and she had laughed and asked him to get a condom the next time. He had gone home feeling humiliated and had not called her for a week. He was not to be in his self-imposed exile for long: his cell phone had rung one day as he was finishing his shift at the hardware store.

"So, you think you can take a girl out and ditch her, do you?" Saro sounded indignant and angry.

"I think we are going too fast," he said.

"So now I am a *fast* girl?"

"No…no, I didn't mean that. I think we just have to slow down. I liked those first meetings, when we kissed and all."

"I thought guys just liked to fuck."

"Well—not me."

"Are you gay?"

"Oh, Saro—shut up. Okay—let's go out again. When are you free?"

"Wednesday. Seven o'clock. My parents will be busy in the restaurant, and I have arranged to study with a friend."

That Wednesday he had armed himself with condoms. He'd never used the bloody things, although everyone in his class bragged that they had, several in one night. Jack was the worst and had been urging Billy to come out to Nella's Roadhouse down on County Road 9. Nella was the town whore, a former postal worker who got fired for absenteeism; now she took high schoolboys on Tuesdays and Wednesdays, when patrons were scarce—she even offered half price on those days. Billy felt bad for not taking Jack up on his offer—a little bit of practice would have certainly helped.

He had difficulty getting his condom on that first time; it kept falling off, or his cock kept going slack with the effort he put into getting 'garbed.' Saro giggled and called him a first timer.

"You seem to be pretty experienced," he shot back, miffed.

"In Toronto, if you did not fuck with the boys, you did not fit in. I fucked boys because I wanted them to stop saying things about me. I did not like what I did. Mahesh was insanely jealous, but he would never tell my parents. We had more to lose if they knew."

He was shocked at this revelation. He was the novice, not her!

Finally, he had the sheath on, but his penis dangled like a limp noodle. Saro took his hanging phallus and sucked him, staring into his eyes with an impish look. He was hard in no time and she helped him inside her warmth. She thrust up and into him a couple of times to get him going and suddenly a gush of energy rushed through him and he was bucking like a wild horse. He lost feeling of latex next to skin and before he knew it, he was shooting his wad.

"Yeuww, watch it!" Saro's annoyance brought him up sharp from the feeling of euphoria enveloping him. "The fucking condom's come loose in me."

He realized fast, as he rolled off her, that he had parted company with his rubber companion. She was fishing the slimy, creamy, elongated thing out from the black hair between her legs and flinging it in the grass. She got up and stalked away to the edge of the mill's fence line. "You need lessons," she hurled back at him.

Suddenly, she was not the virginal exotic nymph he had taken her to be. She was a fiery avatar, bitter, angry, determined. Maybe she was having a PMS day or something. He felt like he did not want to be with her again.

"I'll take you home," he said, pulling on his pants. He packed up the pop bottles and snack packets into a plastic bag. He made to go towards the car when a hand held him back.

"Don't go."

He turned. Saro was back, the anger and fire gone, vanished. There were tears in her eyes. "When we were chased out of Sri Lanka, I vowed never to let anyone get to me. In Toronto, I had to fight to get to the head of my class, not to fall into the ghetto with my fellow country girls who all stuck together and did not step outside their box. I guess I don't realize how unpleasant I've become. Please don't go."

He took her in his arms and kissed her, this time their kisses were passionate, their souls connecting in the place where he wanted to be and their bodies yielding to each other. They fell back on the blanket and within moments were undressed again. He was pleased and excited to see his erection harder and firmer than the previous time.

"Shh!" Saro said, stroking him, making him harder, she reached into his jeans pocket, fished out the pack of condoms, ripped one open with her teeth and slipped it easily over him.

"Now, take me." she said lowering herself down on him.

That had been two short months ago. They had met regularly after that, always coming up here. Her aggression towards him from those earlier times had lessened. It was as if she did not have to put on the tough act anymore.

Saro stirred and stretched beside him, then shot up like a bolt. "What time is it?"

"Coming on six. I guess we have to head back. It's going to be noisy downtown, with the election and all."

She rose and pulled on her capris. She shivered and draped the blanket over her shoulders. "It's turned cold, suddenly."

He felt something missing. They had not made love as they had done on every other occasion since his bad-condom day. And he had got good at preparing himself for that regular event that culminated their meetings, unassisted, too. Today, they had just read to each other from her text book of the *Brave New World* and then she had said that she had not been sleeping well and dozed off. He had felt deflated, his customary erection that arrived whenever they were together, finding no home. Finally, he, too, had dozed until that pesky fly had bothered him.

"You feeling okay? Having a period or something?"

She stuck her tongue out at him. "How about, being unable to have one for a change?"

A cold vice gripped his stomach, and he felt like he wanted to take a sudden crap. "You mean…"

"I'd like to buy a pregnancy test from somewhere. But the bloody pharmacist knows me. Everyone knows everybody in this town."

"Why didn't you tell me? We can drive into Port Mossman."

She looked as scared as he was. "My mother will kill me."

"I'm sorry, Saro." He wanted to reach out to her, but she was hunched over, draped in the blanket, leaning beside the car, her back to him.

"Let's go," he said, reaching a decision. "I'll drop you off and go over to Mossy. I know what they look like."

"You will?"

"Yes."

***

He dropped her off by the waterfront and took the highway to Port Mossman. If he pushed it, he could be back in time for his eight o'clock shift. All the way on the single lane highway that weaved and bobbed through corn fields ripening with cobs, he prayed that a single careless episode would not lead to a whole maelstrom of developments that could alter their lives. The profusion of fertility around him: the fields with their abundant corn, the cows grazing with swollen udders, even the randy horse mounting a mare in Mr. Enright's farm adjoining the highway, seemed to tell him otherwise.

Suddenly, the futility of their relationship came home to him. She was seventeen and he was eighteen—it would not work. A lot of girls got knocked up in this town, and they spent their lives doing low-end retail jobs or down at the chemical plant or becoming stay-at-home moms while their husbands hung around for a bit and then left for Toronto or Calgary or the military or northwest to the oil sands, any place to take them far away from their "problems." Billy did not want any of these stereotypical lives for either himself or Sarojini. His mother had toiled hard enough in this hole. He had wanted to get out to the big city, get a professional job. Yet, he could not ditch Saro—he would stand by her if he was indeed the father of her child. If there was a child.

He pulled up at a pharmacy in a strip mall on the outskirts of the town. The more nondescript, the better, he thought.

The clerk, a bored woman in her fifties, looked at him when he placed the box on the checkout counter. "It's for women," she said.

"I know."

"Your mom pregnant? Or your girlfriend?"

"My sister," he whispered with gritted teeth. *And it's none of your damn business.*

The woman rubbed the package on the bar reader, and it wouldn't scan. A line of customers began forming behind him, and he was too embarrassed to look back.

"Hey, Mabel—price check," the cashier called out to one of her colleagues walking past. She held up the pregnancy test for everyone to see. "How much are these?"

The colleague came over. "That's a new batch—probably not coded yet. I'll get you another, Luv." She winked at Billy and went away. So began his wait, for an interminable period of time, while the clock ticked, the line-up shuffled feet, and the cashier chewed her gum monotonously.

"Unreliable, those things," the clerk said, as everyone waited for Mabel. "My daughter got a negative result—twice. Six months later she had twins."

A woman behind Billy grunted in agreement.

A senior behind her said, "We never used those things."

Very soon there was a debate going on in the line up about the efficacy of pharmacy pregnancy tests.

"Shall I go find Mabel?" a desperate Billy asked.

"Ah, no—she'll be back," the cashier replied and picked up her upturned Harlequin novel, trying to find where she had last stopped reading.

Billy fiddled with the disposable camera display next to the stalled checkout, pretending to show no interest in what was now becoming a group buying experience.

When Mabel arrived, she was carrying an armful of pregnancy tests! She dumped them all on the counter.

"He only needs one," drawled the cashier, upending her book again.

"I know, but none of them seem to scan well," answered Mabel. "Try running them on your scanner."

Mercifully, on the third try, a bar code registered. The cashier smiled. "Maybe this one will work—on your sister, that is. Do you want to put that camera on the tab, too?"

Not wanting to draw any more attention to the pregnancy test, Billy instantly replied, "Why, yes!"

Twenty-five dollars poorer, he literally ran out of the pharmacy to his car, holding the treasured test and the useless camera. Mabel was giggling behind him.

***

Jane rolled over in the king bed and stretched. The sheets smelled musky with a hint of sweat—his. The shower was running, and strands of early daylight filtered in through the blinds of the hotel room. Her mind went back to the sumptuous dinner they had feasted on the night before, to celebrate setting up the books for Bio-diversity Futures, a new subsidiary of Hamilton Industries. They had decided to meet in Toronto where Art was concluding some meetings, and the Four Seasons had been nearby. She, too, had spent the day in the city attending court hearings on her custody appeal for her son. Yesterday had been particularly brutal, but she felt she was close to getting access to her child on alternate weekends. And she had felt like celebrating.

It was nothing but the best with Art: Dom Perignon to start with, a five-course meal that included veal cordon bleu and white wine sorbet, topped off by café au lait fluffed with piles of whipped cream. Over a cigar and cognac, he had invited her to his suite, given that it was too late to drive back to Milltown and they were both quite drunk. They had let their guards down after that, guards that had been slipping from the time of their first meeting.

The sex had been good, hard and physical, and it lasted long—just how she liked it. He had brought her to glorious climaxes many times over, giving her just enough of a pause before mounting her again and again. Now he emerged from the shower, a towel wrapped loosely around his chunky muscular frame.

"Up early?" she purred, wanting him to come back to bed.

"I've got to be in Oshawa for a meeting at nine. And I have to get out of this city. Feel free to order breakfast in bed—it's on the tab. There's coffee over in the percolator, if you like."

She felt deflated. A part of her wanted him, hungrily. Art had kindled that itch in her—the one that ignited infrequently when she met the right man, and meeting the right man was not easy these days. There were lots of offers on the Internet, very few delivered.

"Are we back to being client and accountant then, back in Milltown? And none of this happened?"

He pulled out a fresh shirt and put it on. He dressed with purpose, inspecting the angle of his tie. When he was fully clothed, he turned towards her and his blue eyes twinkled. "I'm afraid so. But there will be other occasions."

She needed more from him then—more than just her fees. A thought struck her.

"That restaurant next door to my office is becoming popular and noisy. And the smell of curry is getting to me and to my clients."

He paused, his jacket about to be buttoned. "What do you want me to do about it?"

"I want that space. I am too cramped where I am."

"Space costs money."

"You will be making a lot on this deal."

He grinned. "I'll take payment in kind. More frequently, shall we say?"

Her lip curled. She had him. "That can be arranged."

"I'll see what I can do." He paused at the doorway. "Have a good breakfast—the crepes here are particularly good."

When he had departed, she felt cheated. It had been too slick. Like he had done this before—several times before—with different women each time. She flung a pillow at the door and dragged herself into the washroom.

Eleven

Frank raised a toast to his team at Macy's pub. The regulars had joined in, turning away from the hockey game on the hanging TV sets over the bar, some dragging their stools over to where Frank and his campaign team—comprised of his office staff and general sycophants—sat around a table in the dining room, celebrating. Even the darts players interrupted their match to join the festivities. The results were in, and Frank had won by a huge margin.

"Here's to Milltown, to our new skating rink, to the new industry coming into this town, and to its hard-working people." Frank slurped the head off a tankard of beer.

"Hear, hear!"

"Yo da man, Frank!"

Something, no someone, was missing. Frank sensed this void as he surveyed the room, his signature plastic smile firmly in place for his well wishers, who paraded by, patting him on the back. It wasn't Frieda, and he was glad that she had chosen this time to be in Calgary to visit with Carrie. No, that woman was better off not being in the picture altogether. If Frieda had not been a product of this town, he would have divorced her long ago. He missed Sue Miller, the only member of his staff who was not at the celebration. She was the missing ingredient. Sue had begged off early and gone home straight after work today, saying she was feeling unwell.

More patrons gathered, like flies around a piece of raw meat, buzzing and chattering. Word had got out that Frank was buying the drinks. Soon, Macy's was bursting. Frank ordered a dozen jugs of ale and an equal number of bowls of pretzels. He jumped up on a table, waving his tankard around to everyone. "Go ahead and help yourselves, folks. Drink up!"

After his third mug, Frank was buzzed and starting to burp and fart. Time to go. Few saw him leave—the pub had taken on a life of its own—free beer would do that. The Leafs were winning again, so the cheers quickly moved from Frank to the much reviled but loved Toronto hockey team.

Frank did not feel that he had achieved victory yet because he had seen that asshole Rick Jones driving Sue Miller home last evening. They had been smiling and enjoying each other's company. That jerk had not even got ten percent of the votes, but he had the nerve to steal the woman that Frank desired from under his nose? Thinking of Sue gave him a hard-on. Frank needed her right now and not in her little cock-teasing ways, but to take her like a real man would. After all, he was the victor today.

He got into his car and headed for her home.

He parked on a side street and walked up to Sue Miller's front door, pulling his golf hat over his head. It was dark, and her porch light was out, so the neighbours in the row of town houses would not notice him. When she opened the door, she was still in the white blouse and body-hugging skirt she had worn to the office, but her hair was tousled and her feet bare. Her eyes opened in surprise to see him standing there; a wave of concern crossed it. She looked over his shoulder at the houses across the street and reached for the porch light switch on the wall beside her.

"Don't," he said, pushing his way inside and quickly shutting the door behind him as light flooded the porch.

"Frank!" She looked angry, intruded upon, and he felt the thrill of danger. Yes, he was in her personal space, trespassing. But would Marty Pierce, soon to be retiring chief of Milltown's police force, dare to lay charges on a newly elected mayor? Especially as Frank had been instrumental in keeping Marty on for another two years to help his last kid through college?

Frank squinted, focussing on the darker interior of Sue's small home. *Tidy, modest, and clean.*

"Frank. You are drunk. You'd better go home."

"I missed you at the pub."

"Congratulations! I guess I still have a job for the next term, eh?"

"Not unless you open up some of those cookies you keep wrapped so well away from me."

"I beg your pardon?"

"Come off it, Sue. This play acting has gone on for too long. I can always get another secretary, you know."

He saw the fear cross her face. *Good, I got the bitch where I need her.*

He advanced, knocking aside a stool. They had moved into the tiny dining room. She backed away from him until she hit the dining room table, a table laid for two. A look of resignation washed over her, and her shoulders hunched.

Her face twisted in disgust. "You'd better make it quick before Billy gets home," she said lying back on the table, between the plates and the cutlery and hoisting up her skirt.

***

Billy rolled his car into the driveway. He noticed that his mother had left the porch light on. Rare, he thought, as they were trying to conserve energy. Conservation was the motto in their home where everything had to be rationed after his father passed away.

He took the disposable camera out—another useless object to junk up his room—who used these things today with digital photography being the popular choice? He was saving money to buy a smart phone; soon he wouldn't need one of these. He had dropped the pregnancy test at Saro's; a discreet pebble thrown against her window and a smart throw of the plastic-wrapped package up to her reaching hands. Tomorrow, they would know.

As he stepped up to the front door, he found it unlocked. *Mom's getting careless. Those neighbourhood kids would be in here in no time if they knew we kept the door unlocked.* He pushed the door open to see a man's bare buttocks thrusting away on the dining table, a woman's legs encircling him at the hips. The man was grunting lustily.

Billy froze when he recognized the woman and the man. The realization was like a blow to the chest, and he staggered back out the front door. Pausing to still his beating heart, he turned back to go inside again but didn't have the energy. He looked in through the window instead. Yes, it was his mother, all right. Her features were fixed as if she were on the obstetrician's table being prodded at her annual exam, which she had taken Billy to once, when he was little, the day the baby sitter had called in sick. Back then, he had been told not to look at what was going on behind the curtain, but today he could not resist seeing what was thrusting back and forth between her legs. Mayor Frank Morgan was in a bath of perspiration, his pants dropped down to his legs, shirt askew and tie over his shoulder.

Billy felt sick to his stomach and gripped the only thing he had with him, the camera.

***

Rick Jones looked disconsolately at the bottle of scotch and wondered whether he should finish it tonight. He had taken a stiff double when the results had been announced half an hour ago. Now he was nursing his second drink as the warm glow of the alcohol's effects began to dull the pain of defeat inside him. It was easy to let go, to sink into the oblivion that alcohol took him to on most evenings. But today, something held him back.

He had never expected to get even ten percent of the votes. He had just wanted to voice his protest about the big guys who were turning this town into their money-making machine at the cost of everyone else. And these poor-sucker citizens were falling for it. *Buy them a few rounds of beer and you buy their souls. Idiots!*

It wasn't the defeat of the election so much as the paper that Sue Miller had given him, and the fact that he had done nothing with it. What could he have done—gone to the press with it? But the two local dailies were owned by friends of Frank Morgan. They would have either delayed the publication or shelved it accidentally, saying they had more important events to record. Put it on the Internet? But who read news on the Net these days—there was so much stuff out there the good information was getting lost and being taken for scurrilous gossip. Besides, construction hadn't started on the rink yet, so a clean-up was still possible. What then?

Sue Miller was also keeping him from reaching for that bottle. For once, he felt that there was a glimmer of hope for him. On a whim, yesterday, he had driven his beat-up 1970 Chevy Malibu sport sedan and parked outside Town Hall, waiting for her to finish work. He had run through half a pack of cigarettes before she stepped out and began her long walk home. He did an illegal U-turn on Main Street and gunned his engine alongside her.

"Want a ride?"

She looked at him and brightened. Then she turned back at the municipal office and smiled coquettishly. "Tomorrow's the election— you are not supposed to consort with the competition."

"Oh, bullshit. Hop in. I'll run you along the lake before I drive you home. You'll still arrive earlier than if you walk."

"A lake-side drive! How can a girl refuse?" She stepped inside.

He liked her hint of perfume that penetrated through the nicotine fumes inside the car. He cut down a couple of side streets heading towards the lake until he hit Marine Drive. Then he accelerated on the strip of road that skirted the lake for several kilometres.

They drove past people strolling on the beach and the boardwalk: teenagers playing Frisbee, mothers sitting back and letting their toddlers roll in the sand, a family running in and out of the water with their dog, the municipal worker combing the beach with her metal detector, oblivious to the world with her Walkman on.

"Remember the walks we took along this beach, oh, so long ago? You and Bob, me and Brenda?" Rick peered cautiously over at Sue, but she seemed lost in thought. Perhaps she, too, was recalling those happier times.

"Bob was never comfortable with those walks. He felt like the poor guy out. He felt that you would rather have had Brenda and me to yourself."

Rick laughed. "And I ended up with neither."

They left the beach behind as Marine Drive merged onto Highway 2. Rick turned off the venerable King's Highway after a few kilometres and headed inland towards the hills. The landscape changed into cornfields, with stalks tall and forbidding and cattle grazing in open meadows, meandering around bales of hay that lay like giant turds dropped indiscriminately from machines that went about their work.

"I wish I had bought a farm when I moved here," Rick said. "I could have converted it to a housing subdivision and joined the landed gentry by now."

"Instead, you threw parties on your boat."

"And the people I loved threw themselves off it."

"Sorry." Her hand had reached out to touch him. "I did not mean to bring back old nightmares. But you did squander a lot of opportunities."

"No problem. I guess I send wrong signals for a socialist. My high life and all."

"You needed to see the high before you hit the low."

"That's why I like driving up and down these hills."

As shadows overcame the land and the fields gave way to little hamlets, Rick turned off the road onto an unpaved stretch that ran downhill. The lake lay before them, a flat darkening blue sheet; its refracted image making it mount like a giant tsunami heading towards the fields that lay before them.

"Brenda fuelled both our appetites for the fast life. One day, when we were in the boat, she wanted me to turn it on full throttle and take off into the middle of Lake Ontario. We were both pretty drunk on Champagne. I remembered the boat heading off into nowhere. It was heady and made us feel invincible."

"Bob never felt that way. He was a plodder. He provided. He was faithful."

"I guess I was mesmerised by Brenda's wild streak."

"It ran in her family. Look what happened to Martha. Both sisters were married to successful men."

"I don't think I was successful. I was too full of 'hail fellow, well met,'" Rick said, shaking his head. "When she realized that I was full of shit, things went downhill."

"Still, her cheating on you must have come as a shock."

Rick pulled the car to a stop by the side of the road. The corn stalks—tall, ripe and dense—hemmed them in.

"I asked her why she was spending so much time in Toronto," he said. "There were arts classes here, too. But she wanted to go to the best."

"It tore my heart when she told me that she was pregnant. And that you weren't the father. I was the only one she still confided in, even though most of the time it was to rub into my face that she was living the high life while I was saddled with a kid and a dull husband whose idea of fun was going bowling on Friday nights."

Rick disengaged the gear again and let the car roll downhill. "We'd better get you home. At this rate, you could have walked home faster."

"I hope this is what you came out for. To talk?"

"Yes, thanks. There is so much more to talk about. But this was a good start."

They drove back in silence, crossing the highway once more and into the town precincts. He let her off at her door. "Thank you again. We should do this some other time."

"Perhaps," she said, then paused as she turned around.

"I know," he cut her off. "I have not done anything with the 'scarlet letter' yet. I'm biding my time."

She looked downcast. "You are not going to squander another opportunity, are you?"

"Leave it with me," he said as he drove off, unconvinced about what he was going to do.

The dogs were barking, and someone was banging on the door, bringing Rick back to the present. He pushed his empty glass away. That would do for drinks this evening. He stumbled through the two piles of books hugging the walls of the passageway—someday soon he would have to build another bookcase in the library and make room for it by getting rid of some useless, crumbling furniture.

He opened the front door. It was Sue's son, Billy, swaying from foot to foot, biting his nails, a plastic bag in his hands.

Rick opened the door wider. "Why Billy—did you come to celebrate my defeat with me?"

"I need to ask you a favour, Mr. Jones." The boy continued rocking on the balls of his feet.

"Cut the 'Mr. Jones' bit. Haven't I told you that already? What's up?"

"Can I come in?"

"Sure." Rick moved aside from the open doorway, and the boy stepped in and stood on the threshold, looking tentatively about him.

Rick backed into the kitchen "I'd offer you a scotch if you were not under age. But I think I have some Coke here somewhere." He rummaged in his almost empty fridge as he heard Billy's steps follow him.

"Mr. Jones…I mean Rick. Forget the drink. I have to be at work soon."

Rick turned around. He had found a solitary can of Coke behind the three-week-old cabbage. He tossed the can at Billy and pitched the cabbage into the overflowing garbage container. "Here."

Billy caught the can and fished in his light jacket, bringing out a disposable camera.

"I want you to develop this roll. I can't take it anywhere to be processed—they might arrest me."

"What's in it?"

"Proof to hang that bastard Frank Morgan."

"You gotta do better than that kiddo. What kind of proof?"

"How about rape?"

A shiver crept down Rick's spine. Suddenly he needed that new drink. "Who?"

"I'm coming to you because you are the only person I can trust…Rick. Whatever you do, please don't make it hurt my mom." Then the lad turned on his heel and rushed out the door, leaving Rick holding the cold, green disposable camera with its stored secrets.

Rick went back into the living room and slumped in his rocking chair. "I'm fucking cursed," he yelled. He reached for the bottle of scotch.

***

After Frank left, Sue ripped the table cloth off the dining room table and threw it into the basement. She would never use that table cloth again; she would donate it to the thrift shop or burn it. She felt dirty and took a shower. What had made her agree to Frank's animal urgings? Fear of her job, a mad desire to see her boss in a vulnerable state, jerking over her body? Now, she felt revolted. Still dripping from the cold water, she draped a dressing gown around and her and wrapped her hair in a towel. She poured herself a stiff brandy from a bottle secreted away for her hot punches during the cold months. Would Frank expect sex all the time now? Even in the office after work? The janitor had a habit of coming in early on some days and that could complicate things. Most of all, she felt cheap and powerless, and by acquiescing to Frank, she had further diminished herself. And if Billy had come home there would have been blue murder.

The thought of Billy made her panic. Where was he? He was late. She drained the bottle into another solid drink and sipped it, the alcohol helping to dull her feelings of revulsion.

She had known that this day was going to come sooner rather than later when she had first given in to Frank's advances. And now that it was done, there was no turning back.

She hoped that Rick would act on the paper she had given him. A big scandal with the mayor was what the town needed, something to flush Frank out and diminish him. That was when she would be in a position to rise up against him. But she would probably still lose her job if the mayor went. The replacement always came with their minions to support them.

She did not know what she was thinking when she had gone to Rick with that evidence. What about all that "avenging of Bob" stuff that had gotten her on this path? Right now, she could not give a hoot for Bob or his boring ways. If he had been man enough, they would have left this blasted place and started life somewhere else. She felt confused, conflicted, and drunk. Maybe Rick Jones would do nothing, like he had always done. Maybe he would just take another drink and lose the paper and life would go on as before. And for those at the bottom, like her—wasn't that their lot anyway?

She put the food into plastic containers, threw the soiled dishes and pans into the sink, and scribbled a note to Billy: "Dinner is in the fridge. Heat it and eat. I'll wash up tomorrow. I am off to bed." She stuck the note under the fridge magnet most used and staggered off to her bedroom, locking the door behind her, as if that would shut the whole world out, Billy and Bob included.

***

Frank Morgan poured himself a scotch and stared at the statuettes in his living room—inanimate objects paying homage to him. There was no life in this house, the air lay dead, and despite the recent victory and the euphoria of having released his long overdue seed into Sue Miller, he was feeling no sense of accomplishment, just a sense of dread and remorse.

Had he overstepped his mark? Power corrupts absolutely. Could he hide behind Art Hamilton on this one? Art only tolerated so much. Art seduced women in style. Frank took his on dining-room tables, desecrating the privacy of homes. Frank gulped his scotch and filled his glass once more.

Tomorrow he would make it up to her. Sue should know a man's drives—besides, he'd had the hots for her for a long time, and if that bitch Frieda were dead, he would have even married Sue. Had she liked what he had done? She hadn't struggled, but just hoisted her dress up and spread her legs upon the table. Perhaps she liked it, wanted him, and feigned disinterest while he took his pleasure on her body. Perhaps, things were not as bad as he thought. Perhaps he could pursue more of these trysts. Perhaps he would invite her over here the next time.

He looked back at the faces of his trophies, some grinning, others frowning and shouted back to them, "Next time, you will get to see me in action!" He knocked back his drink and went in search of a midnight snack.

***

Rick took the whisky bottle over to the kitchen sink and drained the last drink in it down the sinkhole. This was to remind himself that he was on the way to recovery—that he was not into finishing the bottle anymore. Then he staggered over to the couch and sat down, the alcohol having taken him to that gentle place of abandon.

He liked Billy very much. He had taught the boy to drive golf balls. He could never do that with his nephew Andy. Andy, a few months younger than Billy, was always in some kind of a temper. Andy had just kept hitting and missing the still ball perched up on a tee on Rick's back stoop. One day, Andy, after several misses, just picked up the balls and threw them into the lake.

Rick remembered that other time when he had taken both boys hunting. They had spotted a stag down by a waterhole and approached cautiously from downwind. "Wait till you're within thirty yards," Rick had instructed them earlier, but Andy, in his nervousness, loosed a shot way before they were in range. The deer became disoriented then took off, heading towards them rather than away. Suddenly, the animal skidded, realizing its error, and turned broadside to run to the right. Billy was down on one knee taking aim coolly during this turn of events. He released a shot and the deer went down on its front knees. Andy began running forward, firing at the fallen stag, blocking Rick's and Billy's lines of fire. His gun was empty by the time he reached the animal. When Rick and Billy caught up, there was a solitary red stain leaking out from below the left breast of the dying deer.

"You got him, Billy," Rick announced.

Andy shrieked, lifted the rifle, and smashed the butt down on the animal's head, crashing bone and wood. Rick grabbed him and the rifle before Andy could swing a second time. "It's dead now," Rick shouted, but it had taken both Billy and himself to wrestle the broken weapon free from Andy.

When they walked back to the rented four-wheel drive vehicle to get cables to tie the dead animal for transport, Rick put his hand on Andy's shoulder. "We all miss, sometimes."

Andy shrugged off his uncle's hand. "I won't, the next time."

Andy had remained sullen all the way home that day.

Rick drained his glass and looked down at the portable camera. Billy was in some kind of trouble, and Sue was implicated, too, according to the boy's behaviour. Rick hadn't been able to help Billy the last time, after the school shooting when Andy had finally revealed his true colours. Rick wondered if he would have the courage to help Billy now.

Twelve

Sam tried to stop his knees from shaking in front of Rick Jones. Books, newspapers, and magazines vied for space on the faded carpet in the lawyer's study, along with paper plates containing scraps of food, soiled coffee mugs, an empty scotch bottle, and a glass with golden dregs still giving off vapours reminiscent of a back-room bar. Two huge dogs prowled the room, periodically sniffing at Sam's crotch as if looking for their next meal. Sam wondered why Rick did not send his dogs outside into the yard or leash them like they did back in Sri Lanka. Animals were not equal to humans where Sam came from.

"Your lease contract has an escape rider," Rick said, after inspecting the documents. "It says that you can be offered re-location anywhere within Hamilton Holdings' other properties in Milltown during the period of your lease or compensation if they are unable to relocate you. Did you not read the mice print?"

Sam shook his head. "No sir, we were keen to start up. I must have not looked closely. Besides, Mr. Hamilton looked like such a gentleman. My wife thought he was charming, too."

Rick sniggered. "In this country, we slit throats with smiles on our faces."

"Please, Mr. Rick, can you do something? The alternate location they are offering me is too far away from the main street—we will not get any customers. There is no apartment above the new location, and we will have to commute back and forth. We were just starting to pick up the business."

"Have you talked to Hamilton as to why he needs your space?"

"I cannot reach him, sir. He does not answer the phone. I just got this delivered today by courier."

Rick got up and started pacing. Suddenly he paused and shouted at the dogs. "Bill, Phil—get out of here. You're starting to bug me."

Like cowed creatures, unbecoming for their gigantic size, the dogs docilely filed out of the room.

Sam relaxed. A thought struck him. "You know, sir, two weeks ago, the lady who runs the accounting office next door was surveying my restaurant from the street."

"Jane Garner? The newest kid on the block, here, in Milltown. Did you talk to her?"

"Yes sir, I even invited her in. But she said that the smell of our cooking bothered her. Then she went back into her office. She wasn't very friendly."

"She couldn't be the reason…unless…unless." Rick rubbed his jaw, pacing faster, the wheels in his mind clicking as he passed Sam to and fro.

"Leave this with me," Rick said finally. "I'll have a chat with Jane. I don't know the woman at all. But she may give me a clue as to where this is coming from."

"Oh, I am so glad that you are taking my case, Mr. Rick." Sam got up quickly and shook Rick's hand.

"Don't pull out the champagne, yet. We haven't won anything. In fact, I have to admit that I have never won against Hamilton. But I feel pretty darned close to it some days."

***

When Sam returned home, a commotion was going in the upstairs apartment. He heard muffled female voices, shouting. Sam had to relieve Mahesh, who had been holding the fort while he had made his quick run over to Rick Jones' house. It was still before the dinner rush, and mercifully, there was only one elderly couple in the far end of the restaurant having an early supper— regulars now, and quite deaf.

"Ammi and Saro are at it—not sure about what," Mahesh announced, looking up from his pocket video game console. He is trying to look disinterested, Sam thought.

"Have you taken care of those two customers?" Sam enquired, his voice subdued.

"Oh yeah—all they wanted was chicken buriyani and samosas."

Sam nodded, that's what they always ordered, creatures of habit. "Okay—wait here a little while longer. I will go up and check what is happening upstairs. Those two will drive away all our customers with their shouting."

Mahesh cocked an eyebrow. "Ammi has never shouted like that in a long time. I hope that silly sister of mine hasn't done something stupid."

"Stupid? Why do you call your sister stupid?"

Mahesh shrugged and returned to his video game. "There are some things I would rather not talk about. It will only piss you all off."

"Okay, young man, enough of the mystery. You look after those two customers and anyone else who comes in, while I go and sort out our women."

Sam climbed the narrow stairs as the women's voices increased in volume. He could not understand why that accountant woman next door would want this poky place, if that was indeed what had prompted the letter from Art Hamilton.

Sam entered the cramped apartment. Much of their belongings still lined the walls or occupied parts of the floor, unpacked, and had become familiar terrain that they had to tip-toe around. Malani, her hair loose down to her waist and dressed only in her petticoat, was gesticulating wildly as she paced the living room, waving her bare arms about, something Sam had not seen in a long time, and which even then, sent a faint wave of desire coursing through his troubled mind. Through the narrow door into the washroom, he saw a half-clothed Saro sitting on the folded down toilet seat, sobbing.

Seeing Sam enter, Malani shouted at him. Her eyes were dark-rimmed, with mascara or anger, he could not say which.

"Hah, there you are. Ask your daughter what she has done."

Sam went towards the washroom. On the wash basin was an open packet with a cylindrical object that had a blue tip. "What is up, darling?" Sam put his arms gently around Saro and tried to raise her up.

"Leave me alone." She struggled out of his reach, chewing her fingers, sobbing more.

Malani was behind him. "Look at that…that…thing. Your daughter is pregnant. I came into the washroom after my nap to find your precious daughter pissing on that stick."

Sam staggered against the bathroom door as though he had been punched in the heart. Saro went into a fresh bout of howling, loud and uncontrolled. Sam forced himself to go towards his daughter and, exerting superhuman strength, pulled her up. She collapsed into his arms. "*Thathi*, oh, *Thathi*—I am so sorry," His whispers mixed with tears.

"Huh, you'll be sorrier when you have a half-white bastard running around this apartment," Malani threw back at her.

Sam smoothed his daughter's hair, calming her rapidly beating heart. He grabbed a hand towel and wiped her tears. "Don't cry, baby, we will look after you. We will always look after you." He led her out of the narrow washroom into the bedroom that she shared with her brother, another sore point in their lives.

He laid her down gently on the bed. She looked like the four-year-old who had fallen off the mango tree and bruised her leg in their old home in Colombo and who had hugged her daddy for solace back then. He drew the blanket over her. She lay her wet face upon the pillow, finger in her mouth, her sobs subsiding; she closed her eyes from this horrible world, where even her mother had turned against her. Cold fingers of one hand held on tightly to him.

"Your mother is just hurt and scared, baby," he whispered in her ear. *We are all scared.* "Let me talk to her. You get some rest." He closed the bedroom door behind him and returned to face his wife.

Malani was pacing the living room.

"Of course, we have to get it taken out," she said, as if talking to herself.

"What are you talking about, Mala? What about our daughter's health?"

"She is strong and young and foolhardy. Do you want to have a mixed-race bastard running around? Not like in the old country where you can force the father to marry her. Here, they will tell us to get lost. And then what? A single mother on welfare? Not for my daughter."

Sam reached out for his swiftly moving wife. "Sit, Mala. We need to think this thing through. Isn't it her choice to have or not to have this child?"

"It was also her choice not to disgrace us by getting pregnant. Do you know that she was running around behind our backs with this boy? Mahesh told me today."

"Mahesh should have told us up front. His telling us now does not mean anything. In fact, I think that boy is a coward. I don't know how he is going to survive in this country." Sam knew his voice was probably carrying downstairs.

Malani came over and sat next to him. The next moment, she was clutching his neck and wailing, "Oh, why did we come to this country?"

Sam embraced her shivering frame. Between one woman and another, he felt that he was being sucked of his energy. "Mala, when you are calmer, we can talk about this. Now, let's compose ourselves and go down to the restaurant, we need to serve our dinner crowd. Mahesh cannot manage alone. I don't even know if he has just left the place un-minded and run off somewhere."

"Oh, Sam, I am so scared."

"Don't worry, Mala. Remember when they burned the house. We managed, no? We will manage this time, too. Don't worry."

He rose with her and steered her towards the washroom to freshen up before heading downstairs. He felt helpless. He had not told her about the eviction notice yet. He wondered how she would deal with that on top of this setback. And as for Saro's pregnancy, he had no clue how he was going to handle things.

***

Billy had avoided his mother since he had seen her with the mayor two days before. He had scooted off early to school each morning while she was in the washroom, not returned home for supper, hung out at the library after school, grabbed a burger from the McDonald's counter at the service station on the highway, and then headed off to his evening shift, repeating this routine two days in a row, returning late when he would hear her soft snore through the half-open door of her bedroom.

He was angry with Sue. He understood that she had physical needs, too, and with his father gone, she was vulnerable. She was constantly wolf-whistled and chatted up by guys, married and unmarried, at Macy's and other places, yet she had been aloof to all advances, as far as he was aware. Until now. But with the Mayor? Frank Morgan was also her boss, and a married man, even though everyone knew that the mayor and his wife were as good as divorced. And, in *that* way? On the dining room table? Shit, he was never going to be able to eat at that table again. He thought of himself and Saro on the grass outside the mill. They had gone at it like animals too, on some days. But somehow, a parent having sex like that was *not okay*. And what if Rick Jones exposed not only the mayor but also his mother when those photographs became public? Billy would not be able to show his face in school again. The son of the whore, they would say. And school ostracising was wicked, for he had skirted its edges. It was the sniggering in school that had finally turned Andy's screws loose, he knew, apart from the other goings-on in the Hamilton home.

Had he done the right thing by turning over that camera to Rick Jones? Why Rick? Because of all the men who had pursued his mother, Billy would have liked Rick to have won her favour. That he was sure of. That kind but weak man needed something, or someone, to jerk him into action. And that was part of what had driven Billy to head to Rick's house that night with the camera.

He tossed his cup of Coke into the trash can by the door and went out to his car. A light rain was falling, and dark clouds hovered on the north side of the highway. He pulled the hood of his gym sweater over his head. It was time for the evening shift. His cell phone rang. It was Saro. Shit, he'd forgotten all about her in the intervening fiasco with his mother and the mayor.

Her voice sounded feeble, distant. "Billy…I'm sorry."

"Sorry? Saro, I am the one who should be sorry. Sorry I did not call you. How's it going?"

"Billy, I'm pregnant. I'm sorry…" Her voice was trailing, and he strained to catch her, his heart thumping.

On adrenaline, he walked faster through the parking lot, opened his car door and fell into the driver's seat. "Saro…Saro…"

Her voice was crackling on the line, breaking up. "I'm sorry, Billy."

The line went dead.

He sat there as if hit between the eyes with a six by four. He opened the window for fresh air. Suddenly, sex looked like a bad thing. Suddenly, he wanted to drive straight home and forgive his mother.

***

The dining room was fuller than usual today; there were even a few out-of-towners. Sam and Malani had no more time to dwell on their daughter's predicament, as they were busy serving customers till well after 10:00 p.m.

Sam had been so busy shuttling between the kitchen and the bar that he did not fully notice the two strangers seated by the entrance, having only tea. He finally caught a full view of one of them: a tall dark man, as he flicked his fingers, summoning Sam. With Mala busy cleaning up at another table, Sam went over.

The hooked nose was familiar, and, too late, Sam recognized him.

"*Adey*, Selvadurai—come here, man." The tall man smiled, still flicking his fingers. His companion, a short tubby guy with a goatee and slicked-down black hair chuckled, hunching over his cup of tea. Sam looked nervously around for Mala, but she had retreated into the kitchen, carrying a pile of dishes.

"Have you got something for us?"

Sam lowered his voice. "I told your…boss that I will try to come up with something as soon as we are making some money."

"But you must be making a lot of money. This place is almost full, tonight."

"We are lucky on some nights. It is not always like this," Sam said.

The man's voice became nasal and stern. "Listen, baba—you have kept us hanging for too long. From now on, we will be in the area. We will come for you again in a few days. You'd better have a parcel for us. Cash. With arrears." He threw a ten dollar note on the table. "Keep the change."

The two men swaggered out of the restaurant.

Sam had to sit down. There were too many things coming at him: eviction notices, unwanted pregnancies, mob threats. And this was supposed to be a peaceful place, safer than Toronto, safer than all the other places he had been running from. He felt beaten. There was no running left in him.

Malani, returning from the kitchen, prompted him to rise and keep moving. There was no point in wilting in front of her. Then everything would be lost.

Thirteen

Art walked down the white walled corridor to the visitor's centre. He hated these visits, but today he had received a message about his son, and that had required him to make a personal appearance at Sunnyside. The authorities had deemed Andy at risk and were transferring him. There were papers to sign.

"Morning, Mr. Hamilton." Henry gave Art a courteous, toothless grin and opened the visitor's lounge door for him.

"Everything okay here?" Art asked, stepping into the room where a row of chairs faced a transparent glass wall. Two other parents were on phones talking with their blue-overall clad sons on the other side of the glass. Their voices were muted, their faces teary. A bored guard, standing by the heavy metal door behind the young men, stared off into space.

"Andy's been doing fine since he went back to solitary, sir. I think he likes to be on his own. I am going to miss him."

"The weights do him good?"

"Oh yes, he works on them every day. Sometimes, too much. You know he gets obsessive and such."

Don't I know it! Art's thoughts were interrupted when the door on the other side opened and Andy was ushered in by another guard. Art sucked in his breath; his son was looking more and more like his dead wife, a dead wife waving an accusing finger at him.

"Well, I'll be off, Mr. Hamilton." Henry nodded. "Let me know if you need anything."

Art sat on the stool on the visitor's end of the glass, facing Andy, and picked up the phone. Andy stared back at his father and remained standing.

He's filled out, thought Art.

After a further silence, Andy sat down. Art had to admit that the older his son became, the more unsettling he was to face. The guard on duty by the door was a welcome distraction. Art was able to stare down most men, but his son was another thing—perhaps Andy stared into his conscience as well.

Andy picked up the phone nonchalantly.

"How are you doing?" Art said. *He's a little too much out of proportion on the upper body.*

"They are sending me away," Andy said. He did not look very happy saying it. "I like it here."

"You've got into too many scrapes, here. They are sending you to the adult centre."

"Where they will eat me alive."

"There's nothing I can do to delay things. I've tried."

"Why am I always being disturbed when I am just settling in?"

"Change is a part of life. You should accept it."

"Mum's dying was not change. You drove her to it."

Art sighed and leaned back in his seat. They were into the old drama again. The boy just would not let it go. Art gritted his teeth and waited for the emotional berating to begin—his purgatory on earth.

"I didn't steal your car, either, you know," Andy said.

"You did not have a licence at the time. Do we have to go over all this again?"

"Why do you come to see me, if you never want to discuss anything that matters to me?"

"I thought your psychologist and psychiatrist were helping you deal with these issues. They are beyond me."

"That's your cop-out. It was always beyond you. Getting home on time to take me to a ball game was beyond you."

Art could not stop the trigger that clicked off in him. Breaking his restraint, he barked back into the phone, "I was busy earning the money to give you and your mother a decent lifestyle. You both could not get that through your heads."

"Maybe we just wanted you to be home with us—like a regular father. Maybe we did not want an empire builder."

"All I have could be yours, if you will just suck it up, accept remorse for your actions, do your time, and get out of here while you are still a young man. You have only two more years at most, and then you could be out on parole, if you stop playing homicidal maniac. You could go back to school, get a business degree. You will never have to worry about getting a job because you will always have one with me. That is what my time away from you, when you were younger, has earned you. Don't you see it, Andy? It's not all debits."

"I won't be getting out in two years. They are waiting for me in Kingston. I hear stories through the grapevine, you know."

"I'll see that no one touches you. If we have to buy people off, we'll do that to protect you."

"That's all you can do—buy people off."

Art put the phone down for a moment. They were getting nowhere, as usual. When he picked the phone up again, he was resolved to give Andy the message he had come prepared to give.

"Listen, Andy. I can't help it if you do not like me. However, I am your father, and I will be damned if you commit any more atrocities on my watch. If you do not repent at your next probation hearing and accept the treatment that comes with it, I am writing off helping you any further. Got it?" Art stared at his son and saw the lurking fear in the young man's eyes. Maybe somewhere in those complex crossed wires of the boy's brain something was registering. Art was still in control of Andy's life, and Andy must know it. If Art pulled off support—like having Henry mind him here, like getting a set of weights shipped to him for use in solitary confinement so that it would cool his aggression—with perks that other inmates did not get, then the battle for survival with the hard-core criminals in Kingston was going to get that much tougher.

Andy slammed down the phone at his end and left the room. The guard looked enquiringly at Art, blocking Andy's path. Art nodded and rose. The guard escorted Andy out.

***

Art headed down to the chemical plant. Other things were pre-occupying his mind. He had learned to compartmentalize Andy and his mother. Their negative ranting would have driven him off the rails long ago if he had given them much credence. Perhaps it was his very struggle with their opposition to his empire building that had made him so successful in building that commercial edifice.

He did not park at the executive parking lot but drove around the complex to Block H, the furthest building from the rest of the plant. The one they had built in less than a month, working twenty-four-seven with out-of-town contractors. Block H even had its own back-up generator and security access system. Art had been deliberate in making sure that Biodiversity Futures had the least physical and financial links to its larger parent occupying the rest of the premises.

He stuck his face into the retina scan unit and heard the steel door click open.

He walked through two more metal doors and down a long corridor. Through circular glass panels in the doors leading off the corridor, he saw white uniformed staff working around hissing machinery. In some rooms, thick with fumes, staff garbed in protective suits and gas masks moved about like ghosts. Red lights outside these rooms indicated "No Entry." The corridor continued to a loading dock at the back of the building. A nondescript white truck was backed up to the dock, and a row of cylinders waited to be loaded.

Chuck stood on the loading dock supervising the loading operation. The driver and his assistant were signing off for the shipment, while two employees were pushing more cylinders on a dolly towards the truck.

Chuck saw Art step outside of the building onto the dock and paused from his work.

"How's it going, Chuck?"

"Pretty good, Mr. Hamilton. We have another order for next week. This thing is picking up steam."

"And how is the transfer at the border taking place?"

"Works fine. Not too many questions. The paperwork is well-prepared. And the border guys on both sides seem to know us, or at least, they know our clients."

"Good. It's taken a long time and some good work to cover all these details. Glad to see it's all working fine."

Art put his hand on Chuck and drew him aside, out of earshot of the two drivers. "How long have we been working with those two guys?"

"They are new with the firm, but pretty reliable. They've done three runs already and everything has been good."

"No drinking, sleeping, or whoring on the road?"

"Not that I know of, Mr. Hamilton. Duke, the senior guy—I know him from school days—pretty level-headed guy. Ran his own trucking operation for a while. I think we are okay."

"Good—keep me posted if anything unusual happens." Art nodded at the driver and his companion and headed indoors. It always paid to make personal visits to potential hot spot areas, and Art was a big believer in managing by walking around.

He got back in his car and headed home. Now that the heavy chores for the day had been dispensed with, it was time to pack his fishing rods to head down to the cottage. Jane Garner had agreed to be his guest for the weekend.

Fourteen

Rick awoke at 4:00 a.m. He had tossed and turned all night. Even the three scotches, down from his usual four, had not helped him sleep. Perhaps he was "out of pattern." He pulled the blinds and saw glimmers of light on the horizon. The dog days of summer were here. A cool, flat breeze wafted in as he drew back the window. He could make out the shapes of Bill and Phil: they stirred when he opened the window and began to bark. He closed the window again and dropped the blind.

He knew the cause of his restlessness. He wanted to know what was in those photographs Billy had taken. The camera was still lying on his desk, and he had been scared to touch it. He had been scared of a lot of things in his life. He knew it. Alcohol had helped dull some of that fear, but he was running away again, like he had done all his life.

He could take the camera down to a photo shop in Toronto, to an old client who would be discreet.

Suddenly, people around him were looking to him for leadership. The leadership he had tried to solicit with votes from a thankless electorate. He could not let these folks down. The essence of leadership was to give hope, and these people, his people—Billy, Sue, and Sam— were seeking hope from him. Perhaps he was not cut out to be the universal political leader like Frank Morgan, who was charismatic on the outside but empty on the inside and stayed in power propped up by wealthy and influential men like Art Hamilton. If those props were removed, the Frank Morgans of this world would fall, and people would once more return to honest leaders like Rick Jones. And now he, Rick Jones, was being given the levers to pull these palaces of wrongdoing down to the ground—like Samson being led to the weak pillars that had held the artificial edifice of the Philistines aloft. And what was he, Rick Jones, going to do about it?

Who to tackle first? Frank Morgan or Art Hamilton? Rick needed to do some scouting around, gather more information, circle the wagons. He felt also that Sam Selvadurai's predicament was more pressing—so perhaps that was the place to start.

Rick rose, brushed his teeth, flossed, shaved, showered, and daubed cologne, deodorant, and aftershave lavishly. Then he pulled on freshly laundered cream coloured slacks and a white shirt, still in their dry-cleaning wrappers from a month ago. He slipped into comfortable loafers and made a pot of coffee. He sat out on his back deck as the first rays of dawn shot through the tall pines circling his estate garden. He smoked his first cigarette of the day, planned his route, and made a list of the people he would call on.

***

At 11:00 a.m., Rick pulled his car into the rear parking lot allocated to Garner & Associates, Chartered Accountants. The drive into the city, ahead of the traffic and back, watching the opposite side of the highway clogged all the way to Oshawa, had been relatively easy. The studio in Toronto would give him the prints in three days, no questions asked, and discretion assured.

The back door of South Asian Delights opened and Sam, wearing an apron, came out hauling two garbage bags, which he deposited into the dumpster nearby. Rick stayed in his car until Sam returned indoors. Then he went around to the front and entered Garner & Associates. The old accountant, Fitch, had been a bit of a miser and had occupied only two rooms upstairs for his accounting office, which Rick could remember when he had had dealings with the aging accountant many years ago. The once dim stairway, leading off the street door to the offices upstairs, had been re-carpeted and had an extra light installed for guidance up the steep stairs.

Rick swung through the frosted glass door that had a sign saying, "Garner & Associates," freshly painted over what had once been "Fitch and Associates."

A young administrative assistant in steel-rimmed glasses looked up from a cluttered desk, frowning.

"Yes?"

"I'm Rick Jones. I'd like to see Ms. Garner."

"Do you have an appointment?"

"No. But tell her it's me." Rick dropped a worn business card on her desk. "And that I have come about Art Hamilton. I think she will see me." Rick sat on one of the two narrow, wooden chairs, cramped between a coat hanger and a filing cabinet, making his intention clear that he was not leaving until he had met with Jane Garner.

The young woman rose from her seat, wrinkled her nose, and walked down a narrow corridor to the other room, which old Fitch used to occupy. Rick heard muffled voices and then the young woman returned. "It will take about fifteen minutes. Mrs. Garner is on the phone. She can only spare you ten minutes as she has an appointment afterwards."

"Beggars can't be choosers—thanks." Rick gave her a toothy smile, grabbed a *People* magazine and settled down to read, letting the young woman get back to her interrupted work. He saw her giving him occasional glances in between the half a dozen phone calls she fielded while he waited.

At the end of fifteen minutes, he tossed his magazine back on its shelf. "You folks seem pretty busy. Old Fitch never was."

"Mrs. Garner has lots of clients. Many are from the city," the assistant said, coolly.

"You look like you need bigger digs."

"We will be expanding soon," the young woman said, coyly this time, and Rick thought he heard, "and I will be getting a promotion with that," somewhere in the subtext.

"Good for you. You must be fresh out of college."

"I graduated last year."

"Congratulations. It's nice to see Ms. Garner hiring locals."

"Mr. Hamilton recommended me," the young woman said, puffing her chest out.

"Oh, I am sure that must carry a lot of weight. Let me take your card. Perhaps the next time I can phone for an appointment." He reached over and took her card—Jillian Saxon. The name rang a bell.

"Mr. Jones," a voice interrupted his thoughts. Rick turned towards the narrow passageway again and a tall, slim, sharp-featured woman in her late thirties was looking at him. She wore a white sleeveless blouse and dark skirt and a string of white pearls adorned her neck.

He rose, extended his hand, and took hers, cool and dry, in his. "Pleased to meet you."

As he followed her down the passageway, it struck him: *Saxon—Joe Saxon, unemployed accountant; I bet you that's his daughter out front.*

Old Fitch's office had been re-decorated, painted a soft, pale yellow with an eggshell trim. There were paintings of rural countryside scenes on the walls—and Rick recognized the autographs on them as from local painters in the county. A vase of fresh cut flowers sat on the polished walnut desk. The paper files that had littered the place during Fitch's regime seemed to have migrated to the front to haunt Jillian: Jane Garner's office was relatively paperless. The laptop computer on Jane's desk, something Fitch had never owned, accounted for the lack of paper.

Jane sat down at her desk, ushering Rick to the chair in front of it. "Mr. Jones, I only have a few minutes, what can I do for you?"

Rick cleared his throat. Despite her cool professional and accommodating air, there was steel in this woman that he realized would be tough to penetrate. He would have felt better if he'd had a drink in front of him right now. "I appreciate you seeing me at short notice. I am representing my client, Sam Selvadurai, your next-door neighbour."

Jane's eyebrows rose, and a look of mild amusement played on her face.

"Mr. Selvadurai has been asked to quit the building. I am wondering if you received a similar request."

"Why don't you take your enquiry direct to Mr. Hamilton?"

"I will. But I wanted to check with the other tenants first."

"I have not received any such notice."

"Do you have the right to be re-located in your rental contract, Ms Garner?"

"Mr. Jones, this is highly unprofessional, why would I disclose such details to you?"

"You may want to check it, nevertheless. My client barely noticed it. It was so carefully, and elusively, worded."

"Well, my lawyer went over the document thoroughly. I'm sure he would have caught any irregularities."

Rick noticed the school portrait of a young boy on the bookcase full of legal hard covers.

"Your son?"

Jane Garner looked put out by this off-the-cuff comment. She recomposed herself and said, "Yes."

"I haven't seen him around the town. Does he go to school here?"

"He lives in Toronto with his father—for now."

"I see. Nice to have kids. I never had any. Art Hamilton has a kid, who is kept locked up all the time."

"Is there anything else I can do for you, Mr. Jones?"

"Oh, yes. I noticed that you are growing rapidly. This office was never busy like this when old Fitch was around. Are you planning to expand your facilities, perhaps take over another floor, or move laterally?"

He saw her blush, taking in a deep breath.

"I cannot discuss my future plans with you, Mr. Jones. If that is all, perhaps I can get back to my work."

Rick stood up. "Well—I thank you for your time, Ms. Garner. Let me give you one more piece of advice, seeing that I am a lifer in this town."

She rose, with hands on hips.

"Art Hamilton chews up the people closest to him—be they children, tenants, lovers or friends. I thought I would offer you that advice." He fished in his pocket and dropped another business card, his last, on the polished surface of her desk. "If you ever need help in dealing with people like him—give me a call."

She let the card lie there, came around the table, and escorted him to the door. "Thank you for the offer. But I have an excellent working relationship with Mr. Hamilton. I don't think I need your help. Good day, Mr. Jones."

***

The last days of summer were hotter, the grass dry and awaiting the rains, and the water pleasantly warm. Jane glanced up from the dock as the glass sliding door from the house onto the sundeck slid open and Art stepped out, a bottle of white wine sticking out of an ice bucket in his hands. He was bare-chested in swim shorts, tanned, and wearing rubber beach slippers.

He walked the stretch of grass down to the dock and set the bucket beside their two empty wine glasses on the small table between the deck chairs. Jane pulled on her swim suit to cover her breasts. She thought it funny that she could enjoy the most physical sex with this man yet needed to shield her modesty during moments like this.

He poured her another glass of wine and one for himself. Silently, she drank, letting the dryness sink in and fuel the light-headedness she had been simmering in this whole afternoon. The sun was just over the treeline and was descending. Soon she would need her bathrobe that lay discarded carelessly on the deck.

"I hope you have enjoyed this weekend," he said, looking off across the lake, where a solitary canoe sailed by the far bank, its rower languidly stroking, as if tired, or at peace. A barbecue from the adjacent property, though shielded by trees, was sending over wafts of roasting meat odours, making her hungry again.

"Yes, it has been relaxing. I don't want to go back to Milltown. And next week, I will be in court for Jeremy's custody hearing."

"Don't try too hard. Children grow up into people you hardly know."

She looked sharply at him as he said this. But he was sipping his wine and looking out at the distant shore, his thoughts elsewhere. Art had hinted about his personal life for the first time during this weekend alone with her. He had never talked about his wife or his son in prior conversations, although Jane had taken the trouble to find out information about them and was bubbling with questions.

"If I had Jeremy with me in Milltown, I would spend more time with him—prevent him going the wrong way. That was my ex's beef. He was a school teacher—nine to five. And I was churning through 'billable hours' on Bay Street twenty-four-seven."

"The wrong way? How much do you know about Andy?"

"Enough. It must be hard for you."

"Then you must know about his mother too. Do you make it a point to investigate your clients?"

"No more than you do when checking out your accountants." She smiled at him and swigged more wine.

"Andy's mother was a loser. She suffered from depression."

"Does she have a name?"

He flushed this time. "Sorry—Martha. A typical martyr who never stopped being sorry for herself. Infected the boy, too. And now he doesn't forgive me for her death."

"She must have made a strong impression on him while she was alive."

"She made a bigger impression the way she went—over the Falls."

"Is that why Andy made his big statement—the school shooting?"

Art reached for the bottle and filled his glass. He did not offer her a refill.

Jane reached for the bottle gently. Her sluggishness was disappearing with all this talk, and she needed to replace her languor and dull the edge of this conversation. She also needed to see this discussion through to a logical end.

The rower had gone out of view and voices carried over from the barbecue, loud voices, fuelled by beer and sun.

"I struck Andy once. I think that tipped him over. I should never have done that."

"When was this?"

"The day before he showed up in school with my hunting rifle. He took my Cadillac out to impress some girl, without my permission. He did not even have a driving licence. The silly boy did not know that I could track him down with the GSM I had on board the vehicle. He was over in a rundown mill outside town with that twit of a girl and another boy. I went over there in the SUV and hauled him back. I was so mad at him I cuffed him well and good. I still ask myself if that was what tipped him over."

"From what you tell me about his mother and her dramatic exit, he was well on the way to his breakdown." She reached for her robe. The sun had not gone over the trees yet, but she was suddenly feeling cold.

"Better get changed," Art said, draining his glass. "I'll drive you back to town."

Fifteen

A purple vase of cut flowers—red and pink roses and yellow carnations—sat on her desk amidst piles of mail when Sue dragged herself into work three days later. She had called in sick on Friday and taken the weekend to spend time, mostly in bed, to mull things over.

Frank's door was shut, and she heard his muffled voice on the phone. Her heart leapt inside when she thought that the flowers could be from Rick. Then she immediately dismissed the thought. She felt dirty and unworthy of Rick after what had happened on election night. After her "mulling," she had made up her mind to hand in her resignation. How was she going to work in this place knowing that her dignity and freedom were not hers anymore? It would be better to work for minimum wage at the Walmart than step in here again.

She looked at the flowers again. What if they *were* from Rick? Who else could they be from?

Gingerly, she opened the handwritten card placed between the stems sticking out of the vase. She recognized the handwriting and a vice gripped her heart. She felt nauseated but kept reading.

"Dear Sue—a small token to say 'thank you' for the many ways in which you have taken care of me and my work. I am sorry for being demanding at times but put yourself in my shoes before you cast the next stone. I am looking forward to the next four years. Frank."

She sat down, handbag still slung over her shoulders. Conflicting thoughts rushed through her. Frank sounding penitent? If she were a man and had to be deprived of sex from a wife like Frieda, who was gadding off all over the place for months on end, Sue figured that she, too, would be pretty desperate. On the other hand, she had felt violated by his coming to her home that evening. All her determination to write that letter dissipated. Frank opened his office door and strode out.

She felt off guard, hair dishevelled—she normally gave it a brushing once she had settled down—her computer still un-booted, the mail piled on her desk. Frank must have come in early to stage the scene, she thought. She hastily unhitched her bag, tossed it under her desk, and started mussing with her hair.

"Good Morning, Sue." He was all suavity today, but his eyes observed her. "Hope you like the flowers. They go with your hair."

Now, why couldn't you have come to see me that night with flowers. She gave him a weak smile.

He looked down at the papers in his hand. "The press is coming in at eleven for an interview on my plans for the next four years. I have been working on these notes. Can you get them ready for me?"

"Sure." She reached over blindly, anything to keep the myriad of thoughts locked away, anything from having to talk to him about their night on the dining room table. As he turned to return to his office, she remembered to say, "Thank you for the flowers." It came in a gush, a preoccupied afterthought.

He paused in his doorway, that fake smile widening his mouth. He looked like Caesar who had just conquered the barbarians. "No problem. Perhaps we can get together like that again, in better surroundings."

She kept her eyes on the computer screen as it came to life. She felt like a prisoner. She knew she would not type that letter of resignation. Caving in to this powerful man was easier. Perhaps he would be discreet the next time. Perhaps she could keep this charade up and no one would know. And hopefully, Rick would take Frank down soon. Rick was her only hope now—she had no more resources left.

***

The day progressed in a blaze of activity, and Sue did not have a moment to dwell on her muddled thoughts. The press arrived, followed by the local TV station. Frank's cavernous office resembled a movie shoot at one point, with camera lights and wires running all over. The local news anchor sat in a fireside chat setting with the mayor re-elect, talking about the wonderful things that awaited this town over the next four years: more farmland converting into housing estates, more high paying jobs, the ice rink, a new community centre, tourism. If Frank had felt humbled this morning, from the tone of his note among the flowers, he had inflated himself once again and was displaying more bluster than she had ever thought him capable of. *Fuck your assistant and win the election. Who could be more powerful than that!*

At noon, the staff members were treated to lunch by the mayor—sandwiches from the local Tim Horton's. Frank addressed the entire team, about a dozen employees, on how grateful he was for their services and how much he looked forward to "continuing the battle" to make Milltown the best small town in Canada.

Sue excused herself after the sandwiches went around. She slipped a ham 'n cheese and a can of Diet Coke into her bag and walked down to the beach for some fresh air. On a bench on the boardwalk, she kicked off her sandals and gazed over the waves coming in gently from the lake while picking at her lunch. On a whim, she picked up her shoes and ran down to the water and washed her feet. It was an unusually cool summer day, and what was left of the seasonal sun had yet to warm the lake. In moments, she felt her heart rhythm tune into the gentle swells, blotting out everything else. She wanted to strip and plunge into the lake, wash herself clean of the iniquities in her soul. If only she did not have to worry about Billy, she would run down to the VIA station and board the next train going out west, as far west as she could go—Vancouver would be nice, where her sister lived.

The sand sticking to her wet feet was still better than nothing. Drying herself back at the bench, she put her open-toe shoes on and headed back to the office. There was no getting away from some things, no matter how much she day-dreamed.

At 3:00 p.m. the executions began. Three staff members—who had been seen at Rick Jones' rally a few weeks ago, a rally attended by a handful of townspeople, a rally so sparse that everyone who attended could have been marked—got their notices. Sue was asked to send them in one by one. It was only when the first employee, John Meredith, emerged from Frank's office with a ghastly look on his face, that Sue realized what was going on; Frank must have planned on the surprise element by typing the form letter of notice himself during her absence on Friday.

By the time Sally Mortimer, the last to be given her marching orders, left, Sue had a splitting headache. Would she be next? After all, hadn't Frank seen her getting into Rick Jones' car only yesterday? Why hadn't she resigned, like she had wanted to, this morning? At least, then she would have been calling the shots instead of Frank.

Frank came out of his office, the knot of his tie hanging down on his chest. His eyes were red and his lips engorged; he looked like a vampire satiated of bloodlust. "It's been a hard day, Sue, but a productive one." He looked down on her like he was about to pounce. "Now, all we will have left are the loyal ones. Hold all my calls for the rest of the day. I'm sure the union will have a lot to say. I'll deal with them tomorrow."

"Yes, sir," she said obediently, looking down at her screen, holding back the tears that were threatening to explode from her.

She cringed when his hand rested on her shoulder. "You have nothing to worry. You have shown your loyalty to me."

He tossed a file folder on her desk. "These are some CV's of people I am interested in. See if you can set up appointments for interviews starting tomorrow. They will be new positions, ones that could not be filled by the people I let go. I will draft a note to the remaining staff explaining why we had to make these 'changes.'"

***

When Sue left the office at five, a familiar Chevy Malibu was belching across the street. Rick engaged gears and swung over to her side in a U-turn that nearly caused an accident with an oncoming vehicle. Amidst the toots and curses echoing around him, Rick stuck his head out angrily and said, "Come on, get in."

She hung back. "You'll get me fired, giving me rides like this."

His eyes glinted like steel. "Get in, or else you'll get fired anyway."

She meekly complied, drained of resistance, and he took off in a roar down Main Street.

She looked across at him nervously; he was staring at the road ahead, swearing under his breath at anyone who got in his way. He was liberal with his horn until they left the town limits and climbed into the hills.

Sue decided to talk to this angry man who was driving like a maniac. "Frank got rid of three employees today."

"Frank!" Rick snarled. "That's all I hear—the fucker is everywhere."

"I'm sorry, but I've had a hard day, too. Where are you taking me?"

"You'll see," he said and did not talk again until they turned off into a lay-by that was a lookout down into the town below and the lake beyond. Sue breathed deep of the view in front of her—how peaceful, how hidden were the human currents that floated down below when viewed from up here. She turned the window down and breathed in the fresh cool breeze blowing at this altitude.

Rick reached into the back seat and dumped a photo envelope on her lap. "This is why I am mad."

With trembling hands, she opened the envelope and felt slammed back in her seat by what she saw. She wanted to open the door and run out, stumble down that hill. As she reached for the door handle, Rick leaned over and gripped her hand. "No, you are not running anymore, nor am I. This was the biggest kick in the pants I needed."

Suddenly, she wanted to explain, expiate herself. "You must think I am a whore."

"Your son took those pictures."

Sue pressed her hands to the sides of her head. "Billy! Oh my God! That's why he has been avoiding me." She began crying, shaking from side to side. "Oh, Rick what will I do? It's not what you think."

"How was it?" The twist in his mouth told her that he was having difficulty wrestling with his words, too.

"Frank forced himself on me."

"There are laws against rape. Although you did not look like you were actually being violated."

"What else could I do? The man has been after me since I started working for him. It's not like he gave me a choice."

He took the photographs from her. "These photos don't prove a damn thing—two consenting adults getting it off on a table. You could have struggled. You have no injuries."

"Oh, I am past struggling. What good would that have done? And what have you done with the information I gave you?"

"I don't have enough to move in on Frank. And if I use that letter you gave me, it will look like a smear campaign from a poor loser. His buddy, Art, is equally above reproach. Argh! I feel so helpless!" Rick slammed his hands down on the steering wheel and shook himself against it.

"How was Billy? What did he say?"

"He had the presence of mind to tell me that he did not want you implicated."

"Poor boy. What do I tell him?"

"You can tell him you did it for him." He was staring at her as if he still mistrusted what had gone on in those photographs. "Didn't you?"

"Yes. But why do I need to tell him that? I don't want to give him more complexes."

"You could make a clean breast of it. Ask him to forgive you."

Sue burst out laughing bitterly. "Forgiveness. Here is a man who has never forgiven himself all these years asking me to beg forgiveness? Rick Jones, heal yourself first!"

Rick pulled away from the steering wheel. "I have realized that. I threw my last bottle of Scotch away last night. The withdrawal is killing me today. But I think it is time for me to come back."

She reached out and placed her hand on his shoulder. He was trembling more than her. She pulled him towards her. He moved without resistance, his dark features subdued. They remained cheek to cheek for a long time, tears from each other's faces mixing and melding together.

Rick sniffed, still keeping his cheek against hers. "I'll come with you to talk to your boy, if you need me."

"Thanks, but I have to do this one myself." She pulled away and looked into his dull, whiskey singed eyes. He smelled of after shave, cigarettes and sweat—but not of alcohol, for a change.

***

She had warmed his dinner, thrown in an extra sausage, and poured some gravy into a bowl for his mashed potatoes. She hoped that Billy wouldn't be late again tonight, and this time, he did not disappoint her.

When he stepped through the door and tossed the car keys on the side closet, he paused, seeing her seated on the couch, still dressed in her work clothes, waiting for him.

"I thought you would be in bed, Mom."

"I need to talk to you," Sue said, looking straight at him. Billy seemed to wilt. He looked very tired, of a sudden.

"Can we do this tomorrow? I'm hungry."

"We can talk after you have eaten. Sit down."

He looked at the dining table. A look of distaste crossed his face. "I'll eat on the couch, if you don't mind."

She winced. "Eat anywhere, but eat."

She waited patiently while he wolfed down his food, seated on the couch. She brought him a Coke from the fridge.

When he had put his plate in the kitchen sink and popped the Coke can, she called out from her seat in the dining room. "Rick showed me the pictures you took."

There was silence from the kitchen. Then a sigh, one of relief.

"I'm sorry," she said. Tears had sprung into her eyes, and she had trouble keeping her composure.

She grabbed a tissue and dabbed her eyes, but her throat caught, and she could not speak anymore without breaking down. Billy came out of the kitchen and sat next to her.

"I took those pictures to get at him."

"You know that 'getting at him' is impossible. Wherever those pictures go, I will be in them."

He hung his head. "I'm sorry. I did not know what to do. I just wanted revenge, I guess."

"You wanted revenge against me, too."

"Yes. You did not need to give in to him."

"I was thinking of you. Thinking of holding onto my job. Frank fired three people today. I could have been one of them."

"That would have been better than what you did."

"Oh, you are so noble." She found him irritating in his idealism. What was it with the men in her life? Billy was just like his father—naive, trusting, and dull. Maybe when she revealed what she knew, he might soften up. Realize that everyone was vulnerable.

"I got a call from the Sri Lankan girl's mother when I got home," she said slowly.

Billy jumped in his chair. "Saro's mother? How is Saro?"

"She's all right. And she is determined to have your baby. Her mother wanted to know if you were willing to support the child."

Billy hung his head. "Oh shit, Mom—I am sorry."

"I told her that you were planning to go to university. You still plan to do that, right?"

Billy started shaking his head. He was swaying from side to side. "I don't know, Mom. Saro won't talk to me. Frankly, I don't know what to do. I want to be fair by her. And the baby."

"You are like your father. Played fair all his life and never left this place, except in a casket. If that girl was silly enough to get pregnant, then she can look after her child."

"You are talking like a real bitch, now. Where is your sense of compassion?"

She rose and flung the cushion at the door. "All my life I have tried to play fair—and where has that gotten me? On the dining room table of my own house being fucked by my boss, while my son takes photographs. Do you think I want that for you? No, you have to go, get out, get an education and leave this stinking place. No two-bit South Asian girl is going to detract you from that path. Do you hear?" She was raging, cursing inwardly for having broken the calm she had promised herself to maintain during this conversation.

He reached out and grabbed her by the hem of her skirt. "Mom, slow down. We'll settle this, okay? But not tonight."

She sat down again. Her face was flushed, and she felt her heart racing.

"What else did you tell Mrs. Selvadurai?"

"I told her to get her daughter to an abortion clinic—fast."

"Oh, shit!"

"It's no, 'oh shit.' Apart from calling you a few choice names, she tended to agree with me that this baby had to go."

"Mom, it's a life we are talking about here…we feel different about life, you know. Saro feels different. And even though she is not talking to me, I feel the same way, too. You grew up with all this birth control shit, your generation fucked every mother's son and daughter in the planet, gave us AIDS. We are different, you know."

Sue felt smacked. She wanted to strike him but knew that he was talking from the heart. And he wasn't wrong.

Billy rose, drained his can, and grabbed the car keys. "I'm going out to see a movie. I need to clear my head."

"That's it. Walk out when the conversation gets difficult."

"Yes, I am walking out. Neither you nor I are rational at the moment. I need to talk to Saro first before I agree to anything."

He strode out the front door, slamming it behind him, leaving her as confused as when he had arrived home, despite the calm in which she had drawn him into the conversation. She headed to the kitchen cupboard and grabbed the half bottle of Brandy she kept for medicinal purposes.

"Rick Jones, you may be jumping on the wagon again, but I am coming off," she shouted hollowly to the four blank walls of the kitchen as she downed a tumbler full of brandy that burned her insides, hoping it would eradicate the shame, hurt, and disappointment in her soul.

Sixteen

Sam closed early that night. It was 9:30 p.m. The restaurant's regular closing time was half an hour away, but most patrons usually had dinner between six and eight, and the dining room was deserted but for one customer, an old woman who had started coming in frequently during the last month.

She had looked familiar when she first came in. Being a small town, Sam kept bumping into his patrons all the time and did not think much of it. Ever since her first arrival a couple of weeks ago, the old woman always ordered a small bowl of rice, some grilled vegetables, and chicken curry, mildly spiced. After her meal, she would spend a long time over a solitary cup of tea.

He dawdled because he did not want to go upstairs, yet. Ever since Sarojini had dropped her bombshell a week ago, it had been like walking on hot coals around his wife and daughter, like a wannabe Sannasi in Kataragama: you walked past fast, before the scalding took hold. Sam went over to the front door and swung the sign around to "Closed." The old woman made to finish her tea.

"Take your time, I won't be out of here for another half hour, at least," Sam said to her.

She nodded and placed her cup down slowly in its saucer.

"You really speak good English," she said.

That raspy voice! While out on his first walk in this town, eons ago, it seemed, the woman with her shopping basket and the broken eggs.

Sam smiled, feeling vindicated. "I am glad that you like the food in here."

"I like coming here. The food is good, too, after I got used to it. My husband, Harry, and I used to come here when it was owned by the other fella, Spade."

"I hope you don't find our decor too foreign."

As if prompted, she scanned the room to take in the brass Buddha motifs on the wall closest to her; the portrait of Lord Shiva on the opposite wall, in his lotus pose, ringed by subdued blue mountains and rivers; the batik wall hanging of brightly adorned elephants in procession at the Kandy Perahera; the shoulder-height brass oil lamp by the door.

"It's different, sort of mystical. That's what I had to get used to when my Harry died. I'm glad you took down old Spade's. TV—that's all Harry used to watch when we come in here—hockey."

"Oh, I am so sorry to hear about your husband, madam."

"I'm Mabel. Born and bred here. Harry, too. Worked in the chemical plant thirty-five years. Cancer took him five years ago."

"I hear there are a lot of cancers in this town."

"Lots of his buddies went the same way. Can't prove anything, though. He was a smoker. I quit last year—another change I got to get used to." She sipped her tea.

"Can I get you more tea? There is plenty in the pot."

"No, it will keep me awake too much. And then I will think of Harry."

"Well, you can come back here anytime. And you should try our other delicacies."

Sam had a sudden brainwave. "Give me a moment."

He went into the kitchen and picked out some masala vadais, and a handful of string hoppers. He poured beef curry into a Styrofoam cup and sealed it. He added seeni sambol into another disposable container and packed all the items into a larger Styrofoam container and wrapped it in a plastic bag, securing the package with a rubber band.

"This is on the house," he announced, returning and placing the food parcel in front of Mabel.

She looked flustered. "Oh dear, I really, can't…"

"Please, try them. Perhaps you might like something else to eat, when you next visit."

"Oh, I'll like them all, I'm sure. It's just that I have to budget for eating out."

"Ah, don't worry. Check these out, then when you come in the next time, tell me what you liked and what you did not like. Then tell me your budget for the day, and I will fix you a menu to fit with it, hopefully a different menu every time!"

Mabel's eyes lit up. "You will?"

"Sure."

"Tell me about where you come from…"

He recounted his life in Sri Lanka and his family's arrival in Canada. For Sam, it was cathartic, unburdening the bottled-up memories of a life gone adrift. Before they knew it, the town clock was ringing the hour. Mabel rose reluctantly, intrigued by all she heard, and promised to return soon for the next instalment.

After the old woman left, gratefully hugging her goody bag, Sam closed up. He packed some food to take upstairs: a peace offering, if that would at least break the deadlock.

He ascended the stairs slowly, the day's effort suddenly descending upon him. He just needed some peace and quiet, and that, he knew, was not awaiting him upstairs. Still, the talk with Mabel had been rewarding; there were good people in this place, they were just different and cautious of outsiders. If he could melt people like Mabel, he felt that he could soon get into the fabric of this town and be successful.

Saro was watching TV and Malani was darning a torn curtain at the dining table. Her sewing machine took up most of the space. With the flowing curtain occupying the rest of the area, other domestic knick-knacks that had gradually taken up permanent residency on the table were hanging perilously at its edges. He missed the family's large, ornate teak dining table from back home, gleaming with the loving polishing that Malani had given it weekly. That table had gone up in flames with everything else they had owned.

Sam went into the tiny kitchen and placed the food parcel on the counter. He took down three plates.

"Where is Mahesh?" he asked.

"Gone for his Buddhist lecture in Peterborough."

Sam grimaced. That meant that Mahesh had taken the family car and would be gone until way past midnight. His son always had an excuse for being late ever since Malani had signed him up for classes to keep Mahesh centred in his culture: once it had been a highway closure, the next time he'd had to finish some homework with his teacher, another time he'd given a friend a ride home. Sam wondered what it would be tonight. And all the while Mahesh was out with the car, Sam could not fall asleep. And he needed to sleep tonight. The boy also had a bad habit of parking in extremely tight corners, scraping the bodywork.

Sam brought the plates out to his wife and daughter. "A small snack before bedtime?"

"I'm not hungry," Saro said without taking her eyes off the TV. Some re-run of *Who Wants to be a Millionaire*. What a racket, thought Sam, if only I could become one just by answering a bunch of silly questions.

"She has decided not to go to the clinic," Malani said, guiding the end of the curtain through the machine, focussing on her stitching.

Here it comes.

Sam picked up a string hopper from his plate, scooped some coconut sambol onto it, and popped it into his mouth. He was not going to be drawn into an argument, at least not on an empty stomach.

"I spoke to the boy's mother today." Malani continued her sewing.

Her eyes were squinting, but Sam wasn't sure if she was focussed on the task at hand or on some thought in her head.

"And she agreed with me," Malani proclaimed, looking up from her work. The next moment she shrieked and stuck her finger into her mouth, sucking deeply.

Sam saw droplets of blood rim the middle digit of her right hand when she removed it from her mouth.

"Bloody old sewing machine—always grabs me," Malani hissed.

Sam rose quickly and headed for their tiny washroom. "I'll get you a Band-aid."

When he had secured her finger with the tape and the bleeding had eased, he washed his hands and returned to his food. He had lost his appetite now.

"I will put this food in the fridge." He took the plates back into the kitchen. "And then I am going to bed."

"And you are going to continue avoiding this issue." Malani's steely voice stopped Sam midway into the kitchen.

Sam put the plates down on the kitchen counter and turned around.

"I am not avoiding anything. This is Sarojini's decision. It is her body, after all."

The TV clicked off, and Saro rose from the sofa. "And I am having this baby, that's all." She stalked off into her bedroom and slammed the door.

Sam came back over to the dining room table and sat down heavily across from his wife.

"Why don't you let this go, Mala? What has happened has happened. This is her karma. This is our karma."

Malani wrenched the curtain out of the sewing machine, and Sam heard a rip. She threw the curtain on the floor.

"You are constantly prepared to accept, accept, accept! That is why, ever since I married you, we have been going downhill."

"Mala, even your Buddhist teachings say that we should practice acceptance. Things happen for a reason."

"That boy's mother refused to have anything to do with this pregnancy. She told me very rudely that her son was heading off to university in Toronto and nothing, nothing, should disturb him. You call that acceptance?"

Behind Saro's door, they heard a howl, like a wounded dog, or bitch.

"Mala—stop this." Sam rose, the vein in his temple throbbing, the signs of a headache waiting to take over. "I will not talk of this again. I am going to bed."

Sam stalked off into the master bedroom and sat down on the bed in the dark, fully clothed. He kicked off his shoes. The un-curtained window (*ah, that must be the curtain in the sewing machine that will need more stitches now!*) threw in lights from the back lots of the row of shops. A cat slunk across the empty parking lot. Sam lay back on the bed. He heard muffled sobs from the dining room. Through the thin wall separating the children's room from his, he heard other sobs, too. Saro's. Cupboards opened, and hangers were drawn aside. He shut his eyes in futile hope that it would stop the fragmenting of his family. Lights turned into the back lot, and he heard the over-energetic handbrake of his car being cranked into place. *Thank God, at least Mahesh had come home early, and the car was still in running condition—small mercies!* Sam turned over, put a pillow over his head, and blotted out the world.

***

The next morning, he woke to a wailing in the next room. Stumbling out of bed, Sam staggered next door. Mahesh was sitting up amidst a pile of bed sheets, rubbing his eyes and looking confused. Malani stood in the middle of the room, in her housecoat, pulling at her long black tresses.

She looked at Sam with bloodshot eyes. "She's gone. Our daughter is gone."

"Gone? Where?" Sam looked towards Sarojini's bed, adjacent to Mahesh's in the poky room. It was empty. It looked lightly slept in with the blanket tossed over the pillows.

"She probably went to school early," Sam said, trying to believe that himself.

"She never would go without telling me," Malani said.

"Well, the two if you weren't exactly in a friendly mood yesterday."

"Look—even her suitcase is gone." Malani flung open the cupboard. "And all her dresses."

"*Amma.*" Mahesh finally got some words into his mouth. "Why don't you let that stupid sister of mine be? She will cool down when she runs out of money. I know she does not have much cash."

"Stupid is just the word. Pregnant brain—that's what she has got. Sam, we have to go and find her, now. Get the car keys, I'm going to change."

As Sam left the room in his wife's wake, he did not notice his son slump back into the pillows and pound them, muttering "Fuck, fuck, fuck," under his breath.

***

They drove around the town for an hour after discovering that Saro had not arrived at school. They went down to the train station first. The train to Toronto had already departed, and the next one was due in an hour. The train heading in the opposite direction, to Ottawa, was arriving at the station in five minutes, but Saro was not among those on the platform holding their lattes in the crisp morning air.

They next tried the bus station, the women's shelter, and the mission house—all blanks. They phoned her close friends' houses— more blanks. They went around to the coffee and donut shops, to the McDonald's and the Burger King, with no sighting. They tried the mall, but it was still shut.

Around ten o'clock they gave up.

"We must report this to the police," Sam said.

Malani gasped, her red-rimmed puffy eyes widening. "What rubbish—the shame of being in the sights of the police? You know what they did the last time when the house burned down. They treated us as if *we* were the culprits."

"Mala, this is Canada, the police are here to serve and protect, not bully and demand. If we do not get their help, what else can we do other than go back home and hope that she turns up?"

She sat fidgeting, daubing her nose on a hanky. Sam was beginning to feel sorry for his wife. As long as she had been protected by her society and its customs, Mala projected an image of strength. But society, status, and familiar routines had all been stripped away, gradually, sometimes surreptitiously; now she was a hysterical, unhinged woman, hair uncombed and knotted, grabbing an ill-draped sari and wetting a handkerchief with tears of regret.

"Let's go home," he said, turning the car around. "I don't have to open the restaurant until eleven. Let's have a cup of tea and figure out what to do. We also need to rest. No use trying to think when we are tired."

She remained exhausted and slumped in her seat for the rest of the ride home.

***

Mahesh felt the sharp steel press against his chest under his sweat shirt. His father's indictment from the night before, words floating downstairs from the apartment as Mahesh had sneaked out of the restaurant and headed upstairs to see what was going on, still hurt—"I think that boy is a coward. I don't know how he is going to survive in this country."

He hoped that his father would not miss the knife, one of many reposing in the block in the kitchen, but his father and mother had plenty to occupy themselves with today. He was sweating, not so much for wearing a sweatshirt in summer, but because he was treading on strange ground. But he had to go through with it. These white bastards had pushed him and his family enough. He had to show his father what he was made of. He looked on either side of the road; the cops had been active around the school after that shooting last year. No police cruisers were in sight, although the police station was two blocks away and around the corner. A school bus pulled up and disgorged its load of loud students outside the gates. Mahesh crossed the road and blended in with the crush.

He saw Jack and Ted standing at the entrance to the school, beside the orange construction sign: the cement blocks over the drainage ditch had been removed for some municipal work that never seemed to finish. Jack was wearing his Maple Leafs jersey and smoking a cigarette; he always smoked outside the gate, so the teachers could see him and do nothing. Billy was not around, although he could often be found in the company of his friends.

"Yo, Buddha, how's it hanging?" Jack's taunt sailed through the air. Jack took a final puff of his cigarette and flicked the flaming stub at Mahesh. It bounced off his sweatshirt.

Mahesh snapped. The months of taunting that had built into a dam of resentment finally burst. The knife slid out from under his sweatshirt into his hand, and he lunged at Jack. Someone shrieked and students in the vicinity dispersed. Mahesh gripped a frozen Jack by the collar and stuck the knife against his throat, tearing flesh and sending a dribble of blood onto his Leafs jersey.

"Okay, asshole, this is the last day you insult me, got it?"

Jack gulped and nodded, tilting his head backwards from the knifepoint.

"Where is your friend, Billy?" Mahesh said, getting bolder.

"Don't know. Ouch! You're fucking killing me! Get him, Ted!"

"Where is your fucking friend, Billy? He has kidnapped my sister."

Mahesh felt a force hit him from the left side, and he went staggering out of control. Too late, he saw a shock of red hair easing back from him as he slipped off the sidewalk and fell into the exposed ditch. He landed in the squelchy mud and heard nervous laughter from up above. Jack, holding his neck, and Ted, combing back his shock of rusty hair, peered down at him. The knife was no longer in Mahesh's hand.

"Let's finish off the fucker," Jack said.

"Cops," yelled Ted, reaching out to restrain Jack, but he was too late. His companion was in mid air; a moment later, he landed on Mahesh. Both boys went down into the mud. A police siren sounded in the background, but all Mahesh felt was the weight of his larger opponent upon him, squeezing the air out of his lungs, pushing him down into the sewage run-off, the shit and filth of this land.

Seventeen

They came for him in the morning. Three guards carrying truncheons.

"Sorry I have to put the cuffs on, kiddo," Henry said, bending over. "Procedure."

Andy held his hands out lamely, but his mind was split and working overtime. One half told him that he was going to miss this room with its high barred window in one corner overlooking the courtyard. He was going to miss his blue overalls, sticky, sweaty, and creased—they had become a second skin. His old civilian clothes were unfamiliar and tight. The weights on the floor, the ones he had pumped and pumped until he thought his heart would burst, looked forlorn. They had helped him sleep better, better than the drugs. He was going to miss Henry, too. Henry was rough, but he cared. The other half of his mind was measuring steps, looking for weak points, generating adrenaline to burst out when the moment came.

Henry helped him to his feet. "You look like a ghost, kiddo. Don't worry, it's not all bad. Same shit, different home. You'll do fine."

Andy walked ahead, flanked by Henry and another guard, with the third man bringing up the rear. As they rounded a corner, Henry slipped something into Andy's handcuffed hands.

They came out to the main entrance and a prison van from Correctional Services was parked under the front porch. The sunlight was blinding, and Andy eased the prescription sunglasses out of his shirt pocket and put them on awkwardly.

"Let me help you, buddy," Henry said, moving closer while his colleagues went over to the vehicle, where two other men, in federal uniforms, leaned against its doors.

"Listen," Henry hissed. "That piece of paper has names of prison guards and inmates we have brought on side to help you. Your dad has taken care of things. Make contact with them as soon as you get to Kingston, and you are going to be all right. Got it?"

Andy nodded. Henry stepped back, gripped Andy's shoulder and said, "Good luck, Andy, we will miss you around here." Andy heard the catch in his protector's throat. He felt a tear run down from his eye, but his mind was sizing up the two men who were going to drive him to Kingston; both carried holstered revolvers. The older of the two, in his fifties, butted out a cigarette and headed for the driver's side of the vehicle.

The tall blond one, who looked like an ex-boxer, grabbed Andy roughly by the hand and led him to the rear doors, which swung open to reveal a narrow cell inside—no windows in this one. "Get in, fellah. I'll take those glasses and give them to you when you get out at the other end." The sunglasses came off, and Andy was pushed inside. He sprawled on the narrow bench that ran along one side of the vehicle.

The doors slammed shut. Two sources of light filtered in from opposite ends: through a narrow grill on the back door and from a glass panel against the driver's cab which swung shut the moment the two guards were inside. The vehicle took off with a throaty roar.

Andy leaned back, his mind racing. His body jolted against the cold hard wall of this can with every bump in the road. He closed his eyes and waited until the vehicle ceased stopping frequently at traffic lights and picked up speed. He felt them climb a steep incline and merge into roaring traffic. They were on the highway.

He put his fingers in his mouth, depressed his tongue and gagged, vomiting all over his freshly laundered civilian shirt. He squeezed his neck until he felt his head was about to burst. He had practiced this routine while in solitary confinement, in between visits by the guards. Henry had often told him that he looked like shit soon after of those "practices," and his reward had been an upping of the meds which he hated. Still he had needed the preparation for today.

Andy banged against the driver's side wall panel. The panel opened, and Andy pressed his mouth against it, smearing vomit over the glass and screaming in a throttled voice, "I'm suffocating... get me out."

An eye peeped through on the other side then the panel closed. The vehicle did not slow down.

Andy began throwing himself against both sides of the vehicle. Even if he was not making more than a muffled sound, his rocking of the van with this violent movement would soon draw attention. He felt the vehicle slow down, pull off to the right, and stop, its engine idling. He was sprawled on the floor at this point, gasping. The panel opened once more and stayed open longer. Andy rolled across the narrow floor, banging his head against the wall. The panel slid back slowly. The engine switched off.

The back door opened, and sunlight shot in, blinding Andy.

"What are you up to there, fellah? You sick or something?"

Andy kept his eyes on the stick in the man's hands, the holstered revolver. He burped and nodded his head. Then he started pissing, letting it darken his pants and wet the floor in full view of the guard. The man swore under his breath.

"You've been inside too long," the guard said, climbing aboard, grabbing Andy by the collar and hauling him onto the bench. "Fuck, it stinks in here. You're gonna have to wait until we get to Kingston. Won't be long, about an hour."

The guard crouched and started backing away towards the doors. Andy let out a strangled scream.

"Whoa! Stop that! You are not going to your execution." The guard advanced again, lowering his stick.

Andy pounced; the built-up adrenaline acting like jet fuel to send him flying across the cramped space. His handcuffed hands grabbed onto one of the guard's legs, and his teeth latched onto the man's crotch. He bit hard, feeling soft flesh squelch and burst under the fabric of the pants.

The guard let out a muffled grunt and fell on top of the prisoner. Andy felt the air go out of him but kept his pincers tight around the man's shrinking testicles, biting down harder and harder. The guard was moaning, squealing, trying to reach under him for this maniacal monster who was neutering him.

After what seemed like an eternity, the thrashing and squealing ceased, and a sigh escaped from above, like the air going out of a balloon. The man kicked once more and was still, his weight crushing Andy to the point of asphyxiation. Summoning all his strength, Andy pushed up and away and managed to creep out from under the guard. The man, a stain of crimson spreading over the ripped crotch of his khaki pants, smelled of blood sweat and shit; combined with Andy's piss and vomit, the inside of the van could have been the bottom of a cess pit.

Catching his breath amidst the reeking close quarters, Andy fished inside the man's pockets for the keys to the handcuffs but did not find them. The driver must have them. He pulled out the gun from the man's holster. He'd never fired one of these, was it even loaded?

A raspy breathing was coming out of the man; he must have fainted with the shock of his attack. Andy let go the safety catch and was raising the gun with both hands when he saw the wall panel begin to slide open. He had no time to think. He rolled over to the driver's wall, stuck the gun into the—by now—fully opened panel, and pulled the trigger. The gun bucked in his hand, and he heard a grunt on the other side. *So, it was loaded!*

He crouched under the wall panel waiting for return fire. Nothing. He looked at the open back doors, swaying gently in the wind in front of him—freedom! But what if the driver was still out front, waiting for him to come out? Besides, the blond guy was going to wake up pretty soon, eunuch though he probably was by now.

Andy inched toward the back doors, keeping his gun trained on the wall panel, looking for any sign of movement behind it. He reached the doors and jumped down, whirling around to see if anyone had him covered. They had pulled into a lay-by off the highway and cars sped by in a regular, intermittent stream; no one paid attention to him standing by the edge of the road, a gun in his hand, handcuffed, pants stained in urine and likely, blood dripping out of his mouth.

He quickly moved over to the blind side of the van—the side facing the woods at the edge of the highway, out of sight of motorists—and stepped toward the passenger side of the driver's cab. Still no sound of movement in the cab. Shards of glass speckled the ground in front of the van, some had blood on them. Taking a quick gamble, Andy grabbed the passenger door handle and pulled it away, training the gun into the inside of the vehicle. His caution was unnecessary, the driver was thrown back against the shattered windshield, his face a bloody mess.

For a moment, panic struck. He wanted to throw the gun and run away through the woods. His knees felt weak. He sank to the ground momentarily. He was past the point of no return. A sense of power surged through him at that thought. He had killed another human, just like he had set out to do in that schoolyard two years ago. And this time he had killed an armed guard. He felt stronger. A grin of delight replaced his mounting fear. This rush was exciting.

He climbed into the cab, pulled the driver off the dash board onto the double seat and went through the dead man's pants pockets. He found a key ring, and after several attempts, released himself from the cuffs. He peered back through the open wall panel; the blond guy was stirring in the back. Andy retraced his steps to the rear of the vehicle, closing the doors behind him and locking himself in with the recovering guard, with the smell of human detritus. He placed the gun to the man's head, closed his eyes and pulled the trigger. He felt splashes on his face and hands before opening his eyes. The walls of the van were splayed with blood and bone. His body and clothes were splotched with it. Andy sat back on the bench and surveyed the scene.

This is what he had set out to do in the school that day: create a celebration of blood and take himself out before they took him away. Well, that attempt had failed. But here he was, taking out two men, more powerful than him, and still alive to tell the tale. The sense of power engulfed him completely. He saw himself as a marauding invader, wreaking vengeance on all those who had wronged him. And there were more people to whom lessons had to be taught.

He stripped down to his underwear and wiped as much of the remains of the blond guard off him as he could. Then he got out of the van and locked the back doors, returning to the driver's cab via the vehicle's blind side. He pushed the driver down on the passenger seat, took the dead man's jacket that was hanging on a hook by the door, and buttoned it on. He found two spare clips of ammunition in the guards' clothing, which he pocketed. The windshield had shattered into fragments inside and, mostly, outside the vehicle. Andy removed the clinging pieces of residual glass that were bound to fly at him when the vehicle was in motion and turned on the ignition. There was no way he could drive fast on the highway without a windshield. He could see the next green exit sign about a kilometre ahead. He put the vehicle into gear and drove slowly, a rush of wind in his face and some agitated motorists, noticing the van for the first time, tooted at him from behind for slowing them down. Anger blazed in him as they swung past rudely with horns blaring. He wanted to shoot them all in his new-found omniscience, but common sense told him to bide his time.

He turned off the exit and took a country road north. He did not know where he was, probably half an hour east of Kingston. The radio phone on the vehicle buzzed and the operator on the other side said, "Vehicle B34, report your position."

Andy ignored the command and drove faster.

He was passing the last of the farms because small factories and farm machinery outfitters began to pass by.

"Vehicle B34, report your position."

He grabbed the receiver, took a deep breath, deepened his voice and said. "This is B34—still in Belleville. Had to stop for a piss."

"You were past Belleville the last time you reported."

Shit. Andy's brain started revving. The exhilaration was rising in him, too. He wanted to play this game. And outplay them.

"There was traffic outside Belleville. We turned back to take a break."

There was a pause at the other end, as if the working of the operator's brain was being transmitted across in the static that hissed over the open line.

Another voice, older, more authoritative, came on. "That's breaking procedure, B34. Who's driving? Identify yourself."

Andy dug inside the driver's jacket pocket. A lump on the right revealed a wallet. He pulled off the road, fished inside and found a driver's licence.

"Wallace, sir. Mike Wallace. My partner here had to take a leak sir, then there was the traffic again, getting back on the road."

There was more static on the line. Then the first voice crackled, "Give us your position in five minutes."

That was it. He had five minutes. They were onto him.

He revved the van out of its parked position and turned left at the next intersection, heading back towards Milltown, deeper into farming country. After five minutes, the radio beeped again, but he ignored it as his foot was pressed down on the accelerator, trying to get as far as he could. When the beeping got annoying, he switched off the radio. He came to an intersection with a deep wooded gully on the right-hand side.

He revved the engine, put the vehicle into drive, pointed it off the road, and jumped off the driver's side the moment the front wheels left the gravel. He landed on the hard, stony surface on all fours, in time to see the tail of the van disappear off the side and get buried in a blanket of trees and brush.

He had picked his spot well. He could see a farmhouse in the distance and there was washing hanging in the yard. And corn in an untended stand by the road advertising "$5.00. Bag your own."

Ten minutes later, he struck out, hugging the treeline, wearing a pair of tight jeans and a checked red shirt, a bag of corn in his hand. He had obligingly dropped a five-dollar bill from Mike Wallace's wallet in the corn stand. There were four more ten-dollar bills inside to tide him over. He jumped into the ditch when two siren-blaring police cars whizzed by on the road towards the location where he had abandoned the police van.

The game was afoot, and Andy was feeling buzzed.

Eighteen

Billy drove fast, climbing the hills out of town as the sun came over the trees, blinding him. Saro was slumped in the passenger seat, silent. He hoped she would open up when they got to the mill.

He had been surprised by her call at 5:00 a.m. that morning.

"Come to my house," she had whispered after he grabbed his cell phone on its third ring. "Park at the end of the street. I will come out to meet you. Come now."

He had stumbled out of bed, pulled on some clothes, and slunk out of the house without disturbing his mother. As he neared the darkened South Asian Delights restaurant, pink was just lighting the sky over the lake, visible through the giant trees in the park. A figure darted out of the side of the building, suitcase in hand. Sarojini tugged at the back door of the car. She wore a scarf and dark glasses. She tossed the suitcase in the back seat and got into the front passenger seat.

"Drive. Take me somewhere we can talk."

"Tim Hortons is open."

"No. That's too public. Somewhere private."

Billy scratched his head. "We can go back to the mill, if that's okay."

"Yes, that will be fine. Drive."

***

Now she sat forward, slouched, as they drove off the main road onto the cart path that curved its way down to the mill.

The river was low this morning, flowing gently past as they got out of the car and walked down to the water.

"I will always love this place," Sarojini said, raising her arms out and breathing in the fresh morning air.

Billy kicked a dead branch and stood a couple of paces behind her. "I wish you had called me earlier. I missed you."

She turned and fell into his arms. He held her shaking body. Her tears wet his cheek. They kissed, but this time there wasn't the ferocity of absence, the vigour of youth; they were like two old friends hugging for comfort in a storm—practical, familiar, muted.

"Oh Billy, it's been so difficult, ever since *Amma* found out."

Between sobs, she told him what had transpired after her mother's "discovery" in the washroom. He helped her sit down on the grass. He brought back a blanket and slung it over her shoulders as the sun had still not risen over the treeline.

"I'll look after you and the baby," Billy said, sitting down next to her.

"No, you won't, Billy. You are going to be a big guy in Toronto, according to your mother."

"My mother is entitled to her dreams. She is trying to live out her disappointed life through me."

"She will prevent us from being together. She told Ammi."

"She—what? Have you guys all been talking behind my back?"

"Ammi called your mother."

Billy picked at blades of grass by his side.

"The problem is that everyone has dreams for me. I have my own dreams."

She looked askance at him. "What are your dreams, Billy?"

"I've always wanted to get away, fed on my mother's drivel. But now I realize that I could return here and build a better town. There are too many corrupt people here, and I could work to get them eradicated."

"You are being an idealist, Billy. There will always be bad people."

"Yes, but there must be room for good people, too."

They sat in silence for awhile. The sun came over the trees, and Saro tossed the blanket off her shoulders and removed the scarf. Billy revelled in her revealed beauty: the shock of dark hair cascading down her shoulders, the pointed, defiant nose, the dark features that had become angular and more mature since he had last seen her, those shimmering pools of ebony in her eyes that radiated intelligence, warmth, and mystery. He took her in his arms again and kissed her, a long lingering kiss. He began to feel his heart racing and briefly, hers too. Then she broke away.

"I am going to Toronto. There is a shelter there for unmarried mothers. They have agreed to take me in."

"No. You can't do that. Saro, I want to be there when you have this…our…baby."

"When you go to university in Toronto you will be nearby."

"I am not going to university in Toronto."

"Your mother will be disappointed."

"Screw my mother."

"What will you do?"

"I am going to learn carpentry. This whole county needs good builders and carpenters—trades-people—while the university educated ones cannot get jobs. There is a course in Peterborough. I don't need to go away. I can increase my hours at the hardware store, and I can look after you. Besides your parents are here—you have a place to stay."

"Have you seen the inside of our apartment? Mahesh and I share a room. You want to add a baby in there?"

"Then you can come to my house."

"And your mother will throw me out."

"I'll manage my mother. Just tell me that you will stay until I figure all this out."

She hesitated.

"Come home with me this evening. We will have a sit-down chat with my mother."

"How do I know she will even have me over?"

"I'll call her now." He reached into his pocket and pulled out his cell phone. She reached over and grabbed his hand. "No. I need to think. Oh, I am so bloody confused."

He pulled her over, and they sat there on the bank of the river, silent—together, at least momentarily. Billy did not want to talk, and he suspected, neither did Saro, fearing that would lead to another argument and shatter the unity of spirit that had encircled them, one they could not articulate in words.

"Let's picnic here today," she said, suddenly rising and running down to the water. "I want to spend my last summer day like my first, with you." She was shedding clothes, and before he knew it, she was stepping into the water naked, striking out into the middle of the sluggish river.

"You'll catch cold," Billy said, stumbling in after her, only managing to kick his shoes off before the cool water embraced his feet and rose over his shins, wetting his jeans.

His eyes were reverted on her soft belly, which he imagined swollen—at least, it was not as flat as before—nurturing a new life inside it. He wanted to protect that life, protect Saro more than anything else.

She swam up to him and rose out of the water. He sucked in his breath at her wet, dark skin that radiated upwards from the V of her pubis; her black hair, lush and breaking off into wet trails over firm, swollen breasts and their large dark aureoles.

He took her in his arms and let her wetness wash him. He never wanted to let her go.

Nineteen

Sitting in the open sunshine at the edge of the woods, Andy felt his memories, long incarcerated like he had been in a prison, were free to roam again. The strongest of these was the one he had suppressed the most: of the final family trip to Niagara Falls, six months after Aunt Brenda drowned.

His mother had slumped into a deep depression after her sister's passing. She had stopped taking meals with the family, barricaded herself in the spare bedroom and only came out to take a quick meal in the kitchen or to go to the washroom. Whenever Andy tapped on the spare room door, his mother would open it gingerly and peer at him with frightened eyes. She let him in occasionally, when she felt like it; at other times, she slammed the door on him. Whenever he entered, he got the stale smell of old clothes, unchanged bed linen, and burnt candles. There were crucifixes and pages of scripture hanging all over the walls. His mother, despite her Italian-Jewish roots, had never been very religious, but now she had gone overboard.

The last time he entered her room, he noticed how much weight she had lost, her buxom figure was gaunt and her brow lined. Taking a deep breath, he announced, "Dad says that we should go to Niagara Falls. He said it would be good for you to visit your old home."

"I have no home on earth," his mother replied.

"Mom, I don't see you anymore."

"You are beginning to become like him." She pointed at the door.

"Like whom? Dad?"

"Yes. And your uncle Rick. Men. Fakes."

"Mom—just because I go to the factory and joke around with the workers doesn't mean that I am becoming like him. Are you going to come?"

"No!"

His mother had shut him out of her room totally after that. She had even asked the maid to bring in her meals and a chamber pot, which the poor woman had to empty several times a day.

Whenever he passed her room he heard loud praying, like chanting, and the occasional singing of hymns.

His father never spoke about his mother's behaviour and went about his business as if nothing was wrong. Art was often in Toronto during that time.

Then, on one of those rare days when his father was home—Andy remembered it well because he had insisted that his father watch the Stanley Cup playoff game that night with him on television, replete with popcorn and Coke, and Art had complied with a file folder from the office in his lap—his mother's door had opened. She stood there in her transparent crumpled nightgown, her hair a wild sprawl over her emaciated frame, and said, "I'm ready. Take me to the Falls."

Andy shook himself from the memory. What had had been a joyful release of tension for him turned into a nightmare at scenic Niagara Falls. They had checked into a suite at the Skyline Hotel with a view across from and above the tumbling waters. As soon as they arrived, Martha insisted on taking a walk along the boardwalk. Andy accompanied his mother as he did not want her wandering off in her fragile condition. Art said he would join them shortly as he had some phone calls to make back to the office. Andy insisted that his father come with them, but Art had replied coolly, "In a little while. Go along with your mother."

It was a sunny day, and yet, the spray from the falls made everything wet, damp, and cold. Andy realized how much energy his mother had when she suddenly sped ahead of him, bumping into pedestrians and tourists, walking into the rainbow thrown by the gushing waters.

Too late, he saw her grab the cast iron railing and clamber up the fence. People screamed, and a burly tourist tried to grab her. All Andy heard was his mother's scream, "Brenda, I'm coming," as she tipped over the edge.

Andy rushed to the railing and tried to go after her, but this time the big tourist grabbed him, shouting, "Arch, no! Don't be a *dummkopf!*"

He kicked the German good and hard, but the man held on until others jumped in to pin him down.

Then Art was by his side, pulling him away. "Come on, son. You don't want to go there. Let's leave this madness."

That was when the madness on his mother's side of the family totally engulfed Andy. It stuck to him like a keepsake she had left him, like her scarf that he picked up off the boardwalk where it lay abandoned and wet from the spray coming off the Falls.

***

The sun was high, and Andy was thirsty. He had eaten two cobs of corn from his bag, which made him crave water even more. He had come out of the trees and run into a county road heading south towards the lake. There was a deep ditch by the road that he could jump into if any vehicle swung by. He decided to take this road as it should intersect with Highway 401 somewhere. He could follow the highway to a truck stop and hop a ride. He doubted the police would be shutting down highways to look for him.

Just as he began his walk down the road, he heard the chop-chop sound of a helicopter and dove into the ditch instinctively, pulling the tall, loose grass over him. Through this thick underbrush cover, he saw the big bird in police livery, hanging in the sky, seeking prey, moving, pausing, moving closer, then retreating, checking out another spot as it droned overhead for what seemed like hours, before moving away.

He stepped out cautiously and resumed his trek south, only to hear the sound of a car behind him. He jumped back into the ditch. This was not working out. He would never make the highway with these interruptions. And if there were helicopters out already, no truck driver in the vicinity was going to give him a ride: truckers used their grapevines to pass messages among their fraternity about highway conditions, weather, obstructions and delays. . .and about escaped convicts.

The car was slowing down. Andy slid deeper into the ground cover. He felt sand and tasted grass in his mouth. A worm slithered up his right forearm, and he felt earwigs crawling over his face. He wanted to scream but bit his lip until he tasted blood.

The vehicle, a Honda Accord, stopped a few feet away from him, under a tall poplar by the side of the road. A dumpy, dark man with thinning black hair, wearing a black sweater, got out and scurried under the tree. He unhitched his pants and shot a stream of piss into the roots, sighing contentedly. Andy smelled the urine, reminiscent of his recent encounter in the police van, and wanted to retch.

The driver, taller, also dark-skinned and with wavy black hair, got out, stretched his legs and leaned against the car. He was talking into his cell phone. For a moment Andy wondered if the man was speaking in a foreign language. Then a few heavily accented English words caught his hearing. Andy suddenly made the connection with the prison cook who used to talk the same way. The cook had come from somewhere in southern Asia on a refugee ship years ago and had been proud of his odyssey.

Phrases like, "Need payment today," "coming now," "that's not our problem," and "we are not responsible," floated in the air.

Then Andy saw his way out; these guys were from Toronto or elsewhere, tourists most likely. They would not know what was going on in the area. He fingered the police revolver in his pocket. That seductive sense of power floated over him again.

The fat guy zipped his pants and headed back to the car. As the two men made to get back into the vehicle, Andy sprung out of the ditch, his gun aimed at them. "Hold it!"

The beanpole guy froze, his back to Andy, while Fatso, who was facing him on the passenger side, moved with a sudden fluidity that was hard to anticipate. The short man reached inside his pocket and took cover behind the vehicle simultaneously. Andy dove to his left just as a bullet zipped past him. *They are fucking armed.*

In his frustration, Andy released two bullets into the back of Beanpole, slamming the man against the car. With a leap, Andy was behind the tall guy's slumping torso. Fatso was on the other side of the car, somewhere, and could come around either side of the vehicle. A thrill surged through Andy. It was a toss-up, go left or right? He moved the dead man's body to cover his back and went left, around the front of the car. Just then, a bullet zipped under the chassis.

Andy came charging around the passenger door side, gun roaring. He caught a fleeting view of black fabric disappearing around the rear of the car. He also heard a loud groan. This time he took the next corner slowly. The sight that met his eyes made him laugh hysterically. The fat man was bent over, his bloodstained ass staring at Andy. Fatso began to turn around, to cover his rear, when Andy released his last bullet into the man's face jerking it violently to the right and dropping him like a pole-axed mule.

Andy scanned the road in both directions, it was deserted, and the sky was free of choppers, for now. He shoved the two bodies into the car, Fatso in the back seat and the tall guy in the front passenger seat. They were heavy, and he was exhausted by the time he finished. He leaned them back in their seats as if they were sleeping. He slumped over the hood, catching his breath. Then he looked for GPS devices; he was not making the mistake he made the last time with his father. There was a light on the rear-view mirror, and he wrenched it out, snapping the wires behind it. Then he slipped into the driving seat and took off for the highway just as he heard a distant "chop chop" again.

He was shaking with a mixture of emotions: satisfaction, power, fear, all of which were producing a cocktail with an incredible high. *Yee ha!* Now all he needed was a place to hole-out for a few days before things settled down, but first, he needed to see his father. Render an account. Let Art Hamilton finally acknowledge his son's greatness. *And let Dad get me out of this mess, if he can!*

He took the western exit onto the highway, heading back towards Milltown. "Hey fellows," he announced to his dead passengers, "Let me show you the greatest, fucked-up small town in Canada."

***

Andy parked in the back lane behind Hamilton Industries. There was a security gate now, with a uniformed guard behind a glass covered island in the centre controlling swing gates on either side. This was new, no more coasting into Hamilton Industries whenever one wanted. There was also a new concrete, bunker-style building erected by the perimeter, a new one since Andy had been incarcerated. His father was always growing and expanding. A pang of regret hit him. *Was Dad always wrong?* But the other voice in his head was unrelenting. *Your damn right he was, all this time was stolen from me and Mum. Don't let up, kiddo!*

An unmarked white truck pulled away from a loading dock beside the bunker and exited through one of the swing gates. Two men were in the driver's cab; Andy did not recognize them from before when he would visit his father's factory, just to grab some time with Art in-between his father's busy meeting schedule. Even the staff had turned over. Somehow, Hamilton Industries did not look familiar any more. Andy was glad—he did not want this dump as his inheritance. He could never imagine himself doing his father's job; a side of him admired his father's ability, while another deeply resented it.

He picked up the tall dead man's cell phone and dialled his father's private number, the one known only to him and his mother. He hoped that Art Hamilton, the busy business mogul, would not brush him off.

Art answered almost immediately, "Hello."

"It's me, Dad."

"Where are you, Andy?" Art sounded breathless. "There is a manhunt on for you. You killed two guards. Christ!"

"I know." Andy paused to savour his moment of glory. He could hear his father's tense breathing; there was fear radiating down the line.

"Give yourself up, Andy."

"No! I got them both, Dad. They were bigger than me and armed. When are you ever going to be proud of me, Dad?"

"They'll put you away forever for this."

"That's why I am never going to give myself up. And you are going to help me get away."

Art's voice came roaring down the line. "Who the fuck do you think I am? A hoodlum? I don't help escaping jailbait."

Andy sighed. Some things would never change. "I've gotta go, Dad. Keep this line untapped. I'll tell you where to get a hold of me next." He hung up before his father could reply and slipped the car into gear.

He had the tall man's baseball cap pulled over his face and was wearing the man's sunglasses. He had also found a suitcase of clothes in the trunk and had changed into a grey polo-shirt with the short guy's tight leather jacket draped over his shoulders.

As he neared the highway, the tall guy's cell phone rang. *Shit!* He should have ditched it after he made the call to his father. Andy pulled off to the side of the road and slid down the passenger window to throw the phone off the ramp into the bushes below. A perverse curiosity held him back momentarily and made him click the "receive call" button to find out who it was.

A foreign language floated in over the line. It must be the dead guy's contacts. Satisfied that the cops were not onto him yet, Andy flung the phone out of the window. Then he accelerated and headed for the ramp.

A calm spread through him as he drove. He realized that he was literally in the driver's seat. He had never had his father in such a bind. The last time he had been behind the wheel of a car, it had been in his father's "acquired" Cadillac, with all its trimmings, including the dratted tracking device that had located him so easily. Then, he'd had the cards stacked against him: Jen dating Billy, his father on his tail in the SUV, his mother recently passed away, the bullies at school. Today was a different story. Nirvana would be to re-write that scene at the mill, on the day before the shooting.

He passed a police cruiser parked on the side of the highway. Two armed policemen were waving trucks into a weighing station where a line-up of them puffed and purred as other police officers scampered around talking to drivers, taking notes. A car like his was obviously not on the suspect list, yet.

Andy eased his foot off the accelerator as he neared the last exit ramp within the municipal confines of Milltown, the ramp that would take him inland to the mill. That's when he recognized the white truck that he had seen leaving Hamilton Industries earlier. His lip curled—time for some fun before he ditched the car. Time to give his father another headache.

He accelerated swiftly and switched lanes to overtake the truck. When he drew parallel, he glanced sideways and saw the driver and his companion in conversation, oblivious of the Honda that had pulled up alongside.

With a wrench of the steering wheel he cut into the path of the truck. In the side mirror, he saw a look of astonishment cross the face of the driver before the truck careened to the right. He stole another glance in time to see the vehicle hit the guard rail and spin around into the path of a car behind it. Andy took the oncoming exit ramp, swung north at the light, and headed across the bridge overhanging the highway. He looked down and was astounded to see the carnage he had left behind.

The truck was smoking: a white billowy smoke that did not look like the type coming from an ordinary fire, several cars had zig-zagged behind the truck and were attached to each other like fallen dominoes. *Wow—what a pile up!* In the distance, he heard sirens blaring—the cops at the weighing station were heading over. He put his foot down on the accelerator and headed into the hills.

Twenty

Jane Garner was heading back to Milltown, satisfied with her performance at the hearing in Toronto. It wasn't a total victory, but as her lawyer had said, they had made good progress.

The judge had called them in early that morning. She liked it when they could work with clear heads, before the muddles and complexities of the day took control. Her ex, Harry, was in his signature grey tweed jacket with its black elbow patches. Harry's hair betrayed tinges of discolouration. Perhaps his new girlfriend did not massage the dye into his scalp anymore as Jane had once done. Looking at his six-foot two-inch frame, slightly stooped with lines creeping into his face that she had never seen before, Jane was no longer enamoured by his fading good looks. Art had cured her of that.

The judge scanned the papers and dispensed with overtures by both lawyers to help interpret their respective cases. He turned to Jane.

"Ms. Garner—you live away from the city. You have the means, but do you have the time to care for your son, should he relocate to Milltown?"

She looked him in the eye. She had waited a long time for this moment. "Yes, I do."

The judge turned to Harry. "Mr. Garner, any questions?"

Harry raised an eyebrow. "When we were married, I never saw Jane until late in the evenings, long after Jeremy was in bed. She was busy building her 'career.' She is now running her own business and probably sleeps over in her office. I don't know how she will have time for Jeremy."

"Mr. Garner—these papers say that you are now in a relationship with another woman, Tiffany Dench, who herself has three children. Mrs. Dench shares custody of her children with her ex husband. You claim that this is a good household to raise Jeremy?"

"Well, I have a regular nine-to-five-job," Harry said. "So does Tiffany…er… Mrs. Dench."

"When you are not away on field trips," Jane added.

The judge took off his glasses and sighed. But Jane's side-crack had registered. His Honour closed his eyes and began nodding his head.

Then he placed his glasses back on his face and returned to the papers. "Mr. Garner, this recent statement from your son says that when you were away on a… field trip Mrs. Dench and her former husband had a violent altercation in your house. The children took cover in a storeroom."

Harry hung his head. "An unfortunate incident, Your Honour. Had I been there, it would not have occurred."

"But your son has stated that this was not the first time this had occurred."

"Mr. Dench tends to be boisterous when he has taken one too many," Harry replied.

Harry's lawyer jumped in, holding a restraining hand on Harry, almost as if to say, "Shut up!" and took over the testimony, "Mrs. Dench is at the end of sorting out her marital differences with her ex-husband, Your Honour. These incidents will end soon."

After acknowledging that answer half-heartedly and poring through the papers a bit more, the judge went into a lengthy explanation on the duties and responsibilities, the pitfalls and demands of single parent custody. "The boy needs a stable home; that is the most important matter. Access to both parents is secondary."

Jane could see where the sermon was heading and had difficulty breathing evenly. She was screaming inside, impatient to hear the judge make his decision—in her favour, it had to be! Instead, he stumped her, just as she was about ready to shout for joy.

"Mrs. Garner, I would like to have a detailed plan from you as to what time you can commit to your son if he were to move to Milltown. Your financial statements are good, but we are talking about the emotional needs of your son, here."

Jane would have promised him anything then and there, but her lawyer restrained her and spoke in her stead. "My client will provide you this commitment within the week, Your Honour. And we will be grateful if you can reach a speedy and humane decision for the good of Jeremy Garner."

Outside the courthouse, her lawyer, a wizened old veteran of the Child Custody Court told her firmly, "Look Jane—this is the furthest we've got in this case. Don't fuck it up. Prepare to spend some time with your son and commit it to paper. Fax it to me tomorrow, and I will get it in front of the judge by the end of this week. Do that, and I think you will be moving your son out to Milltown before the month is out."

She couldn't believe her ears.

"Getting Jeremy to recount the incidents in your ex's house, painful though they were to the child, was the best thing you did," the lawyer continued, breaking into a faint smile for the first time that morning. Then he looked at his watch. "I have to be off—another case. Don't forget to send me that fax asap."

Now, as she drove home, she felt like she was on the edge of a sexual climax: not quite there, knowing that soon she would fall off the edge, fearing also that the pleasure might be denied her, like had often been the case with Harry.

She went over in her mind all the things she would do with Jeremy: certainly, skiing in the winter, there were so many trails within minutes of Milltown; enrolling him at the YMCA so he could do his swimming and basketball. How about music lessons? But the more she piled on, the more she would be the one carting him to these events. She had to give the boy a full agenda or else the judge might feel she was short changing her son. Harry, being a school teacher, did most of his work during regular hours and could take time off to drive the boy around. Jane's work tied her to her desk and to her clients, even weekends were sometimes not her own. As much as she was content with this morning's outcome, she was feeling anxious about what victory over Harry would mean for her independent lifestyle. And how was she going to factor in Art, who was becoming more than a client to her? She had to keep Art out of this until Jeremy moved to Milltown. Her palms became clammy on the steering wheel when it occurred to her that the judge might take a completely different view on this custody battle if he knew that Jane was dating the father of a juvenile killer.

She was thus pre-occupied as she neared the second Milltown exit.

Suddenly, the vehicle in front of her, a white truck, veered off the road and hit the guardrail. Jane slammed on her brakes and cut sharply into the faster lane to avoid the crashing vehicle.

Too late, she grazed another car on her left which was already speeding ahead in the fast lane. Her car swerved back into the middle, only to meet the ricocheting truck that was completely out of control and bouncing off the guardrail onto the road at a ninety-degree angle. Jane's car broadsided the larger vehicle and her air bag exploded into her chest throwing her against the seat. She kept her foot down on the brake, hoping to slow everything down. Then, something else slammed her car from behind, and there was the sound of squealing brakes, groaning metal, breaking glass and the muted shouts of motorists trapped in the pile-up.

Through it all, a deadly white cloud loomed, seeping in through her shattered windscreen, enveloping her in a noxious, tear wrenching and stifling cocoon, threatening to burst her lungs. She blacked out.

***

Her head was bursting when the bright lights of the hospital ward woke her. As her vision cleared, she saw that there were no other beds to either side of her. Two white-gowned male doctors were making notes and talking in whispers. One was grey and the other younger. A nurse checked a saline drip meter next to her bed, and Jane followed the tubes all the way to her arm that lay hanging over the side.

A sudden spasm shook her, and she wanted to retch. She leaned over. The nurse placed a metal pan under her into which she could see the remnants of her stomach pitch. The retching was violent and came in rapid waves, not like when she had last had stomach flu.

Spent, she hung over the side of the bed, until the nurse eased her back into an upright position. She felt fluid between her legs and realized that she was urinating involuntarily.

"Bedpan…" she croaked.

The nurse dived for a nearby bedpan. "I need help," the nurse said to the two men while she tried to capture as much spillage into the bedpan and save the bed sheets—she wasn't very successful. The younger man pulled out a mobile phone and turned his back on them. The sheets were soaked by the time the bedpan re-emerged from under Jane.

"We need to change you," the kind-faced, but stressed-out nurse said to Jane. Another nurse arrived; one pulled the old sheets out from under the patient while the other slipped new ones in. A screen was pulled around the bed and between the two nurses they managed to get some new clothes on the patient. Jane felt completely powerless; she had lost all control of her muscles.

When the screen was pulled away, the older man, who had been observing the scene with a concerned look, advanced towards the bed. "Mrs. Garner?"

Jane looked blankly at him. She tried to speak but the words got jumbled.

"It's okay, try to get some rest," he said. "I'm Dr. Sheppard. You were involved in a vehicle accident."

His words registered and triggered off the recollection of screaming horns, groaning metal, the crunch of braking glass, the white truck, and the white smoke. Jane instinctively started moving her legs; they moved slowly, there was no pain there, except that her muscles felt leaden.

"You don't appear to have any bodily injuries, Mrs. Garner. Can you move your arms?"

She moved them. The needle from the saline drip pulled and she winced. She nodded indicating that she could move her arms. The only pain was in her stomach which felt as if someone was rhythmically punching it to a four-count.

"And your feet?"

She nodded again.

"Well, that's good."

The spasm came from nowhere. She threw up: yellow vomit spewing out of her mouth and spraying the bed. The clean bed sheets were soiled once more, and the nurse scratched her head. "A plastic wrap for you, my dear," she said, going off somewhere to get one.

The doctor appeared to be unperturbed by this sudden eruption; he just kept nodding his head, as if all this was confirming his diagnosis. Jane wanted to vomit again as the smell of her discharge stifled the air. She retched but there was nothing left inside her.

A stiff plastic cover slipped under her chin and another was moved under her bum by the two returning nurses. When they left, the doctor looked at his watch.

"We think your situation is more related to the fumes you inhaled."

She could only squint at him in enquiry.

"The truck in front of you, the vehicle you collided with, was carrying noxious chemicals. Organophosphates. We think you have been poisoned by the fumes."

Her heart sank. Jeremy! Would she ever see him again? How would she get custody of him now? Sweat broke out on her, and her body started to boil over.

"Jeremy…." she managed to get out; she felt drool escaping, too. The doctor was becoming a blurred image. And her head felt like it was about to split.

The doctor's voice came from a distance. "We will keep you under observation for a few days, Mrs. Garner. Don't worry, we will do the best we can for you."

Do the best? What did he mean? That there was a possibility that even the best may not be enough? Organophosphates. She began to cool down and feel drowsy. Organophosphates, that was familiar. Her fevered brain, alternatively cooling, then heating, then making her want to retch, searched in its recesses for the word. In a flash, like the involuntary twitches and spasms running through her, it suddenly blazoned across her mind as a word in a financial statement she had prepared for Biodiversity Futures Inc. BFI's prime export had been Organophosphates. Now she was eating her own cooking, it seemed.

Twenty-One

It had been a glorious day at the mill, one to erase all Billy's memories, particularly the ones that Andy had tarnished not so long ago. Sarojini and he had just lazed in the sun. She had brought along some samosas and vadais in a container in her suitcase, which they ate sitting in their usual spot on the grass with their feet dangling over the running water. She also had a flask of cold sherbet to slake their thirst throughout the day.

They lazed on the blanket all afternoon, wading into the millpond whenever the mood got them, drying off, and going in again, multiple times. Periodically, as the sun warmed their passions, they made love on the blanket, without reserve, without prophylactics, but with care for the gentle life growing inside her.

"I love you, Saro," he said involuntarily as the sun went over the trees, and they hugged each other with the sudden shift in temperature.

She smiled impishly, suddenly playing coy. "You are quite lovable, you know."

At about four in the afternoon, he decided to tell her about the last time he had spent a day with a girl at the mill. He felt that he had to, because being here with Saro was helping him eradicate those memories, finally.

"I spent the day with Jenny here the day before she was shot," he said, sitting up on the blanket and pulling on his tee shirt. "She had come to help me sort out Grandpa's books and stack them on the new bookcase I had built down in the cellar."

Sarojini rolled over on her stomach and cupped her chin in her hands, propping herself up on her elbows. "Is this the great confession you have been meaning to make?"

The words stumbled out of him, the guilt he could not keep back anymore. Saro had to know, if she was going to be a part of him. "If I had not brought her here, she may have still been alive."

"You were not responsible for her death. Don't go being the martyr. Besides, you're with me now."

He reached out and took her olive-skinned hand, alternatively caressing it and gripping it, as spasms of memory squeezed out of him. "She told Andy to piss-off that day. That's what did it."

"Why did he follow you here?"

"He'd grabbed his father's brand-new Cadillac, to impress Jenny, and followed us as we drove out of town."

Sarojini sat up and ran her hand through her hair. "Well, I don't want to hear any more about that old stuff. I would rather look at the future. Our future."

Billy nodded reluctantly. "Thanks for listening. I had to get that one out. I'd better call Mom and tell her that we will be over for dinner."

A frown creased Sarojini's brow. "Do you think that is wise?"

"Of course. The faster she gets used to the idea the better." He rose and walked over to the car where his cell phone lay on the front seat.

He stepped inside the car, which he had reversed around to face the track heading back into town. As he dialled his mother's office number, he tensed. There was a figure hugging the treeline on the track, heading towards the mill. The call went into his mother's voice mail, she was attending a meeting. Mom? Attending meetings? She was the one who held the fort while her boss attended the meetings. But all this was running in the back of his mind as the figure on the track loomed closer and released that sinking feeling in the pit of his stomach, making him throw down the phone and lurch out of the car, running for Sarojini, wanting to get her to safety, wanting to evade that catastrophic feeling of déjà vu.

***

Andy looked back at the strip mall where he had abandoned the Honda in the very last parking spot. The two inert figures inside sat as if they were taking a snooze from a long-distance drive. It had just gone past two in the afternoon and if he hit a fast stride, cutting through the farmers' fields at the edge of town and running across the fifteenth hole of the golf course, he could make it into the woods again.

He hoped that the room with the trapdoor in the mill was still intact. It was a safe place to hide until he made contact with his father again.

Getting across the golf course proved difficult; given the warm weather, golfers were lined up, waiting their turns to play this furthest hole from the clubhouse. The farmer's field was immediately behind the fifteenth green and Andy had to make his run across it to the clump of trees on the boundary of the course leading into the forest. He sat impatiently, fuming as foursome after foursome finished on the green, replaced the flag, and signalled the next players who were already within short-drive distance. After about half an hour of waiting and seeing most of his father's old buddies go by—he even wondered why his father had not taken up this sport, it may have calmed him down—Andy was about to retrace his path and find an alternate route. Just then, a golfer in the party immediately behind the one on the green, shot a ball into tall fescue on the side of the fairway and all four golfers went thrashing around to find it. The four female golfers already on the green finished their putting, gave each other high fives, put their clubs away and headed off to the next hole. Seizing the gap, Andy crouched and sprinted across the open course, heart thumping, alert for someone to spot him. When he hit the trees and looked behind him, one of the golfers was triumphantly raising the lost ball out of the rough, and the rest of his buddies were thumping him on the back.

The woods led uphill, and he kept to the treeline, retreating inwards whenever vehicles in the nearby country lane went past. He had the squirrels and chipmunks for company. Once, he thought he saw a deer on his right, but he only heard a crash of underbrush when he turned to look.

His mind was filling with dread as he advanced on the mill. It was a safe place, but it scared the pants off him, too. That's where his father had smacked him in public two years ago, before all this shit started. His scene of humiliation. And the genesis for his revenge. What else could he have done. *Jenny, that bimbo!* And after all he had done to attract her—even 'borrowed' his father's brand-new car. How did that asshole Billy's mother's old beat up Cavalier compare? Hadn't his father taken out beautiful women on the strength of his wealth and prestige, even while his mother was still alive? And here he was, Art's progeny, failing with a town chick, even with a Cadillac stacked against a fucking Cavalier! The fear gave way to a searing anger. What he would give to change history!

As he passed the caretaker's run-down shack, he froze when he heard voices coming over the other side of the hill. He slunk back into the trees and slithered forward, straining his ears. When he came over the hill, he could hardly believe what he saw. It was as if history was being remade—there was that asshole Billy, with a girl, a brown-skinned, beautiful girl. *Trust our Billy to lure attractive chicks.* And Billy wasn't even down inside that bloody cellar in the mill like the last time; he was lying with the girl, half naked, on a faded blanket by the water's edge. They were kissing in between their conversation. *Kissing! Fuck!*

Andy grinned deliriously. Hadn't he just been granted the best gift ever? He loosened the revolver in his pocket and waited for the opportunity.

✳✳✳

Billy woke on the floor of his grandfather's hide-hole and felt that his head was bursting. He reached out and felt the dust and sand that littered the stone floor. He heard grunts and gasps coming to him in waves, just like the throbbing in his head. Memory returned gradually. He had been going down the trapdoor. Panic gripped him. *Andy!* Andy had been behind him. He remembered that now: Andy dragging Saro by one hand, a gun in the other. And then the world had exploded on him.

As his vision cleared, he made out a tangle of bodies on his grandfather's mouldy camp bed. The gas lamp was unlit, and light only filtered in from the high window. Billy tried to rise but was pulled back by the sluggish weight of his body. His legs were like rubber, giving way under him each time he tried to get upright. His mind knew what was going on, but his body refused to collaborate. "Lay off her!" he screamed, but the words came only in a gurgle. He heard a laugh. The bodies parted into two separate blobs. They started to gain focus. One pulled up its pants and walked over towards him. The kick to the side of his head sent lights flashing, and he hit the side wall.

"You are not her exclusive fucker any more, Billy boy." Andy's voice sneered down. Another kick landed in Billy's stomach, leaving him gasping for air. Billy focussed on his pain, trying to blot out the sound of sobbing coming from the camp bed as the second figure pulled clothes around it, shrinking, trying to become even more indistinct. His vision cleared.

"If you fight fair," Billy managed. "I'll whip your ass."

Billy braced for the next kick, but it never came. Instead, Andy laughed hysterically. "Who said this world was fair, asshole?"

Billy could feel the blood returning to his legs, but he did not want to spring up until he was sure of his strength. He felt cold metal press against his cheek.

"Feel this, buddy," Andy leered, his face looming within a breath of Billy's. "I could blow you to kingdom come in a flash. But I am not going to. Because you have one more job to do."

Billy lay back on the floor, gaining strength by the minute. He looked over at the camp bed. There was only a whimper coming from that direction now. Andy went over to the camp bed, hauled Saro up, and threw her across the floor. She fell like a sack of potatoes, and Billy crawled up to her to cradle her in his arms. Her eyes stared at nothing. She was in shock; her lip was cut on the side, and a trickle of blood oozed down. She was wearing only her shirt. As he held her close, Saro began to shake, Then, she screamed and screamed, and Billy had to hang on to her with all his might, pleading for her to calm down, not uttering the words but willing her to do so with his mind. She stopped screaming only when she ran out of breath. She continued to whimper like a sick puppy. Her breath came in gasps. Billy placed his hand on her belly. A wave of anger made him nauseous. Would the rape have damaged the foetus? He wanted to slide his hand further, down there, to check everything, but Saro's icy cold hand, suddenly steely in its grip, pushed his away.

"Remember Jen, Billy?" Andy's voice came over from the corner of the room. He was watching Billy comfort Saro. Andy's voice was bitter, as if watching Billy with Saro diminished him further.

Billy continued to stroke Saro's hair, ignoring his tormentor. Now that she was over her initial shock, the sweat streamed out of her body.

"I wanted to do the same thing to Jen, Billy. But you and my asshole father stopped me. You remember, eh? In this room."

Billy remembered. On that occasion, there had been no gun. When they heard Art calling from above, it had distracted Andy sufficiently for Billy to tackle him and slam him against the wall. Andy had fought back like a maniac, but Jen clobbered him from behind with the stool that still lay broken in the back of the room somewhere. Then she ran up the steps, threw open the trapdoor, and called for help. Andy shrivelled under his father's stare as Hamilton Senior descended the steps into the room. The single smack to the side of the face from Art felled Andy like a slave before his master. Andy whimpered and scurried upstairs with his father close behind. The last Jen and Billy saw of Andy, on that occasion, was of him sitting head bowed in the passenger seat of the

SUV that Art was driving. Art slid the driver's side window to say, "I'll send someone to pick up the Caddy." Then he drove away with his beaten son.

But the situation was different now, Billy realized. In the intervening time Andy had become an unrepentant killer.

"What's the job?" Billy asked.

"I need you to drive into town and get us groceries. We are going to be holed up here for some time."

"I've got no money."

"I've got cash."

"They'll spot us."

"You will do the shopping while I keep your girlfriend with me in the car. Any funny business, and she gets it in the head, capiche?"

Billy needed time to figure this out. The trip into town would be a good diversion until he came up with a plan. And he needed to control this plan himself. As much as Andy had a bone to grind, Billy had his own. This was déjà-vu for both of them. He would be damned if Andy won this time.

Twenty-Two

Sam recognized many of his customers from among the people suddenly converging upon the town hall. The mayor had called an emergency meeting for three o'clock that afternoon. Malani was in shambles, had taken a tranquilizer, and was asleep upstairs. There was still no word of Sarojini, and Sam was dreading having to take a trip down to the police station; his phone calls to relatives and friends in Toronto had revealed blanks or landed in unanswered voicemail boxes.

Town folk muttered among themselves as they passed South Asian Delights. Sam went outside and caught some of the broken threads of conversation from the passersby, "…the four-o-one is closed… they say it's highly contagious… infectious, too… it's those damned Tamil Tigers terrorizing us in Canada, now. They found two dead guys in a vehicle at Moxie's strip mall…I don't know what the hell is happening to this country, escaped convicts, terrorists, the mayor had better have his shit together…" This information was news to Sam who was wrestling with his own woes. He decided to join the meeting and find out for himself. If he could have muttered like his fellow townspeople, he would have said, "In this country, they expect the mayor to look after everything. In our country, where was the mayor when everything was burning? Even the police turned their backs on us."

When Sam entered the foyer, a microphone had been set up on a raised platform at one end. The chairs in the front rows were already taken up by seniors, the active ones who came out in droves the moment there was something out of the ordinary taking place—their entertainment in an otherwise placid existence. Mayor Frank Morgan paced the stage, paper in hand, reading glasses perched perilously on his nose, tie pulled low and askew.

When the roar of conversation in the high-ceilinged room had reached its zenith, Frank Morgan straightened his tie and stepped up to the microphone.

"Ladies and Gentlemen. Can I have your attention please?"

The room hushed immediately, except for a senior in the front row who looked at his watch and guffawed, "About bloody time..."

"My dear Milltowners, we have had a couple of serious incidents around the town today, and I want to quell any rumours before they get out of control. What I am going to tell you are the facts. They will be published tonight in a special late edition of the Milltown Gazette.

"We had a prisoner escape today. Yes that 'rumour' is true. But not from the Sunnyside Juvenile Detention Centre—that part of the rumour is unfounded. Sunnyside is safe. Those of you in the neighbourhood need not be worried about your safety. The prisoner who escaped was being transported to Kingston and made his break about 100 kilometres away from Milltown."

"Has he been seen in the area?" one person in the audience asked.

"Who is he?" another one shouted from across the room.

"We cannot reveal names at this time," Mayor Frank replied.

"Is it true that he is Art Hamilton's son?" an even-toned voice asked, and Sam recognized Rick Jones standing by the door with his hand raised. There was a woman beside him who Sam had seen working in the mayor's office.

Frank Morgan flushed at the question. The room burst into tittering and everyone looked towards Rick. "No names at this time," was the mayor's response.

Mayor Frank cleared his throat and continued, reading from the paper in his hand. "Our search efforts were somewhat hampered this morning when a collision caused a chemical spill on the highway. The local police and clean-up crews have been focussed there for now while the RCMP is scouring the area for the escaped convict."

Rick Jones kept his hand raised, and Sam could see the mayor wince even before the next question was asked.

People began looking in Rick's direction, as if he had already assumed Chief Interrogator status. Rick took his time with his next question; he pushed himself off the wall and moved into the centre of the room. "My sources tell me that the truck was ferrying chemicals for Hamilton Industries, or one of its many subsidiaries. Why was the vehicle unmarked?"

Mayor Frank took a handkerchief out of his pocket and loosened his tie. "You will have to ask Art Hamilton that. All I can tell you is that safety crews are at the site and are following the required guidelines for noxious substance spills—just like they did when that cargo train derailed five years ago at Knott's Crossing." Frank mopped his brow.

"Is it true that Art Hamilton is shipping chemicals for pesticides to the US? Chemicals that would not normally be used in Canada?"

"Mr. Jones—if you are so full of questions, why do you not ask that of Mr. Hamilton yourself?"

"And where is Mr. Hamilton? His son is on the lam, his chemicals are poisoning the countryside—where is Mr. Hamilton?"

Frank Morgan stuffed his handkerchief back into his trouser pocket. "We are in contact with Mr. Hamilton. His employees are working along with our safety crews to clean up the spill so that we can open the highway as soon as possible. We hope to have everything ready and clear within twenty-four hours."

"One last question, Mr. Mayor." Rick wasn't leaving the floor so easily. "You haven't told us about the victims of the spill and about the two dead men you discovered in Moxie's strip mall."

"Hear hear," the irascible senior in the front chimed. "You can't get any straight answers these days."

Frank Morgan pulled himself up to his full height. He fiddled with the microphone as he seemed to collect his thoughts. "For the record, the bodies of two men, both fatally shot, were found in a Honda in Moxie's mall early this afternoon by a shopper who parked in the adjacent parking spot. The bodies have been taken to the morgue, and we expect some news soon. They are not locals; that is all I know. At the moment, we do not think that this incident is related to the prison break, or to the accident on the highway. As for the highway spill—the truck driver and his assistant are being treated for inhalation of noxious fumes at the Milltown General Hospital. They expect to be released shortly."

"There was another victim. The accountant, Jane Garner, was driving her car and hit the chemical truck on the rebound," Rick said, thumbs in his belt, rocking on his heels. Sam's breath quickened when he heard Jane's name being mentioned. Was she dead—perhaps then they would not need his space, after all. *And those dead men…not locals…in a Honda…?*

"Mr. Jones—you seem to have more information than I do. Perhaps you should be up here making this press announcement," Frank Morgan said, pulling out his handkerchief again.

In a couple of bounds, Rick was up on the platform. "Then, I will," he said, leaving the Mayor with his mouth agape.

Rick pulled the microphone out of its stand and walked over to the edge of the stage, his height dwarfing the mayor's. "I have been following these incidents closely. We believe that the car in which the two dead men were found was the same car that hit the unmarked Hamilton Industries vehicle. That was part of the Hamilton Industries driver's statement, which our beloved mayor chose not to reveal."

"That has not been verified yet," Frank Morgan shouted, rising on his heels, perhaps regretting goading Rick into taking over the public announcement. "There is no point in spreading conjecture until the driver of the truck is well enough to identify the vehicle."

"And how many blue Honda Accords are you going to find in one day?" Rick asked. "What is more," he continued without waiting for an answer, "we feel that Andy Hamilton is headed back to Milltown. His fingerprints were lifted off the blue Honda."

"You must have some good friends in the police force, Mr. Jones—that is confidential information," Frank said, scowling.

Rick smiled. "I have been in this town a long time, Your Worship. I am owed a few favours, let's say."

The senior in the front seat got up, dusting his hat on his thigh. "I've heard enough of this cover-up shit. I'm gonna get my shotgun. If any terrorist or con comes within a hundred feet of my property he's getting both barrels—that's for sure. Come on fellas, this is a sham meeting. All bullshit! No one's telling the truth."

The meeting started to break up with many of the disgruntled regulars elbowing each other out of the crush, grumbling, muttering, cursing. A coffee at Tim Hortons would be more interesting to them now. Frank tried to maintain order by making a final plea.

"Ladies and Gentlemen, there is no cause for alarm. The police and the RCMP have the situation well in control. We will be posting bulletins on our website and making regular updates on our local radio station as the situation gets clearer. Thank you for coming today." And with that, Frank Morgan beat a retreat through a back door leading off the stage.

As the crowd dispersed, Sam edged over to Rick. He suddenly felt that Rick Jones might have the answers to his own dilemma. The woman from the mayor's office was also making her way over to Rick.

"Mr. Jones, sir—can I have a word?"

"Why, Sam—how are you?" For once Rick Jones did not have his customary hangdog look. He was ebullient, pumped, presumably from his recent few minutes of fame. The woman also reached them at that point, and Rick turned around and said, "Have you met Sue Miller? I believe your daughter and her son are friends."

Suddenly, it hit Sam—she was the mother of the boy who had got his daughter pregnant and started all his troubles, the woman who wanted her son to go to university and leave them all holding the baby, so to speak. He wanted to lash out, call her a white selfish bitch and her son an irresponsible bastard, but the reserve built from years serving customers and being a foreigner in this country held him back. If he let fly, he would be no better than Malani. Instead, Sam looked at her coolly and said, "Hello."

"Sam runs South Asian Delights," Rick said innocently. Sam saw Sue Miller tense, then let out a sigh.

"I've spoken to your wife," she said.

Rick, still ignorant of the undercurrents, rode on his ebullience. "So, you guys know each other?"

Sue cut in icily, "This gentleman's wife claims that Billy made their daughter pregnant."

Sam couldn't contain himself any longer. "And now she has run away. That is what I wanted to see you about, Mr. Jones."

"Wait, wait…I'm missing something here," Rick said, feeling his jaw, eyes darting between Sam and Sue.

"I am sorry I bothered you at this time," Sam continued, ignoring Sue and looking around him to see whether other townspeople were out of earshot, "but my daughter has been very emotional since she found out about her pregnancy. So has my wife." Then turning to Sue, he spat out, "In my country, when things like this happen, people come to help, you know. They don't go inside and close the door."

"How dare you accuse my son of being the father? Schoolgirls screw around with all sorts of boyfriends, all the time."

"Not my daughter, madam. We are not cheap trash like that." A nerve ticked in Sam's temple, and he felt the blood rush to his face. He had trouble keeping his voice even.

"Whoa, whoa—this has gotten way out of control," Rick said, putting his hand on Sam's arm, drawing him aside. Over his shoulder, he said to Sue, "I'll catch up with you later. Obviously three, in this situation, is a crowd."

Sue stamped her foot. "And all I did was come over to congratulate you for putting my creep of a boss in his place." She swung on her heel and followed the mayor's exit through the back door behind the temporary stage.

Rick raised his eyebrows and shrugged. "Well, that's blown it for me today. But come along—let's get to Timmy's. I need the lowdown." He pulled Sam away, and they made for the exit doors to the street.

∗∗∗

The seniors were still chatting in loud groups at Tim's when they left, the old timers were talking as if the world was coming to an end in Milltown. Rick parked across the street from South Asian Delights. He didn't interrupt Sam's recounting of his family's saga. They remained silent after Sam ran out of words, their coffees long finished and lying in the cup holders of Rick's car.

"I thought we had it rough, here," Rick said finally.

"Still, this country is our best chance," Sam said, looking out of the window. "If people will accept us for who we are."

"Listen, I'll do what I can to find your daughter. I'll try to get a hold of Billy—I'm sure he knows what's going on."

Sam picked up the empty cups. "Yes, do what you can. Now I must go and see how my wife is getting along." Sam opened the front passenger door and stepped out.

Just then, the doors of South Asian Delights burst open and Malani staggered out onto the street. She was in a housecoat, her hair loose and ruffled, as if she had been pulling it in different directions. Perhaps she had, for she stood hesitantly, wide eyes darting to either side of the street like a mad woman, not seeing Sam who was directly in front of her and on the opposite side of the road. The last time Sam had seen her like this was when her sister Kamala had died.

"Mala—what's up?" he called to her.

She caught sight of him and looked disoriented for a moment. Then she pulled herself up and screamed at him. "Mahesh! They have Mahesh. *Aney mage putha!*"

He dodged a couple of cars and ran across the road and embraced her quivering body that was about to wilt and fall. His heart was racing, and he did not want to think. "What's up, Mala? What about Mahesh?"

"The police have arrested him. He had a knife…" then she broke into a flood of sobbing.

They stood rocking on the sidewalk. Sam could hardly hold Malani upright, for her limp weight threatened to bring them both down. There was a screech of tires beside the curb, followed by Rick's voice—he had u-turned on Main Street.

"Get in. Bring your wife. Let's go down to the police station."

***

Mahesh shivered in the tiny cell. The temperature was turned down lower than normal to chill out the drunks. The narrow enclosure with its graffiti-covered walls and ceiling-high window facing the street stunk of stale sweat and whiskey, with a bit of piss to top it off. His head hurt, and his wrist was swollen where he had twisted it during his fall into the ditch. Across the narrow corridor, through the bars, he could see Ted and Jack in the other cell. Jack's Maple Leafs jersey was brown with mud, and he had bled some more from the cut on his neck—the jersey sported a brown rim. Ted was busy combing his hair and looking at his watch. Mahesh grinned—it was good to know that he was not alone in this mess.

The door to the outer office opened, and a fat bald man with a handlebar moustache walked in, trailed by one of the police officers who had arrested Mahesh and his rivals.

The fat man was also in police uniform, but his tie hung loose on his neck; he looked harried and annoyed, as if he had been dragged away from more important work. He signalled to the officer who opened

Mahesh's cell door. The fat man stood on the threshold and looked down at Mahesh, his back to Jack and Ted.

"A knife in school is a criminal offence, young man. This is Canada."

Mahesh hung his head. This was not getting any better. Should he stay silent and ask for a lawyer? Should he phone his parents? But he had not wanted to bother them. He had wanted to solve this problem himself. How could he go back snivelling to his parents, like they said he always did?

"They know where my sister is."

"Your sister!" The fat man boomed. "Do you know what's going on in this town now, fella? There's a dangerous criminal on the loose, and we have had a catastrophic chemical spill out by the highway. And I should be worried about your sister?"

"Why are you not talking to them?"

Jack and Ted were smirking behind the fat man's back.

The fat man kept his gaze on Mahesh, unmoved. "I talk to whom I damn well care to talk to. Right now, I am talking to you, young man— why were you carrying a knife to school?"

"Because I am fed up of being called a freak, a Buddha. This is Canada—I know. If you want me to be a Canadian, why don't you treat me like one?" Mahesh was on his feet, yelling at the fat man when the door to the outer office opened again and in trailed his parents and a man Mahesh recognized as the alcoholic lawyer who had recently run for election.

Mahesh immediately felt awkward. His parents should not see him like this, particularly his mother, who looked like she had just got out of bed, her hair loose and a housecoat hastily thrown on.

"Chief Pierce," Rick Jones intervened. "I am the boy's lawyer. I think there has been a misunderstanding."

The fat man turned towards Rick Jones, a smirk on his face. "Jones, you should be over at Macy's at this time of the day. What are you doing here?"

Rick's face reddened. "Let's say that I have temporarily given up drinking."

"Putha," Malani burst out, catching sight of her son. "What did you do?"

"Ammi—I couldn't stand by and see you suffer. Those two guys are the friends of Billy Miller, who's kidnapped Saro. I know it."

All eyes swung on the other two boys in the opposite cell.

"Whoa, whoa," Jack shouted. "Who said we had anything to do with it? We don't see Billy these days. He is involved with his work and his bitch. . .I mean, girlfriend."

Sam's eyes glazed, and he pointed a finger at Jack. "You *are* the fellow!"

"What?"

Sam grabbed the cell bars and shook them, barely able to control his temper. "You are the fellow who stuck a poster on my restaurant the day before we opened."

"What poster?" Malani said.

"I didn't tell you." Sam turned to Rick. "Mr. Rick, this is the boy who stuck a poster on my door saying 'PAKI—GO HOME.' I can show you the poster. I still have it in my back room."

"How can you identify him?" Rick asked.

Sam pointed. "That jersey and that hair. I saw the bugger with my own eyes."

Rick nodded.

"Let's check the writing on that poster, too. We'll need a handwriting sample from you, young man," Rick said, looking at Jack.

Jack blanched and started to cough. Ted looked disgusted and turned to face the wall.

Chief Pierce roared into the dispute. "Okay, okay—enough!"

Everyone quieted down. The police chief signalled for the officer to open the other cell door, too.

"I am letting you *all* go. We have a lot of shit going down here right now. If your daughter is missing, file a missing person's report, then get out of here. My people are strapped today and have no time to launch any more searches."

Then, turning to the three boys, he waved a finger. "And count yourselves lucky that I am not pressing charges on all three of you. Blame it on a jailbreak and a collision that have our hands full. But I have marked the three of you. If I ever see *any* of you in *any* fight again, I will haul your ass in here faster than you can say 'Canadian.'"

He waved his arms to shoo everyone out, then turned on his heels and walked out through another door at the other end of the corridor, into the rear of the building.

***

Mahesh remained quiet during the ride home in Rick Jones' car. His mother sat next to him in the rear seat, massaging his swollen wrist, tears dripping down her face.

Rick was speaking to Sam in the front seat. "I know Billy. He is the quiet type. He wouldn't kidnap your daughter. He probably is out looking for her, too."

Sam interjected, "Mr. Rick—the chief and the mayor said that there are escaped criminals loose. This is not the time for a young girl to be roaming around the countryside."

Malani broke into a fresh bout of sobbing.

"It's okay, Ammi," Mahesh said, unconvincingly. "We will find her."

Sam turned in his seat. "You are not going to do any more finding, young man. Taking knives and chasing people is what happened in Sri Lanka—see where that country is now? You will let the police do their work."

Mahesh turned towards the window. His father was so naïve and trusting. Didn't he know that people were the same people wherever you went? The only difference was the colours of their skin and...and their jerseys.

"Still, you have to hand it to your son," Rick said, chuckling. "Not many people have stood up to Chief Pierce like he did."

Sam replied with a "humph" and was quiet for the rest of the ride home.

Twenty-Three

Rick sat in his study, with Phil and Bill panting obediently at his heels, and went over his notes. He even dispensed with his customary shot of Scotch at this time of the early evening. There was another high driving him: the scent that victory, after years in the doghouse, was near.

Too much had happened today, not the least being the rescue of young Mahesh Selvadurai from the police and handing him over to his grateful parents. The vortex of events had begun earlier in the day, when he had received a call from the hospital around 1:00 p.m. At first, he could not recognize the croaky voice on the phone.

"I've been in an accident." The voice trailed off, then came back again. It was Jane Garner. "Can you come to see me?"

"Where are you?

"Milltown General."

"I'll be over." The undertone in her voice made the hairs crawl on his forearms.

She was in the ICU, in a private room, when he arrived. When he located her, the head nurse barred him from seeing her.

"She's under observation. She should not be having visitors."

"I'm her lawyer," he lied. Suddenly he was everyone's lawyer. Unpaid.

The nurse leaned back, indecision on her face. She looked at the ticking clock on the wall and then back at her clipboard.

Rick cleared his throat. "My client sounded like she was dying. And she does not have a will."

"Make it quick," the nurse hissed, looking down at her papers. "Ten minutes."

When Rick entered, he immediately got the smell of vomit and urine penetrating the sanitizer that hung around hospitals. He couldn't recognize Jane from the crumpled figure on the bed: her black hair was damp and dishevelled, a yellow pallor had spread all over her face, and her flimsy hospital garb was stained. This was a far cry from the suave black-suited woman he had met in the offices of Garner & Associates. A drip was attached to the patient on one side; a tall bedside table with a telephone bracketed her on the other side.

"Jane?"

Jane moved her head. She said something that Rick could not hear. He bent over her. The smell of pungent medication bubbled out of her mouth. "Thank you for coming."

"I'm sorry to hear about the accident."

"I don't have a lot of time."

"What do you want me to do?"

"I want to confess."

"You need a priest, then."

"No. I need you to fix things for me."

"Why me?"

"I want you to make me a worthy mother for my kid."

Rick raised his eyebrows; the situation was getting a bit out of control, even for him.

She opened the clenched fist of her un-tethered hand. There was a crumpled passport-sized photograph in it. "This is Jeremy. My son."

"I recognized him when I was over in your office. You had a picture of him on your desk. He looks like a smart young lad."

"I want him with me in Milltown."

"You alluded to the custody battle the last time."

"Yes. But I have to be a good mother to qualify."

"So?"

"So, I am selling out Art Hamilton to you."

Rick sucked in his breath.

"I have found irregularities in his dealings," Jane said. The last string of words seemed to take the energy out of her, and she retched but nothing came out. Rick reached over and took her hot head in his hands. By the time he eased her back on the pillows she was cooling down again.

"Do you need a nurse?" he asked.

"No. I have called my office. Jillian has a file in a confidential envelope for you."

"Why are you doing this?"

"I want to be a good mother, Mr. Jones."

Rick rose. He paused before exiting. "Did Art Hamilton ever come to see you after the accident?"

"I called him. He was busy with the clean up. Or the cover up. Take your pick." She turned her face to the wall.

Rick tip-toed out of the room.

Now, nuzzled by his pet dogs, he looked down at the contents of the file.

There was a snarl of accounts in here that made his head swim and look towards that bottle of scotch the way Phil and Bill looked towards a fresh bone. But he resisted. *Concentrate.* Pulling back from the detail and looking at the obvious threads, it was clear that Art was up to his balls in shipping some pretty lethal stuff to the US, not in itself a crime if it was being used for legitimate purposes down south. But these customers looked pretty shady to him—no recognized brand names in the insecticide or pharmaceutical research businesses. No wonder Art was keeping this new company, Biodiversity Futures, separate from Hamilton Industries.

He pushed the file back. Why was he reluctant to act? He had pieces of threads of what was going on. They had been coming his way in dribs and drabs—first the letter that Sue had intercepted, then the photographs of Frank's amorous escapade with his secretary, then Art's manoeuvrings to get Sam Selvadurai out of his restaurant. Now this! But they did not amount to much other than a pile of embarrassment for Frank and Art which the two of them would shrug off with the assistance of a good PR agent. Would the younger, more agile Doug Spade on council make more out of these pieces of information?

Did his accidental meeting with Billy this evening mean anything? Rick's mind went back to the encounter after he had dropped the Selvadurais home from the police station.

Rick had forced himself to do his weekly chore that evening, the one he hated, but which he performed more for the sake of his dogs than for himself. As he pushed his grocery cart to the checkout, he saw Billy in the next aisle piling groceries into plastic bags. The boy had his hoodie on even inside the store, in lieu of his customary baseball cap.

"Hey, kid—you making up to your Mom for being scarce all this time?" Rick called out across the cash registers. Billy swung around as if burned. The hood of his hoodie fell back, and Rick caught a glimpse of a gash on the boy's cheek before Billy pulled the hood over again.

"Oh, Mr. Jones." Billy's manner was nervous. "Gotta rush."

Rick sensed that the boy was not grocery shopping for his mother. He left his cart in the checkout line and squeezed through irate shoppers to reach Billy.

"Your mother has been looking all over for you."

Billy kept bagging his groceries, intent on finishing and leaving as quickly as possible, it seemed. Rick tossed in a tin of tuna, that had rolled down the belt, into Billy's plastic bag. "You slumming out with buddies? This diet reminds me of when I was in university. All I could afford was macaroni, cheese and the odd treat of tuna. What's the candles for?"

Billy paid the cashier with crumpled cash. He was short two dollars and promptly removed the can of tuna from the bag. "I'll return this, then," he said to the cashier who was scratching her head trying to balance the bill.

"No, keep it on the tab." Rick passed the woman a toonie.

"Thanks Mr. Jones, I appreciate it. Listen, tell Mom that I am okay. I am just hanging out with some friends for a few days, until I get my head straightened out." He started gathering up his bags.

"I'll give you a hand."

"No, don't worry. Your cart is holding up that line. I've gotta go."

Rick reached out and took hold of the last of Billy's bags. "C'mon, I'll help you to the car."

Billy wrenched the bag out of his hands with a fury that surprised Rick. "No, Mr. Jones. Please! I don't need your help. I have only one more chance to make all this right. Please…!" Then he rushed out the sliding doors cradling his bags in both arms, holding the last one with his teeth.

Rick waited until the exterior doors of the store closed behind Billy before following. He was just in time to see Billy toss the groceries though the open rear window of Sue's Cavalier and slide into the driver's seat. There were two other occupants in the car. He thought he saw a girl in the front passenger seat but the person in the rear was unrecognizable. The car took off with a squeal of tires and made a hasty turn on to Main Street before disappearing from view.

Rick wanted to give chase but realized that his car was at the other end of the parking lot, and he would not get there in time. Reluctantly, he turned back to retrieve his shopping cart, which by now may have been elbowed aside by irate customers who had been standing behind him at the checkout.

Fingering Jane Garner's file, standing by his window looking towards Art Hamilton's property on the far hill, Rick tried to figure out Billy's strange behaviour.

Another chance, the boy had said? What chance? To make up with his mother? Who were the two people in the car? The friends he was hanging out with until he reconciled with his mother's unforgivable and errant behaviour? Fucking the mayor on one's kitchen table, even under duress, must have been a huge betrayal for the kid. Even Rick had to focus away from those disturbing photographs that suddenly swam back into his mind.

"You know what, guys," he said to Phil and Bill who were staring at him, tongues hanging out, contented with the new bones he had purchased for them this evening, that they had quickly dispatched with great relish, "I am bloody jealous that it wasn't me, instead of Frank, on her kitchen table."

He went back to his desk and rummaged among some old files. Something in Billy's words bothered him, stoking an old fire of recollection. The Milltown High shooting was one he had plenty of clippings of. The dead girl's—Jenny Murphy—parents were former clients of his, much to Art's chagrin. The case details did not concern him. He dug deep until he came to the testimony of Billy Miller, and his breath became raspier as he read.

Billy: He shot Jen… Jenny… twice, before I could reach her. I held her in my arms willing her not to die. But the breath was going out of her. When she was still, I looked up, and Andy was standing there. He was shocked and triumphant and confused all in one. I will never forget his look. I wanted to kill him then. I picked Jenny up and carried her into the gym, daring him to shoot me.

Prosecuting Counsel: What did you say to him?

Billy: I cursed him for not giving her a chance. For not giving us a chance to be together.

Rick put down the transcripts, whistling. He needed that drink now. His hands were shaking. He knew what was going down here.

The dogs nuzzled up to him, and he instinctively reached down to stroke them, drawing comfort from their brute strength.

"It's been a long time since we've gone hunting, boys," Rick said, absently.

Twenty-Four

Art walked over to his liquor cabinet and poured himself a stiff one. The sun was crimson on the horizon, hovering on the waterline, as if it would touch down any moment and scorch the lake, turning it into a sea of hot lava.

What a day! Andy on the lam, Jane in hospital, and his lucrative little export business under the press spotlight. Had he taken all the right steps? He paced about his office and went over the day's developments. He had called his PR manager the moment the accident on the highway was reported. He had refused to accept phone calls, except for the one from Jane that had been relayed to him via his secretary. He had promised to call her back but hadn't. He had briefed Frank on what to say at the town hall meeting, but word back was that Frank had flubbed that one—the idiot!

He reviewed the press release that had gone out to the local papers and the one to that pesky reporter from the *Globe & Mail*.

Biodiversity Futures, a wholly owned subsidiary of Hamilton Industries, manufactures custom chemical compounds, under the highest security and safety conditions. We fulfill special orders for clients worldwide. Our products are licensed to be used in approved markets. We regret the unfortunate incident on the highway outside Milltown today. Our driver was adhering to the road rules and speed limit when he was randomly struck by another vehicle that was out of control. Biodiversity Futures is doing everything possible and collaborating with local authorities in the clean-up work. Victims will be compensated through our comprehensive insurance programmes.

Of course, that idiot from the Globe had wanted to know where the contents of the van, which contained a banned substance in Canada, were headed to, and the PR manager had been forced to admit that it was destined for the USA, where in some states, pesticides containing organophosphates were still in use.

The phones in the office had gone ballistic after that, and Art had been forced to make an appearance at the front door of Biodiversity Futures an hour ago to state that he and his staff were doing the best that they could. Despite the many reporters who clustered around him on the front steps, asking for more details, he did not reveal client names due to confidentiality. The Globe reporter had caught him off guard when Art was winding down the impromptu press conference.

"Hey, Mr. Hamilton—I've just come from your municipal town hall meeting, and there was a statement made by a Mr. Rick Jones that the vehicle in question that struck your delivery truck was driven by your son who was escaping from prison today. Can you corroborate that statement?"

Art lashed back viciously, turning so fast that he struck the reporter's microphone boom, sending it swivelling out into the mass of journalists hanging about like flies around a scrap of food.

"I do not wish to corroborate anything. I am waiting for information on my son. I am cooperating with the prison authorities on this matter. My son is a mentally ill young man and needs care and treatment, and I am willing to provide him that. I have always provided him that. Now, if you will excuse me, I have a clean-up to attend to." With that, Art had slammed the front door of Biodiversity Futures in their faces.

Swirling the ice in his glass and watching the sun glint off the single malt liquid inside, he knew that he still had work to do. There were more calls to make, ones that the day's chaos and his jumbled state of mind had not allowed him to make.

He knew he had to call Jane. But what would he tell her? That he was sorry? That her accident was a random event? As random as Andy hitting his transport vehicle? Should Art Hamilton be responsible for all the random acts committed in this world? Andy would be calling soon from wherever he was holed up. And there was also another call he had to make: to his client, the one expecting a white delivery truck to pull into his warehouse in Miami two days from now. Strangely, the news had not been so widely broadcasted as to prompt a call from down south yet.

Art gulped his drink and made the call from his private line. Abbas always picked up his cell phone at any hour of the day. This time, the phone rang and did not even go into voice mail, but was answered by a robotic operator who announced, "The subscriber to this line has discontinued service. Please check your listing and call again."

Art felt his heart contract. He stood for a long minute, working through the permutations of this development. Had he dialled the wrong number in his stressed-out state? Was Abbas in the process of switching cell phone services? Had the client gone out of business? Art was about to re-dial when his private line rang. The display said, "Unknown Caller." Art gulped hard. This must be Andy. He snatched the phone from its cradle.

"Andy?" Art almost yelled.

"No." Abbas' Middle Eastern accent hung heavy on the line.

"Abbas! I just phoned you! Where are you calling from?"

"Listen. There has been a development." Abbas' voice was deadpan. He sounded as if he was reading an obituary notice. "You have to destroy all records of our transactions."

"What's happened?"

"You don't watch CNN?"

Art gulped. "I've…been busy, today. I just found the time to call you to say that the shipment will be delayed. Our truck broke down on the highway."

"We won't be needing shipments for awhile. I was calling to tell you to have your driver turn back, ditch the goods, and take a long circuitous route back to Canada."

"What the fuck is going on, Abbas?"

"Watch CNN. Then destroy all records. I will be in touch." The line went dead.

Art stumbled over to the bar and poured himself a double. He clicked the remote control of the plasma TV housed inside the cabinet under the bar. He surfed quickly to the CNN daily news. The US presidential election primaries were all the rage down there with the new black Democratic contender entering the ring. But scrolling under the headlines was the ticker that said, "Late Breaking News: suspected terror cell uncovered in Miami Beach area…chemicals for the making of pesticides suspected of being used to make bombs…four suspects in custody…investigation proceeding…"

Art sank into the enormous leather chair behind his mahogany desk, shoulders sagging, the drink spilling from his hand. "Fuck…" He stared blankly out at the lake, and it did look like a lake on fire, the flames creeping towards the shore, about to engulf him and Hamilton Industries and all that he had achieved in his life.

His private phone line started ringing again…

Twenty-Five

"I'm going to find Billy," Rick said the moment Sue opened her front door. His Malibu was ticking outside, with Bill and Phil sticking their noses out from each of the rear seat windows.

Sue looked confused. "What's got into you?"

"I saw Billy this evening."

Her eyes widened, and then she sighed in relief, reaching out for his arm with one hand and holding her throat with the other. He took her hand firmly and stepped into the house, standing just inside the threshold. "I've no time for tea or whiskey…or for…" he looked ruefully towards the dining table visible through the open vestibule door.

"Where is he?"

"I don't know." He quickly told her where he had seen her son and about Billy's obvious distress. He left out mentioning the passengers in the Cavalier.

"Billy said he was with friends, but I do not believe him," Rick concluded.

"My son didn't do sleepovers when he was little. He didn't have close friends, except for Jenny…and now, this Tamil girl."

"Where did he go when he needed time out?"

"Mostly to work. Like me and his dad."

"He's not at the hardware store. I checked, and he hasn't been in to work all day."

Sue sat down on a chair, still holding Rick's hand, her face screwed in concentration. "If he was younger, I'd tell you he'd hang out at the mill or the surrounding area up there where he'd go fishing."

"At Old Tom's Mill?"

"Yes—Billy would spend days there when he wanted to be by himself, especially after Bob died. When the place was habitable, he'd be in his grandpa's lair, as he called it. He even built some furniture down there. It's all closed up, now. He was down there with Jen the day before that awful shooting in his school. But I didn't think he would go there again after Jen….you know…"

Rick's breath began to quicken. *Of course, that's exactly where he would be, if everything added up.*

"Do you have any articles of Billy's unwashed clothing?"

"What?" Sue looked even more confused.

"I've got my dogs with me. They are hunting dogs, you know."

Sue sighed in relief and shrugged. "You'll have to check his laundry basket. He hasn't done chores in quite awhile." She gestured wearily in the direction of the bedrooms but made no move to rise.

Rick stepped into the corridor and headed towards the bedrooms. Sue's voice followed him. "Billy's is the one on the right, with the poster on the door."

Instinctively, he looked towards the bedroom on the left with its door half open—Sue's bedroom. The queen bed with a swirly shaped wrought-iron bedstead, the light pink flower patterned duvet, the bedside table with a smattering of creams and lotions, a hair brush, an embroidered pincushion on an armchair by the bed with a lemon green dressing gown draped over it, a bra hanging on a hook inside the open door of a closet, inside which hung various dresses: all the things that had vanished from his house in the years following Brenda's death. Rick paused in Sue's doorway, sucking in the objects in that nest of femininity, reluctant to get to the job at hand.

"His room is on the right," Sue repeated, shattering his reverie, and Rick turned to the other side of the corridor to face a Cold Play poster on another door. This room was smaller and cluttered: a computer table, hockey posters on the walls, a *Sports Illustrated* calendar, books on the bed and on the floor, and a closet with clothing piled inside it. He noted that the table was handmade. *Wonder if Billy made that himself—the boy is obviously good with his hands.*

Rick headed for the closet. A laundry hamper sat on the floor inside it. A ripe smell of damp, stale sweat assailed his nostrils as he opened the lid. Holding his breath, he pushed past the wet socks and underwear— no sense in exaggerating things for Phil and Bill—and pulled out a used tee shirt. He fished out a plastic bag from his hunting jacket pocket and deposited the shirt in it, tying the ends of the bag tightly to keep the contents airtight.

When he returned to the front door, Sue was putting her coat on. "I am coming with you."

"No." Rick scrambled for an excuse. "Billy's still sore with you. I don't want to panic him. Let me earn his trust. I will call you when it's time for you to meet him."

Her shoulders sagged again, and the coat fell off one shoulder. "Why does he mistrust me, so? Are we always supposed to be infallible?"

He reached out and took her in his arms, holding her close to him. "I like fallible people. Perhaps, when he grows up a bit and has a few falls himself, he will learn to forgive."

"Please tell Billy that I love him. I do everything with his interests at heart."

"I think he knows that already. He probably feels guilty that you have to do so much to keep him safe." Rick stole another look towards the dining room table and shuddered. Then he broke away, in case his emotions got the better of him.

He paused at the door. "If I don't phone you in a couple of hours, I want you to go to the police and give them my location."

A look of fear crossed her face. "Why?"

"Just do it. There are predators, noxious fumes, and accidents happening around us. Just do it."

"Is there something you are not telling me?"

"Billy said he needed a second chance. I need one, too. I am asking you to respect that. I'll call you in a couple of hours."

He went out into the cool evening. The moon was out in full, getting bigger now that it was only a month away from the harvest moon.

"Right-ho boys," Rick said, getting into the driver's seat. He fingered the metal of the shotgun resting against the passenger seat, something he had not wanted Sue to notice. He slipped the car into gear. "Let's go hunting," he said to Bill and Phil, who were showing signs of restlessness from all this inactivity.

***

Escaping Rick Jones outside the supermarket had been easy enough, but just out of town, Andy had commanded that they change direction and drive out to Milltown Heights—the swanky neighbourhood overlooking the town and lake—where the rich folks, the ones with the boats in the harbour, lived. They drove through the wooded enclave where the only intrusions were paved driveways cut between the trees, with mailboxes and fire-code numbers at their entranceways. Deep inside, at the end of those wooded pathways, Billy knew there were palatial homes set out of view from the masses who made it even this far up the Heights. They turned in at a driveway sporting fire number 5552. Trees and silence enveloped them immediately on all sides. After several seconds of navigating the winding driveway, they came upon a large white, neo classical building with a portico replete with Grecian columns and pediment. There were no lights on inside the house.

"My father's still at work," Andy said, a pleased tone in his voice. Billy pulled up under the portico in front of heavy oaken doors, expecting a retinue of servants to come pouring out to welcome them in, like in those old British movies on TV.

"There's no staff?" Billy asked, hoping the answer would be yes.

"They go home at five—my father's dinner will be in the slow burner, if he is coming home tonight, that is. I know the drill. Nothing much changes with my father and his solitary life."

"So, what do you want me to do?"

Andy's voice suddenly developed a snarl. "Now, listen carefully, fucker. There is a key in the flower pot on the right. He always keeps it there. You have thirty seconds to find that key, open the front door, go into the house, climb the staircase on the right—halfway up—unless the silly coot has moved it, is a portrait of my mother wearing a blue dinner gown with a tiara on her head. Get it off the wall and bring it here. Remember, thirty seconds—no time for phone calls or anything else from inside. And I still have your cell phone."

"Is there a burglar alarm?"

"Not that I know of. My father doesn't believe in them."

Billy gulped. He groped for time, for an out. "What happens, if the key is not there, or the portrait is not there, or someone interrupts me inside?"

Andy's lip curled in delight. He placed the barrel of the gun against the back of Saro's head, and she flinched. "Then I'll just let fly inside here. This car is going to be one fucking mess if you don't come out in thirty seconds."

Andy flipped open the cell phone and said, "I am counting now— you can go anytime you are ready. And keep the engine running."

***

When Billy left the car and rushed towards the house, Sarojini felt her last support being pulled away from her. She reached out for Billy, but he was gone, and she was alone inside the car with this madman, for the second time. She wanted to scream.

Outside the grocery store the last time, when Billy left, Andy had been strangely quiet. Her mind was pulled back to his assault on her body. It must have been his first time with a girl, because his erection had been well…soft… and she had laughed hysterically at his feeble attempts to get it up. Laughter had been her only defence and release. Andy had slapped her then. And when he came, it had been outside her, quickly. She had felt power over him in that instant as his face flushed, and his semen splashed on her thighs. Billy was unconscious at the time, having taken a shot to the back of the head from Andy when they descended the stairs into the cellar, so she could not call out for help. She had just stared at Andy as he dismounted from her body and stuffed his thing back in his pants. And later, while they waited outside the grocery store, he had kept his eyes averted from her.

But now, Andy was looking at her with more confidence. The gun in his hand was more active than his flaccid penis had been, and he made it a point to keep placing the barrel on various parts of her body, like a doctor checking a patient out with his stethoscope. It made her cringe. She was beginning to feel nauseous. There was also her tormentor's smell in the close quarters of the car that was stifling: stale sweat combined with another sharp, acidic smell.

She had to stay upbeat, not show him any sign of weakness. Perhaps, this running away had been a mistake. After all, her parents had always wanted the best for her: *Thathi* in his kind, understanding way, Ammi in her harsh but well-intentioned way. Maybe this was her karma, as Ammi would have said.

Billy, where are you. Please come to me. But Billy was gone.

The gun barrel was in the small of her back, and Andy was humming a song off-key.

"I'm going to fuck you again. When we get back to the mill," he said, his voice nasal, twangy.

"Make sure you get it up this time." She bit her lip only after the words gushed out of her.

He slapped her head from behind, and lights exploded in front of her eyes. He pulled her by the hair and peered into her face, his acrid, sour breath making her gag. "Bitch, that's if I don't blow your head off next." He checked the cell phone in his other hand. "Fifteen seconds."

She realized that she could not rely on Billy, her parents, the police, or anyone to get her out of this predicament. If this was her karma, she was the only one who could reverse it and preserve her life and her baby's.

***

Billy flew out of the car, even before his tormentor finished speaking. He leapt up the front steps. The flower pot spouted a stout stem of red roses, and he poked around among the roots, cutting his fingers on thorns. The key was barely visible under a large stone resting on the topsoil. He grabbed it in his soiled and bloody hand and made for the front door. He turned the key in the lock, but the door would not give.

"Turn the lock over twice," Andy called out from the car. "See how much I am trying to help you, fucker?" Andy's chuckling stuck to Billy like an oily film as he flipped the key a second time and pushed the heavy door open. Andy was right—no burglar alarms—the rich lived comfortably behind their long tree-shrouded driveways in this enclave.

A vast vestibule with hanging plants and portraits in all shapes and sizes faced him. The floor was marble and patterned in squares of black and white diagonal stripes running opposite to each other. A grandfather clock gonged the half-hour and startled him. It was immediately on his right, inside an alcove. He saw the stairway, carpeted soft mink, leading upstairs on his left and took it in bounds—the maids were going to have to do some cleaning up of muddy shoeprints when they next came in.

He looked for the portrait all the way up the staircase, amidst the pictures of Art Hamilton winning various honours, Art Hamilton playing golf with his buddies, a young Art Hamilton opposite Hamilton Industries when it first opened, Art Hamilton and a former Prime Minister of Canada, Art Hamilton and Mayor Frank Morgan opposite the town hall on Canada Day. No picture of a woman in a blue evening gown and tiara.

Billy's heart began to sink. He wanted to turn back, run to the car, and tell Andy that the picture was missing *before* his thirty seconds ran out. But he was fearful of the reaction. *I'll let fly in here*, rang in his ears and propelled him up to the landing on the second floor. Several rooms ran off here: an office room, a music room, a library. Billy kept throwing open doors scanning walls and moving on. He came to a heavy closed door at the end of the passageway. It wasn't locked. The master bedroom—the size of the entire lower floor of Billy's home. A giant plasma TV on the wall opposite a king-sized bed was all that Billy noticed before his eyes were caught by the portrait hanging on the side wall, all by itself—the woman in a blue gown and tiara. Billy rushed toward the picture but paused, stunned by the woman's beauty: green eyes with cat-like intensity boring into him, silky dark hair down to her waist, a well-proportioned figure with plenty of cleavage and hips, reminding him of '60's actress, Raquel Welch. Yet, unlike the famous starlet, there was an aura of fragility about this woman, a suggestion that the slightest breath of wind would crumble and scatter her statuesque beauty into the wind. *Wow, this was Andy's mother—what a waste—washed down Niagara Falls after procreating a maniac son!*

Billy grabbed the picture off the wall and headed back. He caught a glimpse of a walk-in closet on one side and a white-tiled washroom at its end before he was out of the bedroom and running down the passageway for the stairs. He bounded downstairs in three leaps and struck his shoulder on the wall at the bottom, nearly dropping the portrait. He knew he had run out of his thirty seconds and would not make it back in time. He steeled himself to hear the crack of the gun. *This is what nightmare dreams are like, when you are rushing to get somewhere but are always held up by the next obstacle in a never-ending loop, until you awaken.*

He was outside the front door and stumbling down the porch steps. He wrenched open the passenger side door and stuffed the portrait onto Saro's lap, ran around to the driver's side only to find the door locked. He banged on the glass, wondering what the hell this was all about, when Andy languidly reached over from the back seat and pulled up the inside catch. Billy grabbed the door open and fell down in the driver's seat, spent.

"Good! Twenty-eight seconds, fucker. Great timing. You avoided the big splat inside here."

***

Malani woke up sweating. There was daylight still outside, fading, like her dream. The Tylenol she had taken for her headache, coupled with mental exhaustion, had knocked her out completely after returning from the police station. She stumbled into the living room. The TV was on, and Mahesh and Sam were staring at it. It was tuned to the local news channel and the clean-up of that accident on the highway was being played, again.

"Any news?" she asked.

Mahesh remained quiet and still, staring at the TV, but ostensibly in some other world of his own.

"Not yet," Sam said, looking annoyed for being disturbed from his focus on the screen. Perhaps he was blanking out his worst fears this way, she thought. "Mr. Rick said he would call me later. He thinks he knows where the boyfriend is."

She turned and stumbled back into the bedroom, falling across the bed, trying to hang on to the images of the dream that dimmed by the minute. She shut her eyes and tried to concentrate. The remaining images were grainy: herself, six months pregnant with Sarojini at the bus stop in Kotte in the old country, waiting for her younger sister Kamala to come home from university in the city, amidst rumours that the Black Panthers were on the prowl again, targeting Marxist sympathizers, particularly university students. Of course, Kamala never returned. Malani still could not comprehend why her sister decided to attend the political rally that day. The news came later that evening that there had been a riot during the rally, and black-garbed men on motorcycles had fired into the crowd. Kamala was one of the casualties.

Malani rubbed her eyes, trying to recall another image, the newer one that had appeared in today's dream and was different from the recurring nightmare of her dead sister. Yes, there it was: Kamala was talking to her from a distance it seemed, telling her big sister not to be worried, that she would come again and that she would never leave her. Kamala was also saying that *loku akka* (big sister) should not reject her again, like Malani had dismissed her younger sister's Marxist sympathies when she was alive. What did this mean? Malani, being a Buddhist, was a firm believer in re-incarnation. Could Kamala have been reborn as Sarojini three months after her death? But Sarojini was already on the way to being born at that time, predetermined and conceived.

Malani rose from the bed, rubbed the sleep out of her eyes, and pulled back her lush sweat-streaked hair, greying at the temples, into a bun. She walked out into the living room again, more confident in her step.

"I think Sarojini's baby is my dead sister coming back," she announced to a gaping Sam. Even Mahesh came out of his stupor at her words.

Twenty-Six

Billy slowed the car to a crawl up the trail towards the mill. He stole a glance towards Saro; she was belted and wedged in her seat, staring straight ahead, the large portrait hemming her in like an extra security fence.

"Home sweet home," Andy chirped from behind. "Gotta get ready for our guest."

As they descended into Old Tom's lair, the surroundings did not look as luxurious as back at the Hamilton home, and the air had taken an atmosphere of impending doom.

What had changed? The hurricane lamp still hissed its eerie light, throwing jagged shadows, a glimmer of the moon came in through the window by the ceiling, Old Tom's wall frescos exuded their faded pastoral beauty—familiar sights that Billy had wrapped himself in during years past. But today, with the presence of Andy, the surroundings seemed to have conspired with his nemesis to drag him down.

"Stand the photograph by the lamp," Andy ordered Saro, who placidly complied. "And get those old books out of that corner."

Billy cleared the items so that Saro had the space to place the photograph where the light caught it.

Saro stepped back, struck by the beautiful woman in the portrait. "I wish my mother was as beautiful as her." This was the first time she had come out of her deep silence and said something remotely civil. Billy felt elated.

"She was my goddess," Andy replied, eyes gleaming. "She couldn't take this stinking world for long."

"Mothers are fallible creatures," Billy said, adding quickly, "Saro's and mine, at least."

"You have them alive," Andy said, and his snarl took on a tinge of regret.

"My mother was like that once," Billy continued. "I wish I could have immortalized her in a picture. Then shit happened."

"We grew up is what happened," Saro said.

We have all gotten a lot older in a short time, Billy thought.

Andy had softened his stare on Billy and Saro. It was as if he wanted to sit down with them and have a bitch session on mothers and their vulnerability. Billy's cell phone rang. Andy grabbed it out of his pocket and listened intently. His mouth widened in a cruel grin. "The same place. Remember the last time? Just come to the trap door and lift it. Then come on in. We are expecting you."

When he flipped the phone shut and slipped it into his pocket, Andy's brief moment of softness had evaporated. "Our guest is here," he said, moving towards the entrance beneath the trapdoor.

Billy moved over to Saro, but Andy waved the gun at him. "Stand in opposite corners."

Billy complied, moving to one end of the camp bed while Saro stayed where she was by the head of the bed, next to the bedside table.

Footsteps crunched overhead, and the trapdoor creaked open.

"Come on in," Andy cooed.

Steps descended, and Billy recognized a tired-looking Art Hamilton. His jacket was unbuttoned, the tie loose and hanging down over his crotch, his wavy grey hair was wind-blown.

Art stepped into the centre of the room before recognizing the figures standing at three ends of it. He stared at the portrait by the hurricane lamp for some time, swearing under his breath before sighing resignedly. He turned to face Andy, who was in the darkest corner.

"You called, and I came—like I have always done."

"Good. This time you came at my command." Andy walked out into the light, revealing the gun pointed squarely at his father.

"We seem to be repeating this scene," Art said. "Only, there was no gun the last time."

"This is about getting it right, the second time. Mom never had a second chance."

"Oh, for God's sake, Andy, can you never get past that?" Art unconsciously took a step towards his son as if he were going to smack him again and stopped.

"I will get past it tonight, old man. See the portrait?"

"Yes—I hung it up in my bedroom, so that I had your mother's company with me when I went to sleep at night."

"And she got to watch as you fucked all those other women in the bed you once shared with her?"

"I never…never had…other women in that bed. I guess you will never believe me—but that is true. I loved your mother, but you won't believe that, either. So why did you ask me here? Are you planning to give yourself up? And why are these kids here?" Art turned towards Billy. "I remember you from the last time."

Andy cut in. "I asked you here to apologize to Mom. To beg her forgiveness. These are my witnesses."

Billy found his voice. "I am Billy Miller, Mr. Hamilton. This is my girlfriend, Saro."

"I am sorry to meet you under these circumstances, again."

"My father was Bob Miller. He worked for Hamilton Industries most of his life," Billy said. Andy had suddenly given him the opening he had waited so long for. "My father died of cancer, Mr. Hamilton. And this room belonged to my grandpa Tom Miller—remember? My dad wanted you to convert this place into a museum, but you refused?"

Art's shoulders stooped; he nodded. He looked weary. "This is a day of reckoning for me. Yes, I remember Bob—he was a good worker. I am sorry that you lost your father and Jennifer."

"Fucker, shut up!" Andy erupted at Billy, his voice rising to a hysterical pitch. "This is *my* show!"

Andy turned on Art. "Go to that portrait and kneel in front of Mom and ask for her forgiveness. Now!"

When Art replied, his voice had a calm but steely edge in it. "My communion with your mother is a private matter. You will not dictate how, where, or when I do it. Do you understand?"

"Oh yeah?" Andy's voice had a whine at the edges. "Go on, ask for her forgiveness. You took her to Niagara Falls so that she would jump off. You killed her."

Billy could see Art's face flush, even in the dim light.

"I took her there because I wanted her to face her demons and come through."

Andy laughed. "Shit or get off the pot, eh? Black or white. Because you have no patience for weaklings."

"Something like that," said Art in an undertone. "Did you want her living locked up in her room forever?"

"She was alive in her room. And she wasn't hurting anybody."

The conversation ran out of steam between them. Father and son stared across at each other, lost for words. Then Art shrugged and turned to leave the room.

"Hey, hey! We aren't done," Andy screamed. "Are you going to beg her for forgiveness?"

Art turned a final time. "No. I do not need to be forgiven. I did not harm your mother."

The gun in Andy's hand exploded, and Art staggered backward. Billy saw the look of surprise on the older Hamilton's face.

"Oh yeah," Andy snarled. "Do it, now!"

Art took two steps towards the portrait and collapsed in front of it. Billy had to strain to hear his next words. "Matty—we brought a monster into this world."

Andy screamed and fired again. Art jerked, his head exploding in a shower of red, his body rolling over in convulsions before lying still on the dirty floor. Saro buried her face in her hands and screamed. Billy felt his knees go weak, but he could not go to anyone's aid.

Andy circled the still figure on the floor. "The bastard—unrepentant to the end."

"You're the same, Andy," Billy burst out, unable to control himself any longer. "Do you know what it is to lose a father? Damn you!"

Andy swung around. "I don't need you, you bastard. Or your smart-ass girlfriend."

Billy knew he was going to be the next victim and gathered himself to pounce before the bullet struck. Then, the trapdoor opened, and the hounds out of Hell came charging at them.

***

When Rick turned off the highway onto the road leading up to the mill, he drove a few hundred metres and found a break in the trees to park his car off the side. If the people up ahead were armed, he was not going to be a sitting duck driving in the open. He jumped out of the car and got the dogs out. Just like he had done umpteen times before, when they had gone duck hunting, he pulled the plastic bag from his pocket and held Billy's undershirt under the snouts of Bill and Phil. "We are going to catch bad people, boys." He held their leashes wrapped around his left arm, hefted the shotgun in his right, and set off.

The dogs started on their task immediately, straining at their leashes, pulling him uphill towards the mill. An engine roared behind him, a vehicle turning off the highway and coming uphill, heading in their direction. Rick dragged the dogs into the trees just in time as an SUV roared past. Rick was surprised to see Art Hamilton behind the wheel, a grim and purposeful look on his face.

"Sorry boys," Rick apologized to his dogs, applying the undershirt to their snouts once again. "Seems like there is a party going on here."

He was panting by the time they crested the hill, although the dogs were in full chase by then, sniffing the ground and straining on their leashes, helping him with the climb and rushing him at the same time. They passed the caretaker's house and turned downhill to the bank of the river. Rick had to rein in the dogs again—the SUV was parked in front of the mill, next to Sue's old Chevy. There was no one outside.

"Okay, boys, go slow from here." Bill and Phil slowed down in response to their master's command. *They've been around me for so long, they even whine in admonishment when I fart!*

Rick entered the mill just as he heard a muffled explosion from below the floor. He noticed the trapdoor instantly and paused. The dogs pulled him over to it and sniffed vigorously around the cracks in the floor. Rick rested his shotgun against the nearby wall and tried lifting the door with his free hand—it was awkward with the dogs tugging him. He unwound the leashes from his left hand and, using both hands, wrenched the heavy door open.

Several things happened at once. Another crack rang out, sharper this time, accompanied by raised voices, and the freed Bill and Phil yelped in gratitude and disappeared down the hole in the floor.

"I'll be damned," Rick swore, reaching for his shotgun.

***

The gun in Andy's hand cracked again, and the lead dog was thrown off his charge to fall and writhe fiercely on the floor. The second dog slid to a stop, changed course, and lunged at Andy just as the gun fired again. Andy and the dog went down in a heap, thrashing and kicking. Billy saw the gun fall out of Andy's hand but lost sight of it as the falling bodies knocked the hurricane lamp off its perch and its light spluttered and died. Snarls and groans came from animal and human locked in combat on the floor. Billy ran over to Saro and grabbed her hand. "Let's get out of here."

"Not so fast, fucker." The voice was shrill. The animal sounds had subsided to whimpers.

Billy swung around. In the moonlight that was shining full through the window, he made out Andy: face bloody, clothes shredded, standing menacingly over the second dog that had been clawing him; the animal was in a heap on the floor.

"Run for the door," Billy ordered Saro and turned to face Andy. "Okay, guy, take me."

Billy dove into Andy, tackling him in the midriff and throwing them both back onto the camp bed. The bed broke in the middle and sucked them both into its centre as it collapsed.

Andy was maniacally strong, Billy realized, as he felt bony cold hands circle his windpipe and squeeze. Billy kicked upwards, hoping to connect with Andy's testicles, hitting air instead, and feeling the wind in his throat shut off rapidly. Gasping, he punched into the region of his opponent's face and hit teeth; the impact made him wince. He aimed and hit higher and felt his bloodied hand strike a nose, breaking it. He kept punching, weakening with every blow, but sensing the vice on his throat starting to ease every time he landed. *If I can keep this up until Saro gets away...* He was starting to black out. As he got lightheaded, Art's last words came to him: "Matty, we brought a monster into this world." Billy felt like he was holding evil at bay. Andy even stank strange, his sweat a pungent odour of rotting meat.

Billy tried one more kick, aiming for where he thought Andy's crotch was. Then Andy suddenly grunted and went limp. Billy heard a repeated thumping, like a measured drum beat. Andy let go of him completely. Billy rolled away, and his eyesight began to clear. Saro was standing over Andy's inert body, his grandpa's heavy glass ashtray in her hand. She raised it above her head in a detached fashion and crushed it down on Andy. She repeated it several times until the heavy weight dropped out of her hands, and she fell to her knees sobbing.

When the air had returned to his lungs, Billy crawled over to Saro and put his arms around her. She sank into him, spent. His hands went unconsciously to her stomach—the baby must be kept safe.

***

Rick was undecided at the trapdoor entrance. The dogs had gone in, and he was about to follow when the gun shots rang out. He heard the squeal—one, or both, of his beloved dogs had been hit. Prudence held him from rushing in. He pulled out his cell phone instead while keeping his gun trained on the door.

Sue answered immediately. "It's not two hours yet."

"Get the cops out to the mill. It's horrible, Sue. Tell them to bring plenty of firepower. Don't worry, I'll get Billy out, safe." He hung up.

What the fuck am I doing here, then? Another one of those procrastinations—inactions he was getting fed up with. The shooting had ceased, the dogs were quiet. *Oh shit, they are both gone and here I am like Atilla in my tent, hiding out.*

He cocked the shotgun and took the stairs down quickly. The dark blinded him at first, then the moonlight glowed dimly through the window. He made out shadowy forms sprawled in different parts of the room. Two bodies moved in each other's arms, rocking in consolation, it seemed—Billy and Sam's missing daughter.

Another form emerged from the shadows, slowly at first, a hand sweeping the floor as if looking for something. The moonlight caught the bloodied face, and Rick recognized him: the boy who had crushed a defenceless dying deer with a rifle butt, now about to commit another senseless crime. When he saw the glint of steel in Andy's hand pointing at Billy and the girl, Rick knew he had no choice. He squeezed the trigger of his shotgun. The blast was deafening. The target launched into the air and hit the far wall before sliding down like a deflated balloon along its smooth surface. This time, Andy lay still.

"It's a Greek tragedy," Rick managed to say before he stumbled over Phil's inert form and broke down sobbing.

Twenty-Seven

Rick studied the group gathered around Saro's hospital bed. He was back in Milltown General inside twenty-four hours. Billy, wearing a bandage around his neck, stood next to Saro stroking her hair, conscious of his mother's worried looks in his direction. Mr. and Mrs. Selvadurai sat in the two arm chairs provided in each private room. Rick and Sue had been offered the chairs as soon as they arrived, but Sue had preferred to stand. Rick's feet were killing him from the exertion of the last several hours, but he, too, remained standing. Mahesh leaned against the door, disinterested, sending a text message—that's all he'd been doing, probably advising his plethora of social networking sites about the goings on in Milltown. Rick was sure that a movie deal would be the next big thing to hit this town.

He decided to open the conversation, given it had been his idea to bring Sue to the room.

"I'm sure we will go though more questioning by the authorities in the days ahead, but I am glad that Saro and the baby are out of danger," he said. "The nurse advised me that the hospital would be discharging her shortly."

Sue glanced at her son, then stepped towards the seated couple, extending her hand. "Mr. Selvadurai, I owe you an apology for yesterday. My son *is* the father of our grandchild. I think Billy has more than proved that."

Sam Selvadurai rose eagerly and took her outstretched hand. "Thank you, Mrs. Miller."

"Sue—call me Sue."

"And I am Sam. This my wife Malani. And… *adey* Mahesh! Come here, man, and shake this lady's hand, no. That's my son. He is very good with computers, when he is not fighting in school."

When all the introductions had been made, Sam was grinning. Malani took Sue's hand tentatively and looked towards her daughter.

Sam rubbed his hands together in satisfaction. "Well—we can't all be good friends overnight, but this is a good start, no? Mr. Rick, thank you for all you did to save our Saro."

"Well, Billy here did all the work," Rick replied. "I just cleaned up at the end."

"I am sorry to hear that you lost your dogs. Nice creatures they were, no?"

Rick shrugged. He had not come around to missing the dogs yet, but knew that he would, eventually. "Yeah. I am sorry, too. They were like soldiers to the end. Into the valley of death, they charged, without hesitation."

Sue took his hand, and Rick was grateful.

An awkward silence descended upon the room. Billy, who had been silent up to that point, spoke up. "Now that you have all got to meet each other, Saro and I would like to tell you, once and for all, that we are keeping this baby."

Sam went over and pumped Billy's hand vigorously. "That is very good news, young man. Now, we will become proper Canadians."

"And we will complete our studies if we are able to live with you until then."

"That will make me very happy, Billy," Sue said, tears clouding the corners of her eyes. She went up to Saro and took both her hands. "It's been difficult for me to accept that my son had grown up and embraced a culture different to mine. But I want to welcome you into our family."

Sarojini smiled and hugged Sue—tentatively.

"And we will make sure to feed Saro well during the pregnancy," Malani spoke for the first time. "None of this Canadian dieting for you, my girl. I will show you how to bring a child into this world the healthy way. A baby who went through all that horror to be born, has a purpose in this life."

Sam looked sheepish at his wife's outburst of philosophy. "Er…my wife believes in re-incarnation, you see. She thinks that this child is the re-birth of her sister who died in the political riots in Sri Lanka in the nineties."

"Of course—it must be," Malani insisted. "How else can you describe all these things that happened?"

"Hey guys," Mahesh piped from the door, his cell phone poised and pointed at the group around the bed. "Get closer, I am going to take a photograph to post on my Facebook page. I'm going to title it—my Canadian Masala family!"

Despite her weakened state, Saro extended a tongue at him. "I don't even have my makeup on."

The camera-phone clicked anyway, and Rick imagined what it would look like—a motley crew of people thrown together through a mixture of external and internal events.

Sam, Malani, and Mahesh left shortly to prepare the house for the home-coming of their daughter. Saro was going to need plenty of bed rest. Before leaving, Sam took Sue's hand again and said, "You and Mr. Rick must come to our home for dinner, very soon. My wife and I will cook you the best Sri Lankan meal you will have in this country."

Rick nodded at Sue. "I think this guy might just carry out his threat. I've eaten at his restaurant before."

"Thank you, Sam and…Malani," Sue replied. "I will certainly look forward to that." And for the first time, Malani smiled demurely at Sue.

"Why don't you spend a few minutes with your son," Rick suggested to Sue after the Selvadurai's left. "There is someone I need to see in this hospital. I will be back shortly to give you a ride home."

***

Rick found Jane Garner in the same room as yesterday. Her hospital gown had been freshly changed. The overhead TV was tuned to the local channel that was re-playing the scenes of the police clean-up at the mill. Yellow tape, police personnel, and reporters dotted the spot, a totally foreign terrain from what it had been yesterday.

"It's over," he announced walking in and sitting gently on an armchair. He realized that he hadn't sat since he had got the dogs out of his car the previous day at the base of the mill. He'd even spent the time on the journey back into town in the police bus, hanging onto an overhead rail, talking to a sergeant who had been recording his statement. From then on, he had been at the hospital talking to a wave of people, including reporters.

Jane turned over to face him. Her gaunt eyes managed to smile. "You had quite a lot of action, I can see."

"Yes." Rick was suddenly starting to feel tired. Sitting down had not helped. "I could sleep for a month."

"Sorry to hear about your dogs."

"It's okay." *It's not okay, but what the hell can I say? Everyone is sorry for my dogs. No one ever gives a shit about me.* "How are you doing?"

"I'm feeling a bit better, today. I must be on the mend. But it's going to be awhile, the doctor says."

"That's good to know."

"I feel bad for Art."

"Me too. I don't wish even my enemies to be murdered by their progeny."

Jane looked at the photograph of her son, now on a frame on the side table. A worried frown creased her emaciated face. "We go to strange lengths for our children, don't we? But you can never tell how they'll turn out, can you?"

"No. That's for sure."

"You think all this is worth it? What I am doing to get Jeremy back?"

"I don't think that's negotiable. We do our best and wait for the result. Art thought he had done his best for his son." *And no one asked me how it felt to shoot my nephew, flawed though he was.*

"Are you still going to need those documents from my office?"

"I don't think so. I'm turning over the witch hunt to Doug Spade of the Town Council tomorrow. He is like a beagle in these matters. You'd better report the accounting irregularities at Bio Diversity Futures yourself. You'll need your practice alive to feed Jeremy and make sure he grows up a law-abiding citizen."

She nodded.

"I came to ask a favour," Rick said, rising. "I'm not sure who'll buy Art's real estate holdings, but I want you to drop your request for more space in your building. If you need extra digs, I'll find you another good location. I happen to like Sri Lankan food."

He took her silent stare back at the TV for acceptance and left the room.

***

Sue was waiting for him in the lobby.

"Spoken to Billy already?" Rick asked. "I thought you guys had to go through some plate breaking and hair pulling before you could reconcile."

"Sometimes a hug breaks a thousand plates, pulls a scalp full of hair, and says all the words we need to say," Sue said, falling into step with him.

"A hug says you are human, and that's what you were."

"Frank won't be my boss much longer. I expect he'll resign before the gory details come out. Would you consider running again?"

"And have you as my assistant? No, I'll leave political office to ambitious guys like Doug Spade. He's going to be grinning with glee when I go to see him tomorrow with some 'purloined letters.' I won't be including those photographs, by the way. Doug will have enough to work with.

Rick turned to face her, opening his arms wide. "But I am open to hugs. I am also only too human. And I can't face going home to an empty house without my dogs."

Sue appraised him coolly. "There is a bottle of wine at my place. We could drink it—on the back porch."

Before he could say, "Deal", she swept into his open arms.

Epilogue—30th June 2009

Sam Selvadurai took his morning constitutional on the beach before opening South Asian Delights at eleven o'clock for the afternoon's rush of patrons. He now had an assistant who could hold the fort for him when he needed to take a breather and rest his arthritic fingers. And he was going to need a breather this weekend because it was the Canada Day break and the town would be bursting with activity—good for business.

Already, people from the town and from elsewhere were staking out spots on the beach; umbrellas popped, beach chairs straightened out, picnic bags opened, portable barbecues were being readied, clothes were coming off, and sun-tan and sun-block lotions were being daubed on white and not-so-white bodies alike. By noon, every bit of sand would be occupied by dozing adults or dug up by kids making sandcastles. In the town, across from the park, the steel band was playing, and buskers would perform all day, including in front of his restaurant, providing great entertainment for his patrons.

Even his own kind, South Asians, came out to this beach: in cars, vans, and chartered buses, they loaded up their pots and pans, cricket bats and balls, serpinas and tablas, and made weekend picnics out to this spot where they could mingle freely, without fear of persecution, away from their hard-scrabble lives and poky apartments in the city where they toiled as immigrants or refugees in this new homeland. They, too, were becoming Canadian.

Despite the gaiety and abandon surrounding him, Sam could not help reflecting that he had come to Milltown with his family only eighteen months ago, fleeing persecution. Barely two months ago, in the old country, on a strip of beach like this, his persecutors had fought their last battle and lost. The twenty-six-year civil war was finally over. There would be no more demands for money from the Diaspora. What had been a crazy gamble at the time—coming out to Milltown—had paid off.

But he could never be complacent. Amidst the swaying willows, majestic oaks, and abundant maples dotting the park, hiding behind the happily gathering crowds, the ordered lawns, and the well-maintained houses of this small town, evil had lurked. Evil had been vanquished for now by a few hardy souls, his daughter included, but evil was never far from one's door, *in any country*. He hoped he could frame this picture of Canada Day in his mind for when those dark days re-appeared, for surely, they would.

As if to remind him of that former time, the chemical plant and other buildings of Hamilton Industries, to the west of the beach, lay silent, not just closed for the national holiday, but shut down permanently until the new owner reconfigured and re-tooled the plant. Even though there was a temporary loss of employment, there was great optimism that the new "Green" plant would provide even more employment opportunities for the town folk. The new mayor, Doug Spade—appointed soon after Frank Morgan suddenly resigned and left town to join his wife in Florida—was a big supporter of the environment.

Sam waved at Mabel who was sitting on a park bench facing the water, knitting. She waved back absently and returned to her work, eyes narrowed over the swiftly moving needles. How scared she had been of him during their first encounter on this very spot! He saw his upstairs neighbour, dressed in beach shorts and tight tee-shirt, throwing a Frisbee to her son who had come to live with her a few months ago. The boy ran down to the water's edge to retrieve the spinning disc. Jeremy was always coming downstairs to South Asian Delights to buy vadais or pick up "free" samples that Sam was generous with because the boy said that while living with his father, their apartment in Toronto had been next door to a Tamil restaurant. Thanks to the boy, his mother, Jane Garner, put in a regular appearance with him for a meal on weekends. She still hadn't regained all of her weight from her ordeal last summer but seemed to be wirily fit.

Sam continued his stroll. Mahesh had gone to Sri Lanka for the summer before heading off to university in Ottawa in the fall. From their last communication with him on Skype, he was complaining about the mosquitoes and the heat and the various comforts that were not available in the old country. Sam chuckled. *Good for him—Mahesh will come back appreciating his adopted homeland a bit more.*

At the end of the pier, running at ninety degrees to the boardwalk, the lighthouse beckoned. Sam smiled when he saw this edifice. "After all that happened this last year, you have more stories to add to your collection," he whispered to the silent sentinel.

Midway down the boardwalk, a couple approached from the opposite end, pushing a pram. Sam's heart leaped. Saro and Billy, with their six-week old daughter, Shankari, meaning peacemaker in Hindu culture, who was born on the day the last shot was fired in the war in Sri Lanka. Billy and his mother had both loved the name the moment Sam suggested it. And Malani was delighted too.

Sam quickened his pace. In no time, he was running along the boardwalk, hands reaching out for the light brown skinned infant. The parents looked confused but amused as this middle-aged man scooped the child tenderly from its comfortable nook inside the baby carriage.

Sam held a swaddled Shankari over his head and hurried down to the water while the sun bathers stared at him.

"Welcome to Canada, my child. Welcome!" Sam intoned as he walked towards the water. With the waves coursing over his ankles, he swivelled on his feet, offering the infant a view from one end of the beach to the other and over the gently rolling waters all the way to the

United States of America on the horizon. "This is your land. Our land. We have finally come home, Shankari."

He turned towards the lighthouse, still holding the baby aloft. "Make sure to record this child's story, too!"

On the boardwalk, Sarojini took Billy's hand and shook her head in amusement. "*Thathi* is so over the top at times," she said.

-End-

Acknowledgements

Many thanks to my beta readers who provided me valuable feedback on earlier drafts of this novel: Jake Hogeterp, (the late) Brian Mullally and members of the Pollard Group of Writers, Ben Antao, and Linda Grimaldi

To Jennifer Jaquith for her superb editing skills and for helping me understand Canadian teenagers in schools.

To my indefatigable designer, Joanne Kasunic, who will work on multiple drafts of the cover until everything is just perfect.

And to the unflappable Ken Solilo for his photographs of rural Ontario.

To my advance reviewers who were honest in their opinions.

To my wife Sarah, who did not like the first draft (as usual), but helped me persevere and suggested I wait until time matured perceptions.

Shane Joseph
2019

Biography - Shane Joseph

Shane Joseph is a graduate of the Humber School for Writers in Toronto and studied under the mentorship of Giller Prize and Canadian Governor General's Award-winning author David Adams Richards. ***Redemption in Paradise***, his first novel, was published in 2004. ***Fringe Dwellers***, his first collection of short stories, was released in 2008, and is now in its second edition. Shane's second novel, ***After the Flood***, a dystopian novel of hope, was released in 2009 and won the Write Canada Award for best novel in the futuristic/fantasy category. Shane's 'autobiographical novel,' ***The Ulysses Man***, was published in

2011, and is a fictional chronicle of the Burghers of Ceylon. Shane's fifth work of fiction, ***Paradise Revisited***, a collection of short stories that continues to explore the immigrant experience, was short listed for the Re-Lit award in 2014. He covered his travels in Peru in a novel, ***In the Shadow of the Conquistador***, published in 2015. His latest collection of short stories, ***Crossing Limbo***, was released in June 2017.

Shane's short fiction and non-fiction have appeared in literary journals such as the Book Review Literary Trust of India, The Wagon Magazine and in anthologies all over the world. His blog at www.shanejoseph.com is widely syndicated and he has a monthly column in The Sri Lankan Anchorman newspaper.

More details on Shane's work, blog and public interviews can be found on his website at www.shanejoseph.com.